# Of Immortalized Warriors

# Of Immortalized Warriors

## A Novel

William Mueller

author**HOUSE**®

*AuthorHouse™*
*1663 Liberty Drive*
*Bloomington, IN 47403*
*www.authorhouse.com*
*Phone: 1-800-839-8640*

*First published by AuthorHouse    06/29/2011*

*ISBN: 978-1-4634-0640-0 (sc)*
*ISBN: 978-1-4634-0639-4 (dj)*
*ISBN: 978-1-4634-0638-7 (ebk)*

*Library of Congress Control Number: 2011910765*

*Printed in the United States of America*

*Any people depicted in stock imagery provided by Thinkstock are models, and such images are being used for illustrative purposes only.*
*Certain stock imagery © Thinkstock.*

*This book is printed on acid-free paper.*

To

Young Men and Women

Who with Courage

Honorably Serve their Country

And Commit Themselves to Freedom

I dedicate

THIS BOOK

*"Respect gods before demigods,*

*heroes before men,*

*and first among men your parents;*

*but respect yourself most of all."*

Pythagoras (fl. 6th century B.C.)

Greek philosopher and mathematician

# FIRST PART

## Left and Right

# ONE

I HAVE FOUND THAT when an old friend calls you and, finding you unavailable or unresponsive, leaves imploring you to call him at a moment's notice, and it's life-or-death, the matter is more relevant to him than to you. When it comes to helping someone or doing him a favor most people are able to hold their impatience within reasonable limits. So when I finished reading a report with just enough time to take a cup of coffee, and to visit my favorite website before departing for the Smithsonian, and was told by Joan Moaney, a partner, that James Isner had stopped by earlier and wished for me to give him a call, I felt that I could safely ignore his request.

"Economist?" she asked me.

She gave the business card a second glance.

"He's a professor now."

"I see that," she said. "Don't you want to read the message on the backside?"

"Sure, I suppose."

"Very well."

She turned up her eyes. She gave me the card, turned to a desk by the window with a view of Market Square, and took off her coat. Joan Moaney was a perceptive woman of about sixty-five years. I was sensitive to the fact that she knew we shared a few of the same experiences in life. Her alert appraisal of my casualness suggested that she was keen about my present feelings. When I finally gathered up my papers and laptop computer, she made it a point in her kind, clear voice to see to it that I make time for old friends.

"Dr. Isner is very nice. You should take him out for a drink tonight. He said he is staying at the Hilton right up the street."

I turned away briefly.

"Say is rain still in the forecast? I forgot to check the weather radar."

Joan Moaney smiled.

3

"No, you should be all right on your motorcycle."

"Great, the pickup is in the shop again, so long."

"My impression was it is rather important."

"Joan, I'm running late."

"You'll find the parkway as you like it this afternoon."

"Excellent, a favorable traffic report, too."

"Goodbye, Mr. Cooper."

I had not seen Jim in a couple of years and then only in passing at a professional basketball game; he had always been a good old boy, a true Southerner, and when we ran into each other he had displayed his raucously aggressive voice by calling out my dated tee shirt.

"My God, the Bullets!" he cried, holding up two large beers. "Perfect, I always thought the Wizards was a ludicrous nickname—good to see you, Riley."

"Wow, one always runs into an old buddy at the most awkward time."

"I'm in town just one more day. Let's get together tomorrow night, you free?"

"I certainly am," I replied, as I was pushed forward by the heavy crowd in the passageway.

"I'll shoot you a message when I get back to my seat."

"All right."

I had not known Jim for about twenty years without learning that he kept in his back pocket the mobile phone in which he stored all of his contacts. I was therefore not taken aback when I did not hear from him. It was impossible for me now to persuade myself that this urgent desire of his to talk to me was free from a personal need or desire. Later that day as I walked my dog around the block I turned over in my mind the possible reasons for which Jim might want to see me. It might be that an art-loving girlfriend had implored him to get tickets to the opening reception of the Caravaggio exhibit or that a new dean, seeking ties to the National Endowment for the Humanities, had desired Jim to put me in touch with him; but I could not do my old friend the injustice of supposing him so disingenuous of representation as not to give him a call, so it could hardly be that he maintained an ulterior motive.

Except Jim no one could show a more genuine regard to a fellow Marine whose ideas were recently expounded by the National Geographic Society, but no one could more genuinely turn away from him when academic rivalries, natural events, or someone else's success had cast a doubt on his research. Every man has his ups and downs, and I was cognizant that at the moment he was on the hot seat. It was obvious that I might have found reason without confronting personal casualty in our relationship, but he was a sentimental person and if I hurt his feelings for no reason whatsoever, I well knew his ego and stubbornness could possibly inhibit all future communication; but I was a curious person. I had also my own interest in the friendship.

I had watched with wonder his rise in the academic world of economic theory. His transformation might well have served as a model for any apprehensive military officer entering upon the pursuit of a new career. I could think of no one among my generation who was more in tune with the American dream. This, like a man's right to unfettered freedom in a liberal society, might have been the dominant factor. He was utterly unaware of it though, and yet it must have seemed to him sometimes little short of a tragedy that he had not been able with it to win the Noble Memorial Prize in Economics. I cannot but think that he saw the falseness of contradiction when he studied the two schools of thought represented by the works of Friedrich Hayek and John Maynard Keynes and found out that the former won the prize and the latter was unable to outlive his father. He researched his death and found an obituary in the *New York Times*. If that was it, he must have told himself, he did not really want to be a noble laureate like Hayek; and when the admiration of respected reviewers of his dissertation, writing many comparisons to the revolutionary Keynesian policy of the 1930's (and the antagonists lined up with equal zeal), he must have sighed with relief of one who after long hours of hard work has earned not only a doctorate degree but advanced new horizons in his field of study. Anyone who had recently discovered his ability to challenge certitudes in true believers could deny that at all events he deserved to be a professor at Cornell University.

Jim grew up on high ground in Mobile, Alabama. He was one of ten grandchildren of an enterprising young man who after being the chief engineer of Fletcher-class destroyers at the Gulf Shipbuilding Corporation ended his career the years after World War II as vice president of a multinational petroleum company. This industriousness gave his parents certain advantages. When you search the pages of the World Wide Web for Raymond Isner you saw chairman of the board for Exxon Mobil and secretary of the Alabama Heritage Trust Fund and of Roberta Isner, city council member and words such as "String of Pearls Initiative" and "Mobile-Daphne-Fairhope Betterment Committee." He and his two younger sisters were educated at St. Vincent DePaul Catholic School and Spring Hill College. He was a standout athlete and but for a lingering injury to his throwing arm might very well have signed a contract with the Atlanta Braves. His academic achievement was just as worthy, all the same he let this quality rest in order to become an officer in the U.S. Marine Corps. Jim was even then of a studious habit, inclining to curious diversions outside his military specialty, and he had a certain intractability about him—the likely reason he lost interest in this idiosyncratic way of life—but he was a good son and he knew that it was a privilege to be admitted to Officer Candidate School and receive a commission.

His parents, true Mobilians, moved into an old, but updated, house of Greek Revival design within the Di Tonti Square historic district after Jim was born, but this was a risk for at intervals the Port City suffers from major tropical storms that would cause tremendous flooding and damage, and on three such occasions the family was forced out of their cloistered neighborhood and thrust into the greater city to live temporarily. It was after Hurricane Frederic that Mr. Isner volunteered his boy for cleanup duty, when he was seven years old, appointed chief assistant to the nursing staff at the Catholic Church's hospice. This gave Jim a chance to become acquainted at an early age with the poor people of the world. He was one of the first young people to return home to lend support after Hurricanes Opal and Katrina and the Gulf Oil Leak. You will never hear from his mouth any of the preconceived notions of those who have lived among the slums of the city only during the days after the storm surge.

He knew exactly how men spoke to one another, and the right way women should be addressed according to their principal cultural influence: French, British, Spanish, Creole, Hispanic or African. And there is something captivating in the liveliness with which he handles senators, governors, mayors, executives and well-heeled women. He is cordial without being differential and when appropriate intimate without being impudent. He is always mindful of political sympathies, but shares with them his inner feelings that ascribe to his being a real person. I think it is a shame that, politics having decided that a realistic view of the possibilities is no longer a proper guide for hard-nosed party leaders, Jim, always completely calibrated in his approach to business, should have in his second career confined himself to the narrow reaches of intellectuals and tenured professors. He has a difficult time relating to these people even with his easygoing Southern charm.

I met him first after I completed the Naval ROTC program and was sent to Camp Barrett in Virginia to learn the art and science of being an officer of Marines, and he was then a respectable, good-natured young man, almost six feet tall in his boots and of a slender build, with solid features and a surefooted bearing. He was not handsome, but in a smoothed out way agreeable to look at, with his wide-open, hazel, forthright eyes and short curly hair of light brown; his forehead was rather long, his complexion fair. He looked clean, sincere, and unaffected. He had a bias for action. No one who has read in his early papers the description of an urban assault with a platoon, so vivid and so accurate, can doubt that his compass pointed in the right direction; and until quite lately he was again willing to wear the medals for his service.

He accomplished the first phases of the instruction when men from Annapolis, to show their supremacy, pushed themselves past preconceived limits, and for some weeks during field exercises there was seldom an instructor in which his name did not figure. This particular school, I know perfectly why, has maintained its mantra, for their manuals are respected, and, though many of their recruits have flushed out, they leave with the idea that Marines in battle ultimately fight not for a cause, but for the sake of the men in their own group. Jim ceased playing this highly dangerous game a good many years ago and he has developed a fine taste for Scotch whiskey.

Jim was very modest about his first position of authority. It was to a firing battery within an artillery battalion, and, as is everything he has set about since, in earned respect. He had been sent to the field artillery course at Fort Sill, Oklahoma, and during this he told each one of the instructors how greatly he regarded his example, how much he had learned from his study of them, and how enthusiastically he aspired to follow, albeit at a humble distance, the program his leader had championed. He stood at attention before senior officers as the dedication of a young man entering upon the profession of arms to one whom he would always look up to as his master. Apologetically, fully conscious of his daring in asking so busy a man to waste his time on a recruit's witless question, he begged for criticism and guidance. Few of the responses were deprecatory. The instructors he walked up to, enthralled by his desire and ambition, spent extra time with him. They commended his effort; many of them asked him to their lunch table. They could not fail to be beguiled by his earnestness and impressed by his passion. He asked for their advice with a humility that was true and promised to act upon it with a sincerity that was impressive. Here, they thought, was someone who could be pushed beyond what he thought he was able to achieve.

His training had an interesting result. It made him many friends in outer circles and in a very short time you could not go to the Quantico or Fort Myer officers' club without finding him standing with several captains and majors or chatting up a retired general at the bar. He was so young, so smart, so physically fit, he spoke so earnestly about military affairs and was filled with so many new ideas that nobody could help enjoying his company. He joined an extramural sports league where on Sunday afternoons in West Potomac Park young professionals, lawyers and scientists in government positions and industry lines of work, played softball or rough-and-tumble flag football and discussed current affairs while drinking cold beer. It was soon discovered that he had a gift for explaining complex technical matters. He was so pleasant that his fellow comrades, his superiors, and his new friends, forgave him even the fact that he was driven. He was very busy during this period but was generous with his time, and when they asked him for a favor he could never resist. They thought him not only a rational sort, but an honest guy.

He went on a first tour to Camp Courtney in Okinawa, Japan, and took great pains with his assignment as a rifle platoon leader. He profited by the advice his squad leaders gave him in making larger plans for the three platoons under the rifle company, which directly affected the battalion led by Lieutenant Colonel Reeves. It was only reasonable then that he should at the division's request write a review of the expeditionary doctrine used in the Gulf War and only natural that it set the example for innovation. His tour was successful, but not so successful as to arouse the full praise of his headquarters and service company. In fact it confirmed to them in their suspicions that he had a hesitant soul. He was a bold creative thinker; no warrior spirit, or anything like that: they were quite intent to give an advanced degree to a man who would never thrust a Mameluke Sword into the heart of another man. I know several who shake their heads with bitterness now when they reflect on the mistake they made, especially when considering the unconventional warfare seen by the Marine Corps in Afghanistan.

But they say that he was upset they are wrong. Jim has never complained about the decision which in his youth was the most important of his life.

"I know I'm not a Dan Daly or a Chesty Puller," he will tell you. "When I compare myself with the most decorated Marines I simply shake my head. I was inspired to join the Marine Corps while watching the invasion of Kuwait on cable television, but the Gulf War ended before I finished my training. All I want people to say is that I served my country well. I made my father proud. I always spoke up to my superiors when I thought things could be improved. I think I have good ideas and I can solve problems that plague our ability to fight effectively, after all, my paper made proof against the unwillingness of many colonels: *A New Theory for Advancing Ship-to-Shore Objective Maneuver* was well received by the Defense Science Board, the Joint Chiefs of Staff, and at least five independent studies, and for the contribution I was promoted to captain."

And what, after all, could it have been other than disaffection that made him resign early, though at his farewell party he thanked everyone for their support, and asked them for forgiveness. Well, so it goes with organizations steeped in tradition: while his superiors considered him brave and brilliant, they also described him as "unreliable." Jim, the center of attention at the time of his second publication, had to put up with a hostile work environment; he did, however, like most people, take the beatings and insults, hope for the best and wait for the oppressors who did not like his work to move on or get promoted. He thinks about writing a letter to the commandant, telling him that he is being unfairly disabused and sorry for making such a commotion, but the words he puts down on paper do not ring true and, after a few days thinking about it, decided that it was not worth the fight and soon he became self-critical, and immensely sentimental about the institution that he loved. No one is more anxious to reexamine himself than Jim, and he hopes he is still capable of always being faithful. He does not want to be a disagreeable person, but the innovator in him has a way of always shining through whether it is on a Monday morning or a Saturday afternoon. No one can solve problems better than Jim, and generally by the time the artifact has faded under the indistinct glow of the next full moon, he has forgotten it and moved on with his life. It is only poetic justice that when Jim's next big idea is brought to light the naysayers see in the new work nothing at all that advances the needs of their own cause.

One of the difficulties that a man has to deal with as he goes through life is what to do about the people and organizations with whom he has once been associated and whose deep appreciation has in due course waned. If both parties remain connected in a shared state the relationship stays naturally whole, and in this sense it survives, but if one of them is denied or subsequently rises above the others the relationship becomes strained. Before leaving he makes new contacts and becomes critical of the group, but the elders conserve order; he hears a thousand voices in his head, only one tells him to go forth. Unless he is lacking clarity or courage, he will smile vaguely and with a simple shrug say to them: "I have no self-doubts, no issues to complain about, no misgivings about moving on now. I do not need you anymore."

That of course is what Jim would like to have said if he had no abiding sentiments. He reluctantly accepts invitations to hang out with his brothers at reunions. The meal at which they typically help themselves comes from the galley and is eaten from a number of dishes while standing up; and the beverages . . . . Why do Marines say that simplicity is the final achievement? Have you never traveled to Italy and slept in tents at the end of a runway on a busy airfield? Never mind paying heed to people of quality who know everything without doing or experiencing anything. Of course it is fantastic to enjoy the bravado of the good old days that consisted of sharing precooked rations beneath the thunder of strike aircraft, but it is a little disconcerting when everyone realizes how close the past is to the room they are presently standing in. Jim would feel badly when a comrade tells him that he just made lieutenant colonel and that he earned a Silver Star not for his meritorious service during the preparations for the Iraq War, but for saving the lives of six fellow Marines during the actual military campaign; he doesn't tell him that he wished he had stayed in, and when he compares his life with some of the others, it really does seem a bit sad to him. (Here he takes a shot of whiskey.) He is somewhat embarrassed by his academic achievements and he walks away.

When I encountered him at the annual Christmas party, a black-tie affair, I exaggerated the failures I had in order that he realize that life has its difficulties regardless of the path taken. In the same way when he referred to his research at Cornell University in the most depreciated manner, he was a bit taken aback to find that I had a similar opinion of his ostentatiously enlightened profession. With a wry smile, he spoke of the hypocrisy of the academic world so that he may comfort himself by thinking that my military career possessed as many departures. This was a passive-aggressive defense mechanism rather than a form of sarcasm aimed at the Marine Corps. He was always a hard guy to read.

"So I hear you published an article," he said, "but I couldn't find it on the Internet. A scholarly Greek cultural piece, right?"

I gave him the title of the article.

"I'm rather impressed by your specialization. I didn't think the Marine Corps promoted that kind of intellectual activity. Of course, you employed your military intelligence know-how alongside a dozen or so art-history types."

Automatically, having suffered hypercritical reactions before, I responded at once by explaining that I was out of the Marine Corps and that it was part of a graduate school program, but did not admit that I had taken any archeology classes before getting out: at the same time I acknowledged the crudeness and incompleteness of the findings from the unexpected treasure-trove, my first discovery, putting forward that every page was written from inexperience.

"My God, do you really think it's Alexander the Great?"

"No, the style of portraiture lasted for two centuries during the Hellenistic period. There is nothing at all to suggest that it came from before his death in 323 B.C."

"Perhaps there's some peculiar fact that has been lost in Ancient Greece," he said casually, and I felt that my life had been a long devolution from that one happy moment when we first met at the Basic School at Quantico: "Regardless, although somewhat unconventional, I always thought you were a brilliant shot on the rifle range."

The green-eyed monster seized me and I confessed that I had been preparing myself for a second career. He must have known that my career inevitably wound up at the illegitimate rank of major after a final stint with USAID and offers me advice. I took a quick look at the clock on the back wall and wondered whether my old friend would think I was a wimp if I left the party as early as ten o'clock. I spoke briefly about my work for *The Imperium* magazine and my marriage to a woman from Baltimore I had met at Johns Hopkins so that it should not look like I was wasting away, but he followed me to the door and he said:

"You're a good man, Riley, and I'm sure you made the right decision by retiring—free-lancing is all right. One of these days you'll have to introduce me to the new Mrs. Cooper. I'll walk outside with you."

I took a deep breath of the cold winter air and we shared a final farewell. James Isner suffered from none of the same anxieties. It might sound reasonable to say this considering he had maximized his own situation and had gotten all he could get of people before he moved on; but he did in fact suffer some of the same anxieties, and it would only take so subtle a turn of thinking, a serious lecture or an entertaining conversation, that provoked and brought out this reality. I think it was this kind of negative stimulus, which he described to me as the primary reason why people are motivated by selfishness and the desire to maximize their own lives, as compared to altruism and the desire to do a good job and make the group stronger. Most of us when we struggle to find meaning we have no real depth, but Jim's large brain, always in high gear, never permitted him such idleness—and his suspicions, always in the right place, never denied him such importance.

"Goddamn Johnson," he would say. "He's an egotist, but I love the bastard. I wish I could help him. No, you can't teach an old dog new tricks. It's no good trying to change him. He makes no sense to me now. The fact is, individuals get killed in battle, and he's a freak of nature."

But if he bumped into Johnson at some gathering like the evening parade at the Marine Barracks no one could be more friendly. He slapped him on the shoulder and told him how happy he was to see him. He smiled expansively. His face beamed his acceptance of this particular comrade in arms. Johnson rejoiced in the glow of the wonderful fellowship and it was damned kind of Jim to say he'd do anything for him now that they were both on to bigger and better things for the country. Conversely, if he thought Johnson cold-shouldered him, he would feel a sharp pain in his chest; but Johnson had survived an unusual battle, and Johnson was always motivated by his own needs, wants, and desires but certainly not because the heavenly spirit wasn't acting through him. "Baloney," Johnson would contend, "Jim never fought in a real war." I listened to each side, and found both quite amusing. Johnson had told me that in the old days he had been glad to share a few beers with him at a strip club and spend their thirty days of leave each year sport fishing in the South Pacific. Johnson said that Jim turned into a left-winger. He said he was a communist. He said he was a jerk.

Johnson was wrong here. The most incredible characteristic of James Isner was his magnanimity. No one can be a jerk by being instinctively generous in behavior and temperament. Altruism is the most difficult and paradoxical virtue that is seen by many as the mark of a Marine, as what distinguishes humanity from mere beasts; it needs an enduring culture and morality. It cannot, like pillage or plunder, be practiced at rare moments; it must reign supreme. It also needs a fair reward; although Jim has a good sense of humor, I always thought he took himself too seriously, and I am quite certain that he might have underestimated this key element of human nature. Though I have finished few of his papers, I have read the abstracts of a good many, and to my mind his pugnacity is concealed within every one of their respectable pages. This is clearly the reason for his recent popularity.

Jim has always seriously believed that people think of themselves as worthy of getting into heaven—even if they have no concept of hell—so the idea of selflessness is attractive to him since it implies that a person is performing good deeds on earth. When he published his first paper about behavioral experiments he genuinely believed that economic incentives were counterproductive and immoral, and had a keen way of undermining the moral values that lead people to act altruistically; when later he wrote of material rewards he genuinely believed that substantial parts of most societies willingly adhere to moral rules of their country. He has always been a foe of capitalism, a friend of science, and a rival of religion.

When Jim asked the foe to lunch it was because he was genuinely interested in his thoughts about the invisible hand of free markets, and when he asked the friend of his opinion it was because he was genuinely concerned about artificial praise. When unknown clergymen from the Catholic or Protestant Church came to campus it was not only a necessary preliminary to a discussion that he took them to dinner, it was because he was genuinely interested to understand their objections to his body of research. You had only to hear him talk to an audience to be convinced of his earnestness. When he delivered a public lecture, or sat on a conference panel, maybe informal but equally prepared to defend his position, and faced his audience gravely, solemnly, but with circumspection and self-restraint, you could not but wonder if he was really that committed to the task at hand. Though now and then he was marked by temptations of turbulent passion, it was only to make the argument more interesting when he made his points. His presence was dignified and his voice was purposeful. He was a serious student of economics. He was hardly dull. He was not a quiet, sober man busied in charts, exacting details, and he was fond of delivering exciting talks to students outside the department.

13

Perhaps he knew too much, for when you heard his thought process you felt that you really knew why he attracted the best talent and it was quite natural that his classes were always filled to capacity.

I suppose that is why when Jim spoke before anthropologists or biologists in a group discussion not a single professor he had addressed ever promoted his own books, but there was much interest in his own. His collaborations were numerous. Not only did he develop a good many PhD candidates, but he frequently collaborated with his former students around the world. No school was too small, no research project too abstract, that Jim failed to give it financial support. At times he modified his grants and included them on the team. Most of the schools who collaborated with him have at least passing interest in history, philosophy, and the classics; and few can deny that they maintain a real love for experiencing firsthand the pain and discomfort of field work, especially dredging or digging expeditions.

But this by no means defined his extraordinary management process. He was known to constantly cite how many post-doctorates were working with him and the number of papers published under his leadership, but silently dismissed the notion of any kind of metrics. He was an active member of the organizations that were founded to further the interests of his group of researchers or to relieve failure when missteps or unseen problems brought them to despair. Actually, he was always willing to give help when matters of risk rather than reward was the point of difference and he was never conditioned to believe great ideas must emerge from a single investigator coming up with a discovery on his own. Instead, he could count on it emerging just as easily from a group of intelligent people working hard. He firmly believed that there were only three elements necessary for great discoveries—talented people, excellent facilities, and a manager who actively permitted serendipity and obsessiveness.

He never refused to support his people. He rightly said that no one knew better than he the hard knocks of the business and he could help a struggling researcher turn it around by inspiring him with hope, courage, and confidence. He generally invited the struggling investigator to a conference and seldom failed to get him back to being really focused, that extra edge that he had before. The only stipulation he made was that he should review the findings before the work was published. He was never concerned about aligning recognition with discovery, and welcomed late-night discussions on the telephone, for the history of great discovery was full of ideas that materialize at the most unusual times, and most often at the same time, whether they came from God-fearing individuals or self-described atheists. He figured in many branches of economics, bringing in scientists from many different disciplines, and it was well-known that he was stubborn about his way forward; but no one was more aware of this than his post-doctorate students and colleagues who were persistently unable to come to terms with the fact that their romantic notion of genius might be wrong.

His views on marriage were just as stubborn, for he believed that nothing is better than a celibate life. He had successfully evaded the tradition that many people have found difficult to transgress—an accomplishment I am deeply affected as a result of my unfailing forbearance, especially when provoked by the evangelical ardor of my father. When Jim was in the Marine Corps it was widely known that he had for some years held dear an overseas assignment that brought him close to a married woman of the same rank, and though it was understood that she treated him with winning approval, he never made a bid even after her divorce. This first assignment to Japan reflected his unwonted feelings the strain to which he had been put by the deployment. Later, when he was sent on an extended forward deployment, the strength of spirit he had maintained then enabled him without offense to elude the temptation of prostitutes, who were hoping to exchange an impoverished existence on the street for the security of marriage to a first lieutenant. When he saw in the expectant eyes of one beautiful girl the responsibilities of her large family he told his buddies that a high school sweetheart would always be waiting for him in Alabama and thus prevent him from forming any permanent tie. His behavior weakened his ability to lead men into battle, but he remained no less committed to them.

Later while seeking an advanced degree he sighed a little when he reflected that he may have missed another opportunity of domesticity and the satisfaction of being a father, a good Catholic, but it was a departure that he was ready to make at that point in his life, to fulfill his imagination and dreams. In any event he had noticed that people really do not want to be bothered with the wives of noble laureates. The genius who insisted on marriage whatever the cost only made himself a problem and indeed was in consequence often not able to do the things he would have liked to achieve; and if he had a family at home, he was on his return exposed to responsibilities that shattered the momentum so essential for him to extract the best that was in him. James Isner was a bachelor and now still chasing that dream at forty-one was likely to remain one.

He was a rebel of sorts, and represented what prevailed in America, by good conscience and hard work, which was firmly established in his core values and beliefs. He seemed to have good intentions and was rarely led astray by distractions. He was always going to be a distinguished Marine in my mind and none but a yellow-bellied West Point man could honestly discount his contribution. I felt that to break that special trust—always faithful to the country, the Marine Corps, and each other—would be a disgrace. I sent an instant message to him, spoke to the ghosts of my wife and daughter about James Isner being in town, fed my impatient dog his dinner, and went upstairs to clean up and wait for his reply.

# TWO

**W**HEN AFTER I checked on Riley Junior, and sent him outside to the blind alley to do his thing, a message was waiting for me on my mobile phone, in response to my invitation, that Jim would meet me at eight o'clock sharp in front of the Fish Market restaurant, only two blocks away for me; so a quarter before I went up to the third floor to see if Joan Moaney was still there, which I was pretty sure that she would be working on her book. I thought about casually mentioning to her that it was time to pay the rent on the apartment, but she seemed to be deep in thought, so I let it go and promptly left. Then I walked down King Street, looking frequently into the brightly lighted storefronts, and since I had a few minutes to spare I went into the Torpedo Factory to see if Linda Gogio was in her studio.

Art Night had already begun and a group of well-matched, garish women was crowding around the studios near the entranceway, while a young volunteer, following their movements with speculative eyes, tried to arouse them with a spirited conversation about the vibrant art community: "Eighty studios, six galleries, and two hundred artists . . . ladies please stay." It was a fine evening, mild for late November, and the gentle wind swirling over the Potomac River was comfortable. It made good the decision to go out. I found Linda's studio locked up for the night, so I left. The people on the street moved with a kind of easy unconcern as though the present moment had become a special occasion and since tomorrow was Friday they had an unexpected propensity to slow down and enjoy themselves.

The Fish Market was crowded. In the front room were at least a dozen tourists standing around a stocky doorman and a receptionist; and I had a sudden and agonizing feeling that I should have called ahead or come earlier to reserve a table. The doorman, when I mumbled a few words to myself, put a hand on my shoulder and led me to the receptionist and then into an open area at the bright metallic counter with a vest-clad bartender ready to take my order. A moment later Jim came through the door and I greeted him heartily.

"Let's wait at the bar," I said.

I was glad in thinking that I should make time for an old buddy and I complimented my instinctive judgment. I led him proudly back to the impressive bar of nautical ornamentation, and we passed a good-looking woman on the way; we hesitated before taking a seat and were told by a customer nearby that the two stools were available. It was a room of some size, very loud and active, with a large bay window. We sat down and glanced at the menu and the bartender quickly dropped napkins on the counter before us. As Jim's eyes looked up from the counter and followed one of the napkins to the floor I thought of my regular hangout where there was Irish music, neighbors to talk to and both Harp and Guinness served in a more intimate setting.

"I can recommend the clam chowder," I said.

"Sounds good."

"I'll take a bowl myself," I told the bartender in a cordial and yet casual manner, and then glancing once more at Jim, offered: "And let's not forget to order something to wash it down."

"Now you're talking."

His state seemed to ease a bit.

"Two 32-ounce schooners and why don't you choose the beer yourself. I see that you've gotten new offerings at the tap. Whatever you think a couple of erstwhile, honest-to-God Marines would enjoy."

"What do you say to Budweiser or Bud Light? We rather prefer our domestic here."

When I had agreed to the former and Jim to the latter, he inquired about our standing bid for a table. I waited for Jim to speak up on the subject and yet remained perfectly polite, where he simply turned the bartender's regard back to me. I felt that he was a well-behaved professor perfectly adapted to his environment. The receptionist at the door, a young woman of college age, with a tattooed banana tree on her exposed forearm, hurried over with two seating options for us. The bartender frowned at her with his brusque seniority.

"Erika, why don't you give them a few minutes."

"Very good, sir."

"I think we would like to take a table now," I broke in. "The upstairs room is fine. We shouldn't waste an opportunity on a night like this."

"Yes, of course, sir. I will get your drinks."

"We appreciate it," I continued. "Miss, if you will take my friend here with you to the table, I will wait for the beer to be served."

"Yes, sir."

"And young man, not too much foam, you know, but just right. I want my good friend from Alabama to see that we know what's what here."

Jim smiled and his eyes sought mine: aggressiveness balanced by a little humor was right smart I thought.

When the receptionist led Dr. Isner away, I shouted, "He thinks I'm a good shot, but you should see him—his momma taught him; and she can still beat him in tobacky spittin' contests." Jim turned back briefly and smiled and when he disappeared: "Sorry, I couldn't resist pulling his crank. It's been several years since I did. I'll pay you now."

"You must be military chums," he answered.

This drew my attention to a most invidious realization that my life's journey now constituted the same narrative as Jim's, only less considering each circumstance in turn.

"Oh, he's all right," I said. He smiled. "God bless America. Sorry, I must stop making excuses for myself."

And I knew that James Isner was coming down on the right side of history, at least for the time being, as he is on the front lines of the so-called American Period that has shown to be at odds with itself. But on that point I felt I was quite removed in accepting so abstract an incrimination even though my life still suggested more in the extreme. He looked very good for his age. His curly hair was still golden brown but no longer cut short, which suited him and made his avid face look more boyish. Woody Guthrie came to mind. (I had recently read a biography.) He was not so thin as in his youth and I was surprised that when we greeted his grip nearly crushed my hand. This slight change only added to his potency. It shaped my point of view and because he framed his thoughts more easily than he had before I had a comfortable feeling about him; he filled the table with so much candor and honesty that I had almost the impression that his life was perhaps of unstained virtuousness.

I do not recall whether or not I was being fair to him by my thoughts and recollections, but he was inconsistent sometimes and he talked more than I that I had the feeling that what he spoke of was merely a ploy to lay the foundation. He was well informed about current events and international affairs and he could speak on the topics circulating the Beltway that prevented me from having to explain any nuances of the issues. Many academicians from their specialized interests have the regrettable habit of choosing only those topics they tend to on a daily basis. They form their conversations involuntarily and delve into topics that neither interest nor involve the guests. It makes the intercourse with them somewhat formidable to persons without the proper level of education whose range is limited by their simple needs, and this results in a separation especially in the upper parts of society. Jim was very sensitive to this secondary and usually adverse effect. He would never speak in terms that were utterly accessible only to research types or with a wild fluency in the tongues of strange and perhaps crazy scientists. I was quickly reminded with pleasure and relief that he was just an average guy. No remark pleased him more.

Jim did not have a tendency to use quotes, adages, references of historical import, and figurative language to drive home his points. Unlike his colleagues, who are the most enlightened people in the world, he avoided the necessity of shaping his arguments around great thoughts, from Abelard to Zola, from Ancient Egypt to contemporary America. He was not a devout pragmatist, whose function of thought guides his action. He maintained certain principles and even though he sought clean solutions, he was able to strike a balance between his ideals and practical consequences of his beliefs. His ideas were certainly shaped by history and his deep understanding of our confounding world; they were based upon his own critical thinking, but with an expressive style, and he used his own analysis each time with a sort of instant gratification, as though his prolific brain had just stumbled upon it.

Presently the conversation was of casual things, of our common friends in the Marine Corps, of the upcoming college basketball season. He said Cornell had a pretty good team. He left untouched personal matters. I let him talk and he soon became full of life. He was always cordial, allowing other people to express themselves, and tonight was no exception. He let me expound upon many of his finer points. He stated with frankness that we should try to become closer now that I was out of the military and told me that we should get together more often because of how much he enjoyed my company and what a high opinion he had of my work for *The Imperium* magazine. I felt the same way and tried to meet him halfway. He lived in Ithaca, New York, and traveled infrequently to Washington, D.C., so this friendliness was merely a token anyway. He asked me about the fair city I was living, I asked him about the fair city he was living. He put forward that he actually preferred the North to the South now. We ate the clam chowder and fish platters and meanwhile Jim told me how to properly fillet a fish. We drank the schooners and complimented the waitress for the excellent service.

All throughout I wondered why he had called upon me with such urgency earlier in the day.

After we relaxed, and I started to bring myself to believe that at the height of his career James Isner was growing a bit sentimental and merely wished to reestablish ties with an old friend who was a potential advocate in some obscure circle that mattered to him in order to relieve the complex and intricate situation in which he presently found himself. Regardless, it was well established that our vocations vaguely shared common areas of interest. Had I known that he was in need I should have expected that he would have already brought me into the fold. It began to look as though dinner would end without my finding the quality that rendered my friendship valuable to him.

Perhaps there was no pressing urgency. I knew he was careful, and thought that this meeting, the first after so long a separation, would be used to test the relationship. He was after all mixed up in politics. Much older and wiser now, and trust a plant of slow growth, he was perhaps conflicted by the need to look upon the pleasant, satisfactory meal as compensatory spending.

"Shall we go and have a drink at another place?" I bid.

"I have this one covered."

"I appreciate it."

Subsequently, he followed me downstairs through a rickety stairwell and onto the street, with fewer people around than before; there was a new crowd eager for nighttime entertainment. Three young men and a woman on the sidewalk were laughing hysterically. I gave them a hostile stare, and this precipitated an opportunity for Jim to engage the local population.

"How's it going, guys," he cried, joining them.

I turned away, looking across the street at the people in front of Daniel O'Connell's, and wished I knew at least one of those strangers entering the pub, for it would lessen the burden on this particular social occasion. I was ashamed that I did not call on a few local writers, and was afraid to ask Jim what he had in mind lest he should look down upon me for not taking charge, but was confident enough to rely on the randomness of the night by running into a few mortal souls I knew.

Jim called me back by telling me that he would like to go to the Union Street Public House. The pub is unabashedly fashionable. We stood side by side at the bar surrounded by young people and sipped whiskey.

"You know, Riley, I drank with Captain Theodore Hume here exactly one year before he had a heart attack and dropped dead," Jim casually remarked about the graybeard. "He bought a round of Amrut Fusion from Bangalore and I was immediately hooked on it. I enjoyed a nice dinner with his wife last week."

"Wanda Hume?" I said taken aback for a moment.

"So you know her."

"I suppose," I said with a shrug. "My dad and I saw them when I was home for Christmas about three years ago. He had just retired from the Navy."

"She's younger than I realized, about our age. I dare say she's quite attractive."

"Well, maybe it's time you settled down."

"The idea entered my mind. Of course she had other things on *her* mind. Old Blue Eyes is still very much a part of her life and she is harassed by the media who want information about him. He's been gone over a year already but his popularity seems not to diminish. It is touching if you come to think about it that she should still live in the same house and love him as if he were alive. She told me he was in excellent shape and in possession of all his faculties"—he added with a smile and a wink—"right up to the moment he kicked the bucket."

"I heard he exercised on a daily basis."

"You saw quite a lot of Hume at the time he was first stationed at Dam Neck, didn't you?"

"Well, he and three other guys rented the house across the street. We became acquainted with him. My father complained a great deal but eventually warmed up to him. You see, he went to our church."

"I understand he liked your little community so much he bought a house there, so you must know a great deal about him that other people don't."

"Well, not really. My parents keep me posted. Oh, he has two boys, but because of the difference in age, our families didn't interact much. Wanda is the parish secretary. My mother thinks she's becoming awfully lonely."

There was a slight pause while we sipped our whiskey and looked at the crowd.

"Hume is an interesting figure," Jim said. "At the time of his death, he was the most decorated soldier since the second World War. He enlisted at seventeen and, during a career spanning thirty-two years, was awarded countless medals, including the Medal of Honor twice. Notably, he is the only person to be awarded a Medal of Honor in each of the Iraq wars. He published a memoir a couple of years ago, as you know, but with all this new information coming out now it makes one wonder."

"What are you talking about?"

"Wanda thinks someone has gotten their hands on an unpublished manuscript of his."

"No kidding."

"She's beside herself."

"I bet the Navy is concerned," I pondered aloud. "No, he was a good man who many identify as born of war, freedom, and a philosophy that represents American ideals."

"He was no saint."

I looked at him with narrow eyes and his face twisted with disapproval, and I laughed at the suggestion that Hume was a scoundrel. "Say don't you remember that class we took together at Quantico? You know, where the instructor told us how *not* to disrespect the memories of fallen heroes."

"Well, I doubt there's anything damning in it, but I must confess I think she is getting a bit paranoid."

"I don't know anything about it."

"Anyhow, I don't mind telling you that there are already people writing biographies, but none of them will get the facts right, and every time I read *Gallantry in Action* I think of you."

"I don't know why you would think that."

"Well, the change of opinion is fascinating. I've read several articles about him recently. There is also a couple of excellent blogs covering the story. Have you been following Andrew Hamilton?"

"No, I live in an entirely different world now. I remember reading Hume's obituary."

Jim grinned loosely, but did not respond, but then said, "Riley, I read about the exhibit you are working on at the National Gallery of Art, and think it's somewhat radical, perhaps even judgmental. Doesn't it make you slightly uneasy to maintain that hard shell with me?"

"How so?"

"You're a pundit, right."

"I prefer critic."

"Very well, a critic is a learned person who examines all of the facts before stating his opinion, even now with the changing role of journalism."

"Well," I considered. "You're right in presuming that I get paid for my supposed learned opinions. I've been trying to maintain classical standards according to those set down by my profession, which for the last five years has been working rather well. My duty is to uphold these standards against the triviality of fashion while conveying an ideal of enlightenment to my readers and the community at large. My role is hardly radical but not the work of a blogger either whose task each day is to dilute the authority of journalists in the traditional media."

"Oh, yes, I underestimated you. I've long debated this topic with my students."

"I seriously doubt you're being overrun by contempt."

"One has to listen to the world."

"Sure, but I like to compare myself to John Ruskin who was a writer and critic that redefined British art in modern times. What you get from a Ruskin review in the *London Times*, or any magazine who ran his articles, is not opinion but perspective. He defended Turner who was frowned upon; his treatise produced the principles that art is based upon national and individual integrity and that art is a universal language. Have you ever seen *Ulysses Deriding Polyphemus—Homer's Odyssey*? It is considered the central picture of the British golden age. I think Ruskin's contribution was immense—art reviews became not so much consumer guidance, which tend to be mostly gimmicks, but an assessment of new talent and recent developments for the people who are impassioned by art."

"You don't see it, and the public senses it, to maintain control in this post-web world one has to change. I think you're talking about an era that is long gone."

"Not really."

"All I'm saying is that in a world without borders where anyone can tweet an uninformed response to something, reasoned criticism is under threat and undervalued. The arts like military history are surely taking a hit with newspapers in retreat. Readers, I for one, can no longer look at one source for the complete message. Hume's case is no exception. I've conditioned myself to search for ideas sparking off the beaten track—please forgive me for the old-fashioned figure of speech."

"Point taken."

"Who can really tell what kind of man Hume was?"

"Well, you think you can," I replied acidly.

Jim was not discouraged. I knew I was challenging him and it gave me a good feeling.

"Like you, I think the fundamental principles I finally settled upon when I was a young man were right," he said. "But society needs neither drill sergeants to drum knowledge into stubborn skulls nor gatekeepers to protect itself from the hoi polloi. I think you will appreciate this and that is beginning with Herodotus and Thucydides, writers raised history to one of the supreme arts, because they maintained that history must not only be written as truthfully as possible, but must be also well written. Yet despite their differences, historians are all alike in that they have a strong conviction that history provides lessons which can guide future conduct. More important, they believe historical judgment must be essentially moral. For instance, I found the founding fathers were great men even though I was ashamed that I learned Thomas Jefferson and George Washington lived differently than by the rules established in the Constitution. Also, can anyone deny the Declaration of Independence or Bill of Rights? Of course not. I also think Cornwallis was magnificent. As a young student I was told he was inferior, because he was British and very much unaware of the encroaching French fleet and General Washington's advance on Yorktown with French troops. Cornwallis was certainly not a bad general, just unlucky. There was no such thing as a communications satellite back then. A good many people think now he was one of the best in history. Because my high school teachers told me that to admire George Washington was to prove myself a learned and patriotic young man, I admired our first president, but my God, we were damned lucky!"

"Interesting point. I reckon people should care about the closing military operation of the American Revolution. Many people discuss who the greatest generals were throughout history of mankind, but only a few deserve being mentioned for their skill and knowledge."

"You don't know how insecure of immortality Cornwallis looked when he returned to Britain."

"Winning makes all the difference."

"So does the end justify the means?" Jim asked. "I suppose you think Washington is right up there with Genghis Khan and Attila the Hun."

"Yes and no. Washington was honorable, but I didn't think half as much of Grant as I do now, and I think a great deal more of Robert E. Lee. I still can't reconcile the performances of men such as Hood and Bragg; and now think they were on the wrong side of American history."

"I drove by the statue of Lee today, but what did you think much of in the Civil War that you think much of still?"

"Well, Sherman was very good and McClellan and Burnside were terrible," I considered aloud. "But, yes, Grant is still right up there with Washington and Lincoln among our country's greatest leaders and heroes."

"If you don't mind my saying so, I don't think that is particularly original."

"I don't mind your saying so at all. It is what I had been taught in school."

"Taught! Don't you mean think? I was taught Forrest was one of the best American generals."

"Well, I was taught Abraham Lincoln was not the Great Emancipator; he was Dishonest Abe, a president hellbent on creating a big central government, even if that meant waging war. I think it's all rubbish—what do you think?"

"I told you that I'm beginning to think the country is growing impatient, more restive."

"You asked me why I believed in my own judgment, and I was trying to explain to you that, whatever I said out of learning and in deference to the American dream, I didn't really admire certain generals who had lost battles and the final outcome of the Civil War seems to show that I was right. All of these men were indispensable generals who had deep-seated principles. Grant's weaknesses and various political influences combined to diminish his standing in the first part of the twentieth century, but what I honestly and instinctively liked then has stood the test of time with me and by and large with critical opinion."

"You can't be serious. Society biases us against critical opinion. Quite honestly, I find the status quo unhealthy. What you get as a result is little or no movement and petty partisanship, which, as we have discovered, very easily turns into offensive behavior. You are perhaps becoming a different kind of conservative."

"No, you are."

"I really think that if we isolate or blackball everyone with strange ideas, the United States would be a thinly inhabited country."

"The poor would still sneak across the border."

"Ha, where's your compassion. I still think *The Great Escape* is the greatest war movie ever."

"*Letters from Iwo Jima*," I countered. "Clint Eastwood was excellent, and the battle is shown from the viewpoint of the Japanese defenders, but I think *Patton* is right up there."

"General Patton was a loud, irascible man whose hatred of the enemy is overshadowed only by his own ambition."

"I bet you're still a fan of Forrest Gump."

Jim smiled and turned his regard to the bartender. He then looked in the bottom of his glass, but whether to see if there was any more whiskey in it or to find something new to say in defense of his position, I did not care. I spotted a couple of young women that lived nearby in the townhouse right next to the Carlyle House. Then I stole a glance at my watch, and in so doing considered that I had been a good friend and companion throughout the evening and it was time to say goodnight. Perhaps I had been mistaken and Jim had called upon me only that we might catch up and idly chat of the best or worst generals and top military movies of all time. The course of the evening provided him a trace of a smile. I looked at him with wonder. If a little amusement was his only aim it must be that he was feeling a little down or discouraged. If he was feeling better it could only be that for the moment at least I satisfied a need for him. But he caught me looking at my watch.

"Here try this"—handing me a wee dram—"Ardbeg Ten Years Old is a traditional Scotch single malt whiskey. You'll like this one better—it's complex and peaty, but more evenly balanced."

"I suppose another round can't hurt."

"It's early."

"Not bad," I said, upon taking a sip, "but unlike you I still prefer American bourbon. Recently I started drinking Irish whiskey for the full, sweet taste."

"You can buy the next round."

"We'll see about that—"

"You know, Riley, I don't know how you can deny that there must be something in a man who's able to be a hero of the men who served under him, winning battle after battle, and who's able to hold the ever-changing public opinion. After all, the occupation of Iraq was very unpopular and nobody refutes the two charges most often levied against him: that he was a salesman for his elite unit rather than a general officer, and that he stood by while Iraqi blood flowed down the streets. Of course, I'm here to tell you that a lot of his memoir seems a bit quaint. He flourished in a bad decade and his flaws outnumbered his virtues, especially when he drank, which was often. He was a difficult man, proud and tough, as well as arrogant and capricious."

"His men were the only thing he cared about," I added.

"I suppose that was part of Hume's genius."

"Yes," I said.

"I wish you had been here when we toasted him on his fiftieth birthday. It was really something else."

"How did you get invited again?"

"Accidentally. Well, it wasn't only military, you see, it was a thoroughly diverse gathering—business, academia, politics, religion, international; I think you'd have to really go a long way to find gathered together such a collection of nice people as received invitations from Wanda Hume. It was awfully moving when Bishop Murphy offered a prayer at the table. He chose a passage from the first book of Samuel, where David defeats Goliath with a sling and a stone. I don't mind telling you that there were a few tears shed by his men that night."

"I hope Hume didn't cry, too."

"Almost, but no. He was himself, rather quiet with Wanda present, you know, and well-behaved and grateful, of course. Wanda made sure the big, gruff football star didn't get started at the dinner table but when we went to the bar she left, and his energy was contagious. I slipped away while he was swapping stories with the remaining few. He was holding his unlit cigar and having a ball. Before I left I asked him what was the significance of the prayer. He wouldn't tell me, he just smiled a little. He asked me if I was a former Navy SEAL, and I said, 'No, I'm a veteran of the Marine Corps,' which seemed to please him a little. Then I asked him if he was surprised by the occasion. 'Yes, indeed,' he said, 'very surprised and appreciative.' The fact is, I suppose, he was still upset by having his nomination for rear admiral rejected in the wake of that Congressional inquiry. He loved soldiers and soldiering—he used the term frogmen when he told stories; Wanda was in her glory and wanted everybody to see him when he was at his best, but of course she left early when he grew impatient with her. I wished him well in his retirement and then shook hands with him."

I looked at the door.

"I'll be driving down to Virginia Beach on Saturday to have lunch with Wanda. Do you want to tag along?"

"I don't want to intrude," I said.

"We can visit your family."

"I was just there at Thanksgiving."

"Suit yourself."

"Well, I really should be going. It was great seeing you again."

"I shouldn't have anymore to drink myself. I have to give a talk tomorrow at Georgetown. You might be interested in the subject. I'll get you into the conference if you like."

"Oh, no thanks. I have a deadline tomorrow."

We walked out onto the street and I took a deep breath of the cool air. It then occurred to me that I missed the chance to mention the subject of my current assignment. I had thought that if I spoke about Schliemann's nineteenth century search for the Trojan War, or more generally about the quest of historians and archaeologists and even doubters to get at the truth of wars during the Heroic Age, I might set off an intellectual trigger in his brain. When we turned the corner and I started up King Street, he said: "I'll walk up with you instead of waiting for the trolley." We marched up the street and after a pause where I tried to muster an opening statement, he asked me:

"So whatever happened to his first wife?"

"Whose?"

"Hume's."

"Oh, I don't know," I said.

"A thought just occurred to me. People still seem to look at marriage as a social obligation. It is not an obligation. It's a sacrament. If you are religious it should be an ideal."

"You think the institution is very bad?"

"Yes, it's pure sacrifice!"

"Are you starting to question your faith?"

"Why do you say that? To obey is better than sacrifice, right. You know, I have a feeling he was extremely unfaithful to her."

"Perhaps."

"You think he always loved her?"

"Oh, I don't know, but what's your point?"

"Do you know why the devil she left him?"

"I recall he had enough and left her."

Jim gave a short laugh.

He did not pursue this last point. We had reached Market Square, and turning to look at the lighted fountain I extended my hand to him. He was looking for the trolley, and it was a clumsy farewell. I knew that this was intended to be an exploratory meeting. I was not concerned if I had disappointed him. What he wanted of me was still unclear, but for whatever reason the thought that there was a secret manuscript began to slowly grow on me, and as I walked across the street and into an inner courtyard until reaching Pat Troy's I wondered if I had been too disagreeable for fraternal sympathies.

The evening left me in neither a completely discordant nor antagonistic mood but it was quite evident that he had created for me a role to play. He was a committed person who pursued tirelessly his most important objectives.

I entered the pub for a nightcap. After the indulgent hullabaloo of discourse it had a pleasant silence and luminosity; it was an idyllic Irish setting. Most of the patrons at this hour were people I recognized, but on this night I did not look to start up a conversation; nevertheless all of them smiled at me as if telling me to take the easy road where the green grass grows in a field by the river, and so I sat down to wait for the venerable Mr. Matz to pour my usual pint of Guinness. With shy discretion two or three nearby watched with appreciation the steady arm of the professional, so that if you were ignorant you might have thought it was a curious antic or perhaps red-carpet treatment for a regular. I am no longer young and foolish, and now am full of wisdom, but here no one cares about such things, because experience, intimately an expression of one's theory of life and the ideal one cherishes, was everywhere and drowned in darkness now. You had the feeling that the people who frequented this place were no longer full of passionate intensity as on King Street, racing young men who have a strong throb of the artery and ask not about mankind's forgotten wars, but this is no country for old men who are caught in that tender music most young people disregard, disbelieving old wind-broken trees who have witnessed blood-dimmed tides and the occasion of goodness vanquished. You felt that these patrons came here night after night for similar reasons and knew the bartender as well as I do. Our own Mr. Matz had drifted around the country after the Army and worked in some of the worst bars in Washington, D.C., but you would never have figured it had you seen him walking his dog along the streets of Old Town. He was not overweight, red-nosed, and talkative as one expects a bartender to be; he was plain and simple, neat but not fashionable, a man who was an offspring of the greatest generation; he served in Vietnam and had seen all the phases of the moon. He was much like Joan Moaney who in later years became business-like, quiet, bristly skeptical and very patriotic.

The apartment I returned to was on the second floor of an old brick townhouse, a modest residence sandwiched between the Old Town Writer's Flat and a former trial attorney who specialized in tax law. It contained a sufficient living room, two small bedrooms, and an updated bathroom and kitchen. The rooms were painted with an antique white and on the walls were watercolors from Iraq and Afghanistan, disarmingly humanistic perspectives of combat operations and remarkable buildings against deep blue skies; there were hardwood floors covered with colorful Persian carpets, interesting vases and artifacts, and all the furnishings were of natural colors. There was about the apartment a nostalgic atmosphere of my nomadic years, and when I looked out the window I expected to see a long caravan of horses and camels rather than a procession of automobiles and buses. The windows featured wooden shades of a dark brown stain.

# THREE

I HAD SEVERAL THINGS to do when I awoke the next day, but my dinner with Jim and the lingering memories of the past, the feeling that a context attendant upon preceding events was needed to work things out, that my family, I did not know why, had stirred up thoughts even more strongly than usual. I stood looking out the shuttered window at city hall that was decked with Christmas wreaths and I felt that I must travel back until the mind could dissolve everything I could make of this affair. It was as though all the people who had at one time and another influenced my progression to manhood inveighed my thinking to reflect upon the formative years of my life. The bustle of this historic city, which I did not know well before my retirement, or know if even imagined for its own memories, now exposed by the traditions of another holiday season, gave my stimulated mind a sound footing to be curious. The wars I had experienced seemed to have lost their reality and I saw them as though they were taken from Homer's imagination and I a solitary beholder looking back and trying to visualize the last fling of the Heroic Age. But I could linger awhile now and ask a question or two about the authenticity of recent events, and of bona fide battles. My mind was being obscured by neither darkness nor maddened by those drumbeats when the ceaseless cascade of orders seems to rob it of ample time for reflection and judgment, but clear and quiet as when I painted Marines and locals by ruins.

I firmly believe that my life is more real now than it was at twelve years when for all intents or purposes I set out on my journey. Yet I learned in school that empires did rise and fall, that before there was a Roman Empire there was a Mycenaean civilization that collapsed, that the Trojan War really did take place, and that Aeneas did suffer through this bitter war only to have the last laugh as the founder of Rome. When one starts out, one's only hope should be that the roads are full of adventure, full of knowledge. Life like warfare may have seemed worthier then, possessed more solid virtues, and as I was told in school possessed more substantial heroes, but upon revisiting Greek mythology I wonder. The Trojan War cycle, a collection of epic poems and the culmination of Greek mythology, starts with events leading up to the war: Eris and the Apple of Discord, the Judgment of Paris, and his abduction of Helen, the most beautiful of all women and wife of Menelaus. Agamemnon, king and brother of Menelaus, led a united campaign of Greek city-states to Troy and besieged the city for ten years because of Paris' insult. After the death of many heroes, both Greek and Trojan, and the ruse of a Trojan horse, Troy fell. In other words, Helen, the queen of Sparta, was not only beautiful but she made off with her husband's treasure as well as his honor, and the Greeks wanted the gold back. I do not know if that is the fact, but it certainly means nothing has changed. Like today rulers regularly skewed or inflated the case for war, but all of the ancient texts and artifacts conserve this simple truth: wars were sometimes low-intensity, often devious, and always sordid. Homer maintained these truths better than anybody even though Troy fell centuries before his time. Kings of past times were obstinate; they fought too much, many of them drank too much, and wanted too much. Their curses were common curses of Mankind, and their decisions were often afflicted. Yet they were distinctly modern.

I do not speak of the rank and file, young men and women of simple ways, nor of contract mechanics, cooks, teachers, computer technicians, engineers and so on who have become inherently essential to military units, but of the deciders (generals, national politicians, and corporate boards of which I knew nothing about until I grew up), who fear God as simply as they love the smell of death. The ingenuity and heterogeneity of the masses who served the country in Iraq and Afghanistan was almost unthinkable. We carried out the mission and performed well, both winning and losing battles, but the wars were long as the sunny mornings many, so when time was on our side we created diversions. There were no green keepers in Iraq; yet inside the Green Zone a new storage compound contained a nicely kept putting green, which was covered with artificial turf. There was also a well-kept bowling alley attached to the cafeteria at the fortified airport outside Baghdad. Enlisted folk enthusiastically took to the carefully built lanes of polished wood and automatic pin-setting machines; faithfully we watched the spirited contests on our computers via vast networks and streaming video.

You may think that we had it pretty good, and that we pursued entertainment for its own sake. Sure, we indulged ourselves in diversions.

I, for one, liked to listen to songs by Bruce Springsteen and Tom Petty (and was deaf to the world with my earphones on) while some of my comrades escaped reality in video games. One could argue that this only exacerbated the situation; however, it was essential and everybody kept the mission in their minds. It was difficult, and to return was the ultimate goal. In addition, people who were condemned to spend several years of their lives within two hundred yards of one another at remote bases wrangled endlessly and, seeing each other every day and being surrounded by sandbags and concertina wire, found no reason to be friendly or courteous; they became egotistical, bullheaded and disturbed. It was a life that only became worse in Afghanistan as a result of the constancy of focus and the lack of connectedness. We were there to fight, to eat, to sleep, to exercise, and then to fight some more. People were not so much like they were back in the garrison and it seemingly only grew more perverted through the lens of gun oil, intensity and action; and disturbed people are not so easy to get on with. It may be that Marines hold up better than others in this kind of environment, but our tribe accepts one another without the old suspicions and we try to have a little fun. What is more, our manners, though stubborn, are large-hearted. Some would disagree with me on this last point, but I like to think that we are more prepared to compromise, especially when faced with ruin.

I chose this lifestyle after a comfortable existence on the outskirts of Norfolk. My father was a professor at Old Dominion University. My mother was a librarian there. She came from an impoverished but landed family, and the only assets she brought to the marriage was a future share of the proceeds of farmland presently lying fallow (as it was chuck-full of stones but attached to the farm was a modest federal subsidy deemed a divine right by her late father), and seven sister-in-laws. Of these only two remained in the area when I and my three brothers entered upon the scene and yet all of them were familiar as a result of heated conversations at the dinner table. Meanwhile, as deliberation and disagreement settled in for the long haul among sisters, I suppose my parents considered the budding communities in the southern part of Virginia Beach an affordable middle between their busy university life and their desire for a nice family setting by the ocean. I liked the expansive beaches with which they were heavily utilized.

My mother was a young, affectionate woman, but of a staunch Calvinist upbringing, and though married for less than three years to an erratic son of another farmer who also received a subsidy for every crop of tobacco that he did not grow, preferred books and sophisticated things. When a renowned professor from the University of Virginia, with a name that already in the 1960's was celebrated in DNA research, took the chair of the new research department of Genetics, Evolution, and Environment at Old Dominion University, though my father knew of him (chiefly, I surmise, to take advanced courses from him in the new sphere of biology), he was quickly offered a position and moved down from Princeton, New Jersey. No one thought they were a good match. My father said it was accepted as perfectly unreasonable. My father's mentor had a different perspective, and, I was never told why, they decided to get married within two years of their chance meeting at the checkout counter of the university library. I still remember the discussion that ensued when my older brother Frank asked if my mother might show us what a real tobacco plant looked like; a field trip to a local plantation was reluctantly given to us, but it did not occur until after my two younger brothers Arnold and Robert were old enough to fully understand. My mother wanted to be sure that her four boys had bigger dreams and aspirations, and my father could not agree more:

"Boys, man is born to do whatever he wishes, but not if he doesn't get a solid education, or have faith."

My father used to take us to church every Sunday morning, and my mother always made sure that our homework was completed before bedtime, but if my father thought we had the impression religion was more important than eduction he was much mistaken. My mother knew better, and silently considered him old-fashioned.

The community of Nimmo consisted of wide boulevards that serviced shopping centers and large mercantile establishments, with townhouse complexes and single-family subdivisions, many of the latter were isolated and built on long winding roads; and from this ran a certain number of short dead ends, recently developed, that looked out on one side into marshes and on the other into fields. Our house looked out onto one such field. My brothers and I eagerly took to the open wilderness and over time our expeditions led us to a majestic inland body of water called Lake Tecumseh. When I was old enough to be allowed out by myself I used to spend hours wandering about there looking at insects and frogs, and fishing on the lake.

It was on Lake Tecumseh that I first encountered Theodore Hume. I had just finished sixth grade and school was out for the summer. Right after getting home from school I took a fishing pole and tackle box and went down to the lake. The sky was blue and the air hot and humid, but the Atlantic Ocean made sure that it was absolutely perfect to celebrate and just relax. In the summer residents and outdoor enthusiasts canoed and kayaked on the lake, which through a series of channels linked up with Back Bay National Wildlife Refuge. Although not expressly forbidden young people from the adjacent naval base brought out their watercraft with much exuberance, motoring themselves around the lake in order to pull one, two, or even three persons on water skis; but now there were several people jet-skiing back and forth on the far side of the lake.

I heard the roar of the engines and the discharge of their voices, drowned out a little with the throttles turned wide open, but in which from recent memories and associations of the red buoys I quickly realized that a race was about to begin. They wore black wet suits and sun glasses, and their hair was similarly long. They had a strong, eager and innocent appearance. I do not think they were very rational, but they were coherent. I remember counting about ten of them, and though they were not the same size for the most part were equally proficient with the pivoting handle-poles. There was no one else on the lake and they took little time organizing themselves at the starting line.

Afterward, sneaking along the edge of the lake and then from behind some large bushes, I tried to get a closer look at the racing machines, which were parked on the beach just beyond the makeshift finish line, and when I came out one of the men spotted me. He stopped and said hello to me. Another man appeared from out of nowhere. Initially I was startled and quite nervous. Both men turned to get a better look at me and then with wide smiles spoke a few words to me. The first man was referred to as Ted and was very big with a reddish-brown beard and he had just opened a can of beer rather loudly. The other man seemed small in comparison, and was not as impressive looking, but both of them were calm, good-natured, and very cool.

A thought occurred to me that I should go but while they exchanged a few precursory words with me Hume looked at me in a friendly way, with a smile in his pale blue eyes. I felt that for a minute the other guy would have kept up the conversation but he turned nonchalantly away when I started to ask too many questions. I realized I should not run the risk of being outspoken so I let him carry the conversation with his Texas drawl and his aura of blunt certainty as he led me over to the line of jet skis and explained to me the closed-course racing contest in ever greater detail. I was still carrying my fishing pole and tackle box, and this changed the discussion to a subject I was very familiar. His enthusiasm for fishing was infectious and caused the other men to join the conversation. I told them that I mostly caught white and yellow Perch in the lake, but on one occasion when fishing from a rowboat with my older brother managed to net some Blueback Herrings. In addition, I told them the lake was full of crabs and clams. Their sentiments were summed up when one guy uttered, "Fishing from a jet ski offers me more freedom than my 18-foot boat." I finally told them that I must be getting on (fortunately, for I had already learned how to break away from a gathering of my prying aunts at holiday parties and would otherwise endure agonies of shyness while I talked about school and whatnot), but I bid that I would like to try riding a jet ski if my father allowed me.

Ted nodded and smiled as I departed, but he appended his farewell with an earnest remark that he would stop by and introduce himself one of these days. I suppose he was just trying to be neighborly, well-intentioned but in those days we did not mix with the Navy. My father said it was unconscionable to have all that unbridled energy so close by, but of course Virginia Beach was a Navy town. Yet even bar owners gave a faint sigh of relief when an aircraft carrier deployment finally had gotten underway and Virginia Beach sank back into its usual peace.

When I went home to dinner, my father and three brothers playing basketball in the driveway, I commented that I had watched a wild jet ski race on the lake and was unable to catch any fish as a result.

"New neighbors," remarked my older brother.

"Yes," said my father in explanation. "The Houghtons' house has been rented out."

The old lady's name was Vera Houghton; she was eighty-five years old, awfully miserable with tidy gray hair and a small sallow pale face. I suppose she was finally resigned to the fact that she would not return to her home, but to me it seemed appropriate. She was without a husband and children. This made people think her rather pitiful and my parents, being good people, were more than glad to look in on her. Being a widow of a Navy commander, she did not lack resources to keep up the house, but we took care of her trash each Wednesday and from time to time completed odd jobs for her. After she was omitted to the hospital that brought her to a nursing home Mrs. Houghton arranged to have the house put up for sale, but upon reconsidering the matter at length, decided instead to hold on to the house.

"I just met them," I said in reply as I associated the trailers parked on the front lawn the night before. "I saw the same trailers down at the lake."

"That a fact," considered my father.

"Why, it would be cool if they are Naval officers," Frank added, upon taking a jump shot.

"No, I believe they're enlisted," said my father. "Your mother spoke to Mrs. Houghton about it already. One of the boys is related to the Murray family."

"How many are they again?" asked Arnold.

"Apparently four," my father replied. "But it seems as if there's a lot more."

"I'm pretty sure they're Navy SEALs," I said.

"Wow, no kidding," said Frank.

At that time in Nimmo, though the operations assigned to SEAL Team Six may never be known to the public, everybody knew about their compound at Dam Neck and their spectacular actions to save Grenada.

"I'll have mother give Mrs. Murray a call," said my father with a vague frown. "Let's clean up for dinner." He turned and went inside the house.

"Mrs. Houghton is not coming back?" asked Robert, who was still trying to comprehend the situation.

"Yes, I think so," Frank said. "She may be back after she gets better."

"I asked them to show me how to ride a jet ski," I declared proudly, upon seeing my father disappear.

"No way," said Frank.

"Yeah," I said. "Freestyle is done standing up. It will take some practice. But I think I can do it. Do you think Dad will go for it?"

Frank laughed and then Arnold and Robert joined in.

"Oh, come off it guys."

"Riley, there's no way."

"Mr. Ted Hume said he would stop over and say hello."

"Ted who?"

"He's the guy I talked to mostly today."

"Well, if it helps the cause, I will offer to come along with you. Personally, I wouldn't waste my time on the sport," added Frank, who played nothing but basketball now that he had a fair chance to become a starter on the freshman team. "Anyhow, I still think he'll say no."

"They said they have a ramp and one of them does back flips with only one hand and one foot on the jet ski."

"No way," said Arnold.

"I'm not kidding you," I said.

"I wouldn't mention that," said Frank, laughing.

"You should have seen the speed in which they raced around the lake."

"I'd chill out if I were you," Frank said casually before turning to go inside.

"You're probably right."

So I did. The best thing you can do during the summer is to keep out of trouble. At twelve I had already found that I liked my freedom, and stirring up trouble only led to more chores around the house, or bible classes at the church, which I preferred not to go to; but the notion of flying across Lake Tecumseh excited me to distraction.

When I consider the celebrity that Captain Hume afterward achieved I cannot but smile as I remember the way in which he was initially considered in the Cooper household. When he died a year ago and a ferment arose among certain members of Congress about his burial in Arlington Cemetery the present commander of the Naval Special Warfare Developmental Group, Hume's successor twice removed, wrote to the Secretary of the Navy pointing out that he was a plank owner and not only had served the country well, especially the last dozen years of his life, in the Middle East, but had shown there as a result of an extraordinary mission the potential of going back to the time-honored strategy of offshore balancing and bottom-up support to our partners that still offers the best formula for dealing with new threats such as terrorism, nuclear proliferation, or a traditional great-power rival; it was only becoming then that his bones should be in the same graveyard where under shade trees heroes of the Civil War and both World Wars rested in peace. Was Hume a brilliant, farsighted, creative, tireless, magnanimous, great man? Or was it true that during the course of his career he lied, cheated, blustered, manipulated people, gave bribes, exhorted protection money, served up insults, and pursued vendettas? There was no sympathy on Capitol Hill when, the Speaker of the House having somewhat curtly refused the Pentagon, Wanda Hume sent a dignified letter to her congressman in which she expressed her deep sadness that she would not be able to carry out the final wishes of her dead husband and was left with only one option and that was to have him buried among his family in El Paso, Texas. Unless the crowned leadership of the Navy staff at the Pentagon has very much changed since my day I do not believe they immensely liked the idea of "declassifying" information, but as I afterward found out, they had never known the persistence of the second Mrs. Hume.

# FOUR

THE FOLLOWING SATURDAY after watching the 43rd Scottish Christmas Walk with Linda Gogio, I returned home and found a letter from Wanda Hume. It was your typical holiday greeting card that bid me warm and friendly wishes for a very happy Christmas, but included a note that ran as follows:

> *Dear Riley,*
>
> *I spoke to your mother this week after having a nice lunch with Dr. James Isner and I am so glad to know that you two are good friends. Your mother has been very kind to me this past year. With a loving heart and willing hand, she helped me greatly after Ted passed away and is so pleased to know that you can assist me during this period of enduring pain and personal crisis. You knew Ted before he was my husband and have your own memories of him. Ted told me some of these stories about his first days here in Virginia Beach. I have a photo of him standing next to you at Lake Tecumseh. He took great pride when you decided to stay in the Navy, and joined the Marine Corps. I'd be very pleased if I could persuade you to work with me and help me redress his honor. I wonder if you have time to visit me during the holidays so I can properly explain everything to you. Please send word through your mother. It will be fun to talk of old times. I only pray that when Ted left us, he knew how much everybody cared about him.*
>
> *Sincerely, Wanda Hume*

As I've said earlier I had already met Wanda Hume and she but nearly interested me; however, I do not like having to go through my mother; that alone would have been enough to make me decline her request; and I was frustrated by its general disinterest in me which, ostensibly not a valid

41

excuse, made the reason not to lend a hand to a family acquaintance all the worse, namely, that I should not help her because she did not think I was appealing or attractive. This only gave me reason enough to let it go. Besides, I had no manuscript of Hume's. I suppose it must have been my short history of ghostwriting, a brief memoir for a fellow USAID employee working in Afghanistan and another for a fellow Marine who had seen some very bad days in Iraq, but I was then just retired and needed the extra money while studying at Johns Hopkins University and even if I was dabbling in this genre I seriously doubt Hume would have considered me. How was I to become that privileged person to write the life story of the greatest military hero of recent times? I hesitated only because Wanda had spoken to my mother and I am sure it was a good thing to do. It was certainly strange, but it would not be a burden to do it if I could, and after all it would be hardly inconvenient to see her while I was visiting my parents.

The letter arrived at noontime and after eating a sandwich during halftime of the annual Army-Navy football game I decided to call Jim. I presume as soon as my telephone number flashed up he answered his phone. If I was not a sane person I should immediately have suspected that he was waiting for my call, and Jim's potent voice shouting '*Yo*' so confidently would have confirmed my suspicion. No Marine could honestly be quite so happy being down ten points to Army.

"I hope you don't always pick up on the first ring," I said.

"Absolutely." His laughter transcended the announcer's voice on the television broadcast. "But I'm glad you called. Typically I get a dozen or so calls during the game. It's great fun. Everybody here seems to think I went to the Naval Academy."

"I can see why, Jim," I responded, "but I don't think you're the sort of person who makes a tradition of the rivalry. Besides, aren't you waiting with great expectation for the BCS championship game?"

"Well, Alabama is *not* the best team in the country."

"Ah, yes, Bear Bryant's football factory is still in high gear."

"You bet, brother."

"I suppose the Bear, in his hound's-tooth hat, is still deemed a quintessential coach to people down there."

"Yeah, but I wish upstate New York had good football."

"Look here, I've just received a Christmas card from Wanda Hume with a funny little note inside it."

"How is it funny? She told me she was going to call you. I bet she thought it over and went with a more casual approach."

"Casual? I think she's being rather cagey, don't you?"

There was an inflection in Jim's voice such as I was trained to pick up as if he were telling a white lie to his mother or a new girlfriend that was not familiar with his playacting. I decided to call his bluff.

"Not so fast," I said. "I'm not completely ignorant so please do not keep this attitude of utter nonsense. What is it you want of me?"

"This has hardly anything to do with me."

"Bullshit."

There was a measured pause that by chance coincided with a Navy fumble, but it was recovered as quickly as it was lost. I waited for Jim to respond to me.

"Are you busy on Wednesday?" he asked. "I'd like to come and see you."

"All right, if you think it's that important. But I don't know why you won't just spit it out."

"I need to show you something. I think you will appreciate it."

"About what time?"

"Probably around two—it'll be a day trip with a quick visit with Percy de Burey and I need to get back for an evening lecture."

"De Bury? I thought he was dead."

"Ha, he's got one foot in the grave but very much still alive. He'll be at the World Bank signing his latest book and I just can't pass up an opportunity to meet him. You know, he was the first economist to examine both the Industrial Revolution and hunter-gatherers, then as peasants and laborers, from the perspective of understanding why some societies were so willing to trade their ancient poverty for amazing affluence while other societies were content with the status quo. He learned that by the end of the eighteenth century, the average person's consumption in England was still about fifteen hundred calories a day and hunter-gatherer societies in Africa and South America were enjoying twenty-five hundred calories or more. Primitive man ate well compared with Western civilization's preeminent society. His book is titled *The Malthusian Trap.*"

"Just call me."

Smiling I hung up the telephone and sat down on the couch next to Riley Junior. He looked up briefly at me before returning to his usual mid-afternoon slumber. I thought perhaps I should have been more cordial. Then I thought how free hunter-gatherers seem to be—free from possessions and laws and most social duties and even money—but it is a hard life without sentimentality. Surely, my old Marine Corps buddy could not forbear that. I gave Wanda Hume's note a second glance.

I remembered clearly the day in which the photograph was taken. I happened to be taking a long hike not far from Lake Tecumseh when I came upon a certain Malcolm Brown, the clever and tall son of a high school football coach with much swank and natural powers. Perhaps to relieve the boredom of structured life he was trying to connect with nature on this pleasant afternoon. His recent birthday party was assorted and fun. My mother insisted upon my going to the party with Frank. Kids from the neighborhood and school played games with liveliness and an easy awe without concern of gender.

Yet I maintained a distance from the older crowd, suiting both my own preference and my brother's resistance, and I found that Malcolm Brown neither played the games nor hung out with any of us to whom he avidly acknowledged, but he liked our company and enjoyed the feeling it gave him of being the center of attention. When on this occasion I crept up behind him and knocked off his baseball cap he was of course very angry with me and demanded that I pick it up and apologize. My impression earlier in the day was of him stepping off the school bus, showing off somewhat, and in those days I always objected to showoffs. Consequently, neglecting my age or size, I refused and he said, "Well then, I'll have to make you pay for it."

He proceeded to do that and I fell down to the ground on my back but managed to get my arms around his legs, and while being recklessly hit I was kicking his ass very hard. One of his contacts popped out, and I think I won that round. As we faced off I saw Hume, and a few of his friends, make their presence known on the lake. Seeing them thundering along the shoreline I mentioned I had taken a ride with them.

Malcolm Brown, putting on his pretense of indifference, proposed that we should go over and talk with them when they returned to the shore. I demurred, for I had not seen Hume for at least nine months and I did not really want to share the friendship with anyone else (though the former I kept to myself); and if he insisted I could not believe that Hume would support or encourage another as he had done with me. But there was another classmate of his arriving, a certain Michael Seldes, with a reputation of academic prowess so spontaneous that, instead of mastering this realm as the laws of man and society decreed, he devoted his energy to the cultivation of highly potent cannabis. His energy to meet Hume was unbounded and the moment Malcolm Brown made the suggestion he said it would be totally cool. Both of these boys were considered to be very smart and popular. The last intruder of the afternoon was a big fat friend of Seldes and it appeared that his admiration for Navy commandos was so intense that he was prepared to walk across the lake to see them.

"I know you don't do favors for others without being asked, Cooper," said Malcolm Brown. "But you should consider this a privilege."

"I count six of them," Michael Seldes interrupted. "I think they could manage easily."

I could not see myself going to greet Hume in that company and tried to throw cold water on the idea.

"I can empathize with your pain," I said. "He'll hate having a bunch of kids demanding rides like this. It'll only bore him to death."

"That's what he lives for and why we should not waste this opportunity to see him now. We can't expect him to live much longer. My old man says Navy SEALs live on the edge, you know to keep an advantage. He also says that they go around the world eliminating evil in a way which gives him much pride and that kind of feeling has always been one of the greatest enjoyments of the American people. My old man told me that he wished he took that route in the Navy. Of course he didn't have a choice. Today he's pestered by all sorts of people at school who want him to teach football by the book, and idle fathers who can't understand why their sons do not get more playing time, and silly hysterical mothers. But Navy SEALs are very cool. I can't believe your old man tells you to keep away from them but for those times he thinks you should be neighborly. I mean, these guys might get killed on their next mission. You have to think in these terms. Obviously, you're different."

"How so?"

"I think you are quite out of your head."

"Oh, bug off," I said.

"Your brother says you excel in all kinds of strange activities. But what, I don't know. Now I see a sort of intensity in your eyes, which is very difficult to describe but I like it. What is it you're groping after? Perhaps we can help you." As the three boys laughed I wondered if they had seen me hiking across the wildlife refuge on a compass course, regardless of the marshes or flooded rivers, sleeping outdoors alone, canoeing as far as I could between dawn and dusk, climbing over Navy fences, or perhaps just seeing that I didn't give a damn.

Of course I thought he was wrong; but as I looked at them I perceived that Michael Seldes and the fat boy thought he was right; so it seemed best to say no more.

We walked over together. Lake Tecumseh and Back Bay were separate bodies of water about two miles from Nimmo, and between the two were thick, woody swamps. A small canal was dug, I suppose, about 1970, plain and understated, but substantial; it was created from the Ash-ville Bridge Creek, with an intent to improve drainage and navigation in which soon became part of the sprawling Back Bay system, and there were many people who made use of the man-made connection. A few years ago the clock was turned back and the two bodies of water were returned to their separate, natural selves. I suppose it is still possible to canoe or kayak back and forth but one might have to portage over the berm, somewhat of a hassle, but certainly a worthwhile effort, and from what I understand the water quality has gotten better and you had a much better chance of catching larger fish now. My father occasionally complains that the berms act like a dam and only worsen the flooding in the residential areas that always flood easily. The lake was once open to the Atlantic Ocean, better-known as Brinson Inlet to bird enthusiasts for the thousands of migrating waterfowl that used to seek shelter there. Storms and shifting sands eventually closed the inlet, which is still self-contained on the grounds of the Dam Neck naval base. Clear blue skies seemingly always spread over the calm lake and the wide fields, and the edges were of the same ageless quality. There were many masses of wildflowers in the summertime, and I am glad my childhood universe has returned to its original state.

It was no wonder that I thought that it was a perfect place of escape. It was just the kind of place in which a distinguished warrior should have spent the idle afternoons of his formative years. Wanda Hume had never stepped foot in this nature reserve. She preferred the ocean and was a woman of discriminating taste, I estimated, with bright brown eyes and a topaz complexion with golden-brown hair. She dressed sharply and wore different styles in each of the four seasons. Her figure was shapely and she was neither tall nor short, and she looked fit, ambitious and competent. She might have been Theodore Hume's first wife, then only a girlfriend who managed an extreme sportswear store in Kitty Hawk and had a peculiar disaffection for sitting on the beach.

Dotti Moore was introduced to us by the team's targeting operations officer and a young woman, who stood up as we were allowed into their controlled area. They were Lieutenant John Grass and his wife. Malcolm Brown and Michael Seldes immediately assumed the portentous affability that persons of rank assume with their elders or superiors in order to show them that they are not in the least conscious of the very fact that they were going to enter eleventh grade in the fall.

Then Theodore Hume came over to us. I had seen a glimpse of him on the local news broadcast. (SEAL Team Six was singled out for the accidental death of a fisherman as well as safety concerns at their facility.) But it was with awe that I saw him in the flesh again. He was more angular than I remembered and very slender, his face was no longer covered with a heavy red beard, he was well-shaven and his appearance was almost superhuman. His eyes were very blue and the hair of his eyebrows blond. He looked like a hero, a mythological being, transcending earth-born mortals by courage and daring; he smiled readily and his white teeth and marbled skin made his appearance strong and potent. I had never seen him but with a beard, and his face was both fierce and composed. He was dressed in a black, well-cut swimsuit of some special kind of fabric and his tee-shirt, wet or perhaps two or three sizes too small for him, showed a ripped, powerful torso. His massive right hand held a bottle of Perrier and he looked a little like one of those lightly armed Peltasts on summer holiday in ancient Greece.

Dotti Moore gave him a quick glance as he came over and smiled proudly; she must have been satisfied with the cleanness of his appearance. He shook hands with each of us in turn and said something friendly. When he came back to me he added:

"I want to show you something, Riley. I hope you don't mind getting a little wet today."

I was a little surprised, for he spoke as though we had been great friends, and I was happy these guys would now think I had not been bragging a short while ago when I claimed to have known him well. But I wondered if the casual friendship of last summer had been forgotten.

"I don't know how long it has been since I last rode," I said to be brave.

The others looked at me for what I suppose was no more than a few seconds, but for what seemed to me quite a long time, and then a diversionary tactic: he threw down the bottle of water. It was so sudden that nobody could have considered the purpose of it, and so perfect in that when everybody turned their regard away from me I could hardly believe my eyes. In a moment he was once again the center of attention, astutely mindful and highly responsive. He decried the taste of the florid water and with smiles all around we followed him over to the jet skis.

This also was in what could only be described as deflecting attention. Almost thirty years later I now believe that he always had a sense what another person felt without having to ask him. I think it was an emotional connection. For a minute or two, I pondered whether or not it upset him to see me embarrassed that day. At least, I think he was. On the shore of the lake were six modified Kawasaki JS-400 models. In a semicircle in the middle was Petty Officer Hume and around him were a few of his fellow frogmen with their girlfriends wearing colorful bikinis and brightly flushed and evidently having a good time. We stood close by and listened to him talk about the watercraft. All of the jet skis were fitted with conspicuously large engines dubbed the X-2 that was officially introduced the following year in the two-seat model. The 650-cc engines were expertly incorporated by Seaman Eddie Cody and he was proud to confirm the larger two-stroke engine produced almost twice the power. I wondered how he had managed to get his hands on the new engines well before the general public; his bright eyes and sharp insights betrayed the fact that the jet skis were "serviceable." The conversation came to a conclusion after a lengthy discussion of an R&D effort to fabricate a four-stroke engine that with the help of superchargers could produce up to 260 horsepower. This smasher would not be unveiled until 2003 when Kawasaki officially released the Ultra 250X, and Sea-Doo the RXP, and I would not wager a bet that the Naval Special Warfare Developmental Group was not one of their first customers to receive the new model.

Dotti, like the women of most Navy SEALs, was in excellent form and she did not let the men do all of the talking; so that, however much we clearly wanted to hear what her boyfriend was saying about these most divine engines, we had a hard time following his narrative. She was confident and intelligent. Though Theodore Hume's insecurity about his marital status and his feelings of mortality compelled him to let her speak up during the course of their relationship, she managed notwithstanding to reduce the intensity of his position often enough by sudden or repeated shifts to evade the inevitability and yet she was soon engaged to him after an animated talk about life and the painful possibility of a permanent breakup in the fall when he was scheduled to begin a fleet commissioning program at the University of Oklahoma. This was an opportunity offered to him by name because of his outstanding qualifications and motivation to move into officer ranks. It had taken her just six months to size up this young man from Texas and even then she had not had time to really get to know him or react to other dominant males. She liked everything about him so much; they seemed like a good match; she loved things to be exciting.

Until now the most salient and impressive stood at the center of the group, but Lieutenant John Grass and his wife began to move closer to Hume. He engaged Hume in conversation on the topics of funding and contracts management, a sphere in which he seemed to be very knowledgeable and capable, and my attention being thus distracted I watched the outranked petty officer. The conversation became sidetracked and the seamen began talking amongst themselves. Lieutenant Grass then began telling Hume how to properly hold the throttle and giving him a tutorial of a technique he really ought to practice. He listened to him with what looked like polite interest, putting in now and then a word in a voice too low for me to catch, and when the lieutenant made a joke (both cracking funny, pointed remarks in turn) he perked up and gave a loud laugh that seemed to say: this dude isn't such a crashing idiot after all.

Remembering the past, I inquisitively asked myself what Hume might have made of this afternoon, his colleagues and their attractively active women, easygoing and so discreetly competing with one another, and the pristine nature reserve in which they raced. I wondered if he had missed those days. I wondered if the subtle emotions I saw that day with his superior amused him or if the kindheartedness or gratitude of his manner masked downright derision. Perhaps he felt the keen eyes of four young men who were coming of age, for he gave a good example. The question of whether true compassion exists at all, or whether it is inherently motivated by self-interest swirled about my brain for a while presently and yet oddly an answer seemed to appear from out of nowhere, and then suddenly, unmistakably, as Hume should be wired up, I recalled that he had reached out and put a hand on my shoulder. The instinctive gesture in that heavy, experienced hand was more than comforting, it was encouraging; I did not know it at the time. My expression had imparted a smile.

When Malcolm Brown joined in the conversation at the center of the group, Dotti turned to me.

"You knew Ted before today, didn't you?" she asked me in a soft voice.

"Yes, last summer."

She reached into a duffel bag to find something and then turning back and looking at me said:

"Ted likes to capture friends for his photo album. I think he would like it very much, you know, if I could get a picture of you two guys by his jet ski."

"You think?"

"Come here."

"You dog, Riley," said Malcolm. I turned and saw his envious eyes staring back at me.

"Great idea, Dotti. See if you can get a shot of us from over there with the view of the lake." Hume raised his voice a little more. "Guys, clear out of the way; this will only take a second."

This was the sort of simple human response to which it was difficult to find a cause, but I felt that one was embedded into the folds of his brain.

"Considering the clouds I think it turned out all right," Dotti said.

Theodore Hume took a quick look at the picture.

"What do you think, Riley?"

At seeing me smile we split up into smaller groups and after standing about nervously for a couple of minutes Theodore Hume joined us. I had been talking to Michael Seldes and the fat boy and for want of anything to say was looking out toward the shimmering ocean. I turned to him.

"We were just talking about how fast a boat can really go out there," I remarked.

"Good question." Hume looked up and then at the others and a huge smile lighted up his face. "We chew on that question every day, right guys?"

Nobody was paying attention. But Dotti came up to us with fresh energy. Her voice was high and song-like.

"Say Ted, I'm sure the boys would love to take a ride on the boat. You said you were going to take it out later this afternoon."

"What a great idea, better than a jet-ski ride, but we'll have to pick up you guys from the beach south of the base," he said plainly.

There was excitement in the air as we filed into the back of Hume's vehicle on the other side of the berm. It was a black four-wheel-drive SUV, with dark windows and a trailer for two of the jet skis. It was the sort of vehicle that a Navy SEAL would manifestly drive around Virginia Beach. It was surprisingly tidy but the scuba diving gear gave it a military feel.

"We'll load the jet skis at the landing," he said, looking back at us with a simple facial gesture. "Then we'll stop at the 7-Eleven for sodas. It'll take us no more than thirty minutes to launch the craft."

I admired him for laying out a plan of action, and Dotti Moore, when he turned back around, put her hand on his shoulder and kissed him on the cheek in appreciation. She then gave us a quick, bright smile.

"This is so cool," said Malcolm Brown and Michael Seldes, almost in unison.

"I can't wait to tell my mother," added the fat boy.

His buddies followed from behind in their vehicles, two of which pulled trailers, and while they loaded and secured the jet skis onto the trailers I had a look at the miscellaneous items the vehicle contained. As combat swimmers embody, I ran my eye around quickly to see if there were any assault rifles, but could not find anything resembling a weapon; I saw, however, other tools such as net-cutters and a complete diving suit and breathing set with particular features, which looked especially nifty; I guessed that they are needed because frogmen have to swim fast and far while avoiding detection and perhaps the dull color, lightweight materials, plastic fasteners, and the closed-cycle rebreather with bag and tubes permitted stealthy tactics when approaching the target. But all of the diving equipment was clean, simply organized and in such perfect order, that I had the impression that Dotti must have maintained the gear for him. I also remembered seeing both an ordinary and a full-face mask and inside a traveling bag there was a special version of the latter with a heads-up display capability. This was something you would find in a James Bond movie, like *Thunderball*, which portrays an extended underwater battle, and there were a number of technical manuals in the side compartment. The trunk had the look not of a Navy SEAL's vehicle, but of a refined civilian with a recreational purpose who was fully capable of accomplishing tasks that regulations forbid an amateur from undertaking. I had a suspicion at the time that if Hume read anything at all it was *Sports Illustrated* or *Playboy*, of which I found neither stowed away, and I was too young to appreciate the significance of finding a worn-out copy of *Meditations* by Marcus Aurelius.

When the men had dropped us off we stood quietly on the beach and sipped our sodas. But Dotti Moore was a woman of action and it must have occurred to her that I, the prime reason for the invitation, had scarcely had a chance to have a little fun, for at the water's edge, whirling around with a large, bright smile, she cast a Frisbee at me.

"I was so glad to hear that you and Ted had gotten to know one another. I bet your dad just loves him."

I looked at her for a moment before giving chase to the flying saucer, with that level, ironic gaze of mine. I had the opinion that if Theodore Hume were here he would have either distracted me or tackled me to the ground.

"I suppose," I replied. "Well, we haven't really seen him around much lately."

Malcolm Brown whistled from afar and called for me to throw it his way.

"He's been overseas," she said, "but he'll do anything for young people."

"You should have seen me trying to ride it the first time. I think it took at least twenty attempts before I was able to stand up on it."

"I wish I was there," she said. "I could have helped you."

"It's harder than it looks," I acknowledged with chagrin. "I tried over and over again and I could never get myself to stay poised on it."

"That's all right," she said.

"No, it's not," I retorted. "You don't understand, but it does take a great deal of strength."

"Was Ted patient with you?" she probed.

"Oh, yes, very much so."

"I teach the basic course, and I always tell people that a good disposition is the most important element of a successful instruction."

"Good thing he wasn't charging by the hour. But I got the hang of it."

"Oh, good."

Dotti excused herself for a moment and Malcolm walked casually over to me. Michael Seldes and the fat boy were looking at something on the horizon. I thought I spotted a gray silhouette duck behind a wave.

"Nobody does anything without regard to reward or the benefit of recognition, and I know your old man has been giving him a hard time."

"What's your point?" I said.

"Funny how people in the military act sometimes, with their strange feelings of obedience and duty, but it can't have anything to do with that. So how many times did he take you out on the lake anyway?"

"Oh, come off it. You sound like a cheat. I think you should stay here, and forget the boat ride." I considered the words I remember shouting out that day, on such principles of sharing and generosity. Even at that age I had a strong sense of what was good and bad.

"So how many times?" he demanded again.

"Three, I'd say. But who's counting."

"You dog."

"I wish I could go out more often, but I don't think Frank cares so much for it. My dad says that I have to go with Frank. Dotti's pretty cool, don't you think?"

"As a rule, girlfriends of Navy SEALs are sweet."

"They seem to get along very well."

"Oh, come off it. You don't know anything about girls."

The special operations craft broke through the breaking surf, sat down and turned about, and we quickly boarded it at the stern and then raced out to sea.

# FIVE

**T**HEODORE HUME HAD taught me to ride a jet ski. That was a fact, and that was indeed how I first met him. And I remember well the day I purchased my first jet ski, but I also know well it was not a common occurrence in our little suburban cul-de-sac of Nimmo in which I existed and when you saw most kids speeding along on bicycles down the street and around the block you found me on the lake zipping along the shoreline until out of sight.

It was still a matter for glowering facial expressions on the part of my father who said a mountain bike should be good enough for me, and for discerning fear and some anxiety on the part of my mother who refused to go down to the lake and watch me. I had become in little time the envy of the boys whom I was playing with in the neighborhood. It gave a neat opportunity for standing apart of everyone else when I arrived at that age where girls were getting interesting. I had persuaded my parents to let me buy a used one with my savings at the beginning of the summer, just after my fifteenth birthday, and though my father was against it, since he said I should be focusing my natural abilities on baseball or soccer, he yielded to my ungovernable enthusiasm more willingly because I was of course making good grades, staying out of trouble (though somewhat paranoid that my rebelliousness might get out of control and lead to drugs and then to crime and evildoing), and lastly and most important paying for it myself by delivering papers. I researched the matter thoroughly and then a few days before the end of the school year he took me down to a local boat dealer to pick one out for myself.

Frank, seventeen now, was equally determined to find freedom in Nimmo and soon after getting his license he had purchased a pickup truck that was used to transport the watercraft around town. My personal freedom would depend upon not only Frank but also one of my younger brothers to load it onto the truck, but Robert at just ten years old was hardly any help and as a result my triumphant excursions to the lake were sufficiently humbled when seeking out Arnold to help me lift up one end of the watercraft that I seemed at the end no nearer to being totally free than before I purchased it.

One day, however, thinking that Arnold who for a twelve-year-old was getting too smart to give his older brother a helping hand without something in return (the art of quid pro quo being his new mantra), I took off and walked down to the road that led to the boat ramp which I knew was perfectly reasonable to assume that some good-hearted people might do me a favor. I asked a young couple preparing for a canoe ride, but my entreaty fell on silent ears. Then I waited at the landing in the midday heat and became very hot and bothered. After I had been there waiting for about an hour, though I began to think that God did not intend me to have personal freedom, but was determined (still unable to bear the thought of giving up yet something else to Arnold, each occurrence strengthening his newfound confidence) to get assistance all the same, to my surprise I saw a black SUV coming along the road by the lake pulling a trailer.

I immediately sat upright and stepped forward on the gravel road, following the vehicle in a detached way around the lake and up and over the large berm as though I had been for a hike and were just resting there consumed in contemplation of the idyllic surroundings. I kept the corner of my eye on the dark windows which were reflecting light toward me, but I felt that the people inside were watching me, and though my head was turned away from the direction in which it was traveling I finally realized that it was not Hume's vehicle; but as the SUV passed me I heard a woman call out my name and, stopping a short distance away, the driver rolled down his window.

"Dude, hello there," he said. "I thought I recognized you but was unsure about it."

It was impossible under the circumstances to maintain my appearance of casualness and, smiling broadly, I said that I didn't recognize the vehicle.

"Yes, I bought a new one after I graduated."

The woman had walked around the front of the vehicle as Theodore Hume stepped out.

"Riley, you've grown so tall," she said.

"You think so?"

"Oh, yes."

At this point I knew them as the Humes, recently commissioned Ensign Hume and his beautiful wife Dotti.

"Ted wanted to come here," said the latter. "But I prefer to ride ocean waves whenever I get the chance."

"Well, I like it here," he said with a smile. "Today we are doing it my way. We arrived here just this past week. I see nothing has changed."

She put her hand on my arm that gave me a warm and friendly feeling and when I returned her smile an odd sensation. She looked over at her husband with her lips pursed and with her eyes opened and there was in her face something that even then I recognized as singularly different. Just then I had an impression of a rather delicate swashbuckling woman.

I was bemused. Self-assertive women I did not know made me dreadfully embarrassed, and yet I could not take my eyes off of her. The impression of her appearance was felt deep within me. I do not know if I noticed then or only remembered afterward that she wore tight athletic shorts and a white dress shirt from the men's department, underneath a black bandeau giving shape to her body, and a baseball cap, adverting the local Triple-A affiliate, the Tidewater Tides, I recall, of the International League, sat tightly on her head and held back long straight fringes of dark golden brown hair.

"Yes, this is lovely," she said, looking across the water which shimmered in the midday sun. "Riley, do you still like to hike and explore around here?"

I felt that this inferred an admiration for my former avocation.

"I have already mapped out the entire area," I said.

"This is my first ride of the summer," Theodore Hume said suddenly. "I'm really looking forward to it, and wish I could offer you a ride today, buddy, but we are short of time. What would you say the temperature of the lake is?"

I looked away momentarily. I could no longer contain myself now.

"I have my own ride now," I said. "I've only had it a couple of weeks and usually get my brothers to help me get it into the water."

I equivocated a bit there, but I made my offering with my conscience by leaving out the request for help: except right then when I looked down.

"That's great, Riley," Dotti said.

"Say you want to ride with us?" he asked in a good-natured way, looking at Dotti. "I'll make a run to your house. It will take only a few minutes."

"Oh, yes," I said. "I'd love to ride with you guys."

"All right, excellent."

Theodore Hume jumped into the vehicle. "I'll put our jet skis in the water first and then we'll go."

I stepped aside with a big smile, and Dotti and I followed the vehicle to the landing area as he backed up and eased the trailer into the water.

"The lake is much warmer than the ocean," I offered. "I'd say it's up to seventy-five already."

"Here take the ropes," he said.

I ran and they rode by me as I erupted with energy. I was very hot when, notwithstanding my excitement, I met them in front of my house. It was very rebellious under such circumstances not to preserve the disapproval befitting my father's deterrent example, and when I turned up the driveway and for twenty or thirty steps actually was worried that my mother might be home in the middle of the day instead of at the university.

Theodore Hume walked up the middle of the driveway with his right arm waving and shouted: "This way, Dotti, back up slowly." I realized nobody was home and began laughing so hard that I positively forgot all about my standing orders not to use the jet ski without seeking permission first. The jet ski sat on blocks at the side of the garage.

I thew off the tarp, my expression no doubt wearing an air of contemptuous disobedience, and received without embarrassment the words of congratulations on my selecting a jet ski of such fine qualities, which made me feel very proud.

"I want to see if I can pick up this end by myself," I said, and he grabbed hold of the heavier stern while Dotti watched us from inside the vehicle.

Then, wanting to rest a minute, tired but anxious to leave, I grabbed my vest and sat down right next to my jet ski. Theodore Hume breathed uneasily. We chatted. I did not of course realize it then, but I know now that there was a right smart forthrightness in his manner that put one at one's ease. He talked with a kind eagerness, like an equal struggling over the issue, and his blue eyes were lit all the time by his engaging smile. I did not know why it gave me confidence in myself. I should say it was a little clever, if cleverness were not a terrible quality; it was too ingenuous to be clever. It was manipulative rather, like that of a good parent who wants to do right by their children, but is quite aware that you will resist; he knows all the same that you won't be really upset and if you don't fully understand the full meaning about it he will quickly pull you aside and tell you himself. But of course then I knew that he was concerned about my safety.

Presently Theodore Hume, looking at his watch, said that we must be going and suggested that we all ride back together in the front seat. Remembering suddenly it was just the time that our sitter would be arriving from her position at a daycare center to look after us until dinnertime and I did not want to run the risk of being seen by her; so I nodded my head and climbed off the trailer, as she would in all likelihood not notice me inside the vehicle.

Dotti Hume slid over to make room for me, and Theodore Hume took the wheel, somewhat pleased with himself, which made me think that he was having a good time and enjoyed my company, so I felt comfortable being with them, and looking at me he said:

"We'll drop your baby in the water, Riley. We have time for three laps around the lake."

"All right. Can we take the racecourse? I'd very much like that."

"You bet, mate," he answered.

We drove off down the street, and in a few minutes I was pressing the ignition of the engine. Feeling very confident in myself, I opened up the throttle and stood up immediately when the jet ski jumped forward and then after turning around throttled back without falling. I think I bragged a little when I returned home, but nobody saw me return with the Humes.

Next day at about noontime I washed and waxed my jet ski after cutting the front lawn. It was Saturday and it held the promise that even though my father was busy with errands and whatnot he would allot time before dinner to take us to the beach, and my mother thought of the weekly ritual during the summertime a good social pattern in which the family assumes a position of ascendancy over individual interests. In anticipation I rubbed the jet ski down with a special wax and then, opening the engine compartment, checked the vital organs until I was completely satisfied that everything was in working order.

The sky was blue and the air, baking hot and yet fresh, moved, as it were, with the undulating waves. The beach was brilliant and required heavy protection against the sun. The sun's rays seemed to push the ocean with such force that it was like a Greco-Roman wrestling match.

I rode back and forth along the shoreline, waiting for others to join me, and presently saw three jet skis come. I saw that the riders were boys about my same age who attended another middle school. I sat down and waited for them, floating easily at a shoal about fifty yards from the beach, and we rode around together. One guy complimented my technique and another my ability. We rode recklessly into towering peaks, clinging with grim determination to our handle-poles, but triumphant, and one guy said that as soon as we felt sure of ourselves we must go down the beach and ride with the older boys.

"I want to try the waves at the point," he said.

I knew exactly what he meant, and was a bit nervous thinking about it.

"They're awesome there," he added.

"I'll wait and see," I said. "Do you think we can manage the currents, and the ten-foot waves?"

"Rather," said another.

"I heard a couple of the jet-skiers are Navy SEALs and we can ride alongside them."

"Let's go for it," the first said.

"I don't see why not," I said.

"Yeah, baby!"

After the outcry the leader of the three gave me that presumptuous look of contempt, and I was humiliated. I knew that if I wavered irresolutely and decided otherwise now he would laugh. I looked straight ahead as he rode by me in vain hope that if I did not look at him he would not see the faltering confidence in my eyes. I was tense. I thought that if I decided to turn toward my family sitting on the beach the ugly truth would quickly reach the ears of everybody at school, and I considered whether it would not be better to control the nervousness that could no longer be concealed. When we rode off together for the breakers, all three of them said that if the current flows were too much I could make the decision for them to divert to the beach. (I had already shown them that I was a better rider.)

"Do you know who taught me to ride? The guy who jumped over that wave there. He's in SEAL Team Six!"

When I sat down to dinner I debated whether or not to slip in casually the tidbit that I had by accident run into Theodore Hume, but unbeknown to me Robert had followed us up the beach.

"Who were those boys you were riding with this afternoon?" asked my mother. "I thought I told you to stay close by so we could watch you."

My father, chewing his steak in which he found delectable, looked over at me.

"Just some guys from Redhead Bay," I said without emotion. "You know, one of them plays on the varsity basketball team and he's only a freshman."

"What's his name?" asked Frank. "I may know him."

"Riley," interrupted my father, "I was hoping you would spend time with Bob and Arnold today. They asked if you were going to take them for a ride."

"Yes, sir."

"I'm not going to say anymore," he added, seeing to it that dinner did not turn into an unpleasant affair.

"He prefers to ride with Mr. Ted," uttered Robert, with a devilish grin.

"So that's it," said my mother.

My father let it go—wise to the fact that the Navy commando no longer posed an imminent threat to the family and our new neighbors were a young, quiet couple—but involuntarily looked sullenly at his plate.

I began to withdraw, but in self-realization of my shamefaced outward appearance and to show my respect when my father remarked that helpers were needed at Bingo Night, though it was not expected of me (for I was an altar boy at St. John Apostle Church, in line with family tradition), I agreed to help out the Knights of Columbus, his time-honored fraternal order. Arnold and Robert quickly asked to be helpers, too.

My father was pleased with me for setting a good example and my mother asked if I wanted the last slice of cake.

"Yes, I think I can make room for it," I said appreciatively.

"Why does he get it?" Frank complained.

"Yeah," groaned Robert, which was followed by a louder utterance from Arnold.

"Because Riley needs to put on some weight," my mother replied quickly.

"Oh, please," sounded off Frank.

"Can't you see I'm still growing," I said, grinning comically at my older brother.

"And I'm not," Frank said.

"Enough is enough, boys. Last night it was your turn to have the last piece," brokered my father. "Tomorrow it will be Arnold's, and then Bob's."

My mother gave me the slice, which I ate with the attitude of one who, impelled by a carrot being dangled by a stick, performs an act that is motivated solely by fear or greed. It was a wonderful strawberry cheesecake. Brenda Hoover made the best desserts in the world. But when my mother asked us what we would like our sitter to make for dessert tomorrow if one had one's druthers, I refused to respond like a stubborn mule; all the same, the "carrot on a stick" was an unconscious process in the Cooper household. My father discharged us and I carried my cantankerous feelings into the backyard.

But a few days later when I saw that my brothers had gone outside I went into the kitchen. Brenda Hoover was washing the dishes in the sink. Something was baking in the oven.

"Say, do you think dad will let me go down to Cape Hatteras with the Humes this coming weekend?" I asked her.

Brenda Hoover had become our babysitter when I was ten years old. She was then almost eighteen, and over the years had given me advice when I needed it, and now the seven years that separates us seems meaningless, but back then the difference was huge. She had dressed me, bandaged scrapes and bruises on my arms and legs, helped me with my homework, and talked to me when I was bored silly or when I moved about the house restlessly. Likewise, for each of my three brothers, Brenda took a personal interest, and she was fun to be around. I don't know how she became such a good cook but perhaps it was a result of baking so many cakes and pies for church fund-raisers. The Hoovers were in our parish. She has since traveled around the world and I think she was a teacher at a missionary post on the Amazon River right after graduating from Virginia Wesleyan. While going to college there, she never missed an afternoon with us. My parents paid her a very good hourly wage. At the time, while pursuing her master's, she worked part-time at the Toddler Playhouse in Nimmo; and she still sings in the choir on Sundays. She knows who everybody is in town, who had married whom, what anyone's ailment or problem is, and how many kids, what they are called, and what they best do to become good Christians. But Brenda had yet to get married herself.

When Brenda ignored my question, I asked her again and she looked briefly out the kitchen window before turning around to speak to me.

"It's a good thing he didn't move back into the Houghtons' house," she said. "I would try to find someone your own age to hang out with this summer. Why don't you spend more time with Arnold and Bob?"

"Rather not," I said.

I already found out that Brenda was keen on my incipient tendency to explore the great outdoors by myself.

"Well, you shouldn't be seeking him out. He's a bad apple."

"How's that?" I inquired.

"I see. You saw him at church last week, and now that he has married a local girl he's a respectable person, right? The impudence of him coming back. I don't know why your father doesn't put his foot down. Oh, yes, of course."

"What are you talking about?"

"Boys seldom rebel against anything that does not deserve rebelling against."

"Say what?"

"Your father is a good man and only wants to see you grow up into a fine young man."

The aroma was distracting me and I pressed the light switch on the oven with my finger and bent down to take a quick look inside.

"Don't open that, young man." Brenda turned to the dishes in the sink but could not help herself: "Dotti could never keep a boyfriend. She's had a good many, too. I reckon being a cheerleader helped. She's doing quite well now. I'm not so sure she will be any good for him. Teddy is just the type of man who needs a good wife." When I tilted my head, discerning the incongruity, she abruptly changed the subject: "Your mother told me to make two cherry pies. I heard there was an uproar about seconds. There will be plenty to go around tonight. You boys eat like kings around here."

"You said Dotti is from around here. Did you go to high school with her?"

"Oh, yes, I knew her well. Dotti transferred from Princes Anne at the beginning of our junior year. Her father was a soldier in the Army. He fought in Vietnam and when he came back he moved the family to Fayetteville, North Carolina. He had lost an arm and was forced into retirement and he was out of work a long while before landing a job as a painter at the naval air station. We played softball and field hockey together and she was an excellent pitcher. Our coach was upset with her when she decided not to play in the spring of our senior year. I understand that counselors moved her to Nimmo High to keep her out of trouble. Perhaps that had something to do with it."

"You said she was a cheerleader," I said with the curiosity of a teenage boy.

"Yes, she cheered for the basketball team, and did quite well with that, too."

Brenda was a large woman with strong arms and legs, but fairly attractive, and I do not suppose she could have also wanted to be a cheerleader during high school.

"I wasn't surprised to hear that Dotti got married, only the guy she picked."

"Is it really true she was a professional windsurfer?" I asked.

"Yes, for a couple of years. She was an instructor at the Rogue Warrior, too. The owner had her help out in the store, and when they expanded to other sports, and locations, she was quickly promoted to store manager. That's when she stopped."

I knew the Rogue Warrior as a sporting goods store that we passed by on our way to Cape Hatteras, near the Wright Brothers National Memorial. It had a sort of independent spirit. On the day before a hurricane you saw on the horizon people surfing the cresting waves. My father very much disapproved of that kind of recklessness, and on one such unfortunate time as we stood in traffic with thousands of other tourists who were forced to vacate the long chain of barrier islands before the storm arrived he tried to get our minds onto something else. Even after the Rogue Warrior became a chain store up and down the East Coast, it was still frequented by young people who came from miles around to ride the celebrated breakers with their surfboards, sailboards, and jet skis. Many visitors who came to the famous first-flight memorial usually stayed a bit longer to see what was going on and, much like our family when we crossed the road to get a closer look, watched them with awe.

"Why, what made her take that kind of job?" I asked, my curiosity leading to nosiness.

"Why didn't she stay a windsurfer?" said Brenda. "What would your father say if he caught me talking about someone else's business like this? Well, I can resist everything except temptation. There wasn't a person who she didn't consider a rival and compete with. No matter who they were. She was loved by everybody, it was a passion for overcoming that drove her. They tell me many men went to the store just to see her. It must have been horrible, but then again the store was hugely successful. That was when it began with Roger Bernard. It was the sort of place he was likely to go during vacation, your typical British expatriate working in the United States, but I understand he went in for directions on his way down to Ocracoke Island, and saw her. And all throughout the week he never missed a day there, hanging out with all of the college dropouts and drifters, and of course he was older and had a certain confidence about him, and him with that cute accent and showing an affection Dotti could hardly dismiss. Oh, I was laughing at her; and the gossip it generated. Well, it got to be so that the owner told Roger that he wasn't welcome inside the store anymore and when that didn't work he told him he wasn't allowed on the beach, but even that didn't stop him, which is quite typical according to your dad."

I first met Roger Bernard when he worked for my father, but as it turned out his assumed name was Sir Roger Lewis and the title by which he is presently known had been given to him when he became the administrator of the British School of Classical Studies at Athens. Later, after his foray at Old Dominion, he was presented that academic plum. Essentially, his life followed three plots. He was a scientific intelligence agent with MI6 right out of college, but he also dabbled in Greek archeology, and he graduated from Liverpool with an advanced degree in genetics and microbiology. He lived in an apartment complex near the university and spent a great deal of time during the summer months at shared beach houses. I think Brenda had a crush on him as he was a tall, older guy with wavy brown hair, somewhat sinewy, with a dark tan and bashful green eyes.

Thinking of him now, he may not have been a spy. He was always very unassuming and when you saw him walking at a measured pace across the courtyard of Old Dominion, his white shirt and a conservative blue-and-gold striped tie cast over his shoulder, you could not but smile at him. Anyway he made one tactical mistake, but in retrospect it was fundamental to his assimilation: on Sunday he used to attend the oldest Catholic—not the oldest Episcopal—church in the Tidewater area. But everybody knew that he wanted to be made chair of the research department, and it was evident that he was qualified to be heir to the throne, but my father said not until he was good and ready, and though Dr. Bernard as an objection went to the private tennis club frequented by the president for a year my father remained cussed. He cut him down when he held staff meetings. A rapprochement was effected and Roger Bernard maintained his swagger, but my father only lent his upstart protégé meager support and some protection so far as to make sure his research project was adequately funded.

Oddly enough the scheme he hatched almost worked. The department staff grew to think my father distrustful, and I have no doubt that he was swollen-headed and despotic. At home my mother complained of his short temper and his brassy voice—when he was talking to my brothers in the backyard you heard every word he uttered in the front—and our neighbors thought his behavior combative. He was much too hard-line; when he talked to them it was as though he were not party to them at all; they said he had become bossy. But if he thought his blown-up-larger-than-life importance was legitimate—extending from his function of guarding and overseeing the department's research program in the Molecular and Cultural Evolution Lab, his leadership opposing Richard Dawkins' "Selfish Gene" theory, to his willingness to do anybody else in the department a good turn when they conformed to his rituals, hierarchy, and unyielding lines of reasoning—he was mistaken, for natural selection explains everything about us: our brains, eyes, and yet what it postulates is indeed simple (and everyone but him seemed to get it at the time). His efforts at leadership were met with insincere collegiality.

I remember the time when the dean's secretary was calling on my mother at work and she passed on to us at dinner that Dr. Bernard might be stopping over to see him.

"A car just parked under the basketball pole," complained my brother Frank, looking out the window.

My father took a deep breath and everyone got up from the table.

"He said he wants to speak with the Professor," Frank reported a moment later.

"I know what this is about."

There was another moment of confusion. My father was not at a loss to know how to deal with such a confrontational act, but my mother, who knew all about the situation, who knew how to welcome guests at the house, and who was typically untroubled by commotion, I think felt a tad anxious. My younger brothers, who were still round-eyed souls, welcomed the visitor and quickly engaged him in conversation; but when Frank returned to the scene he made Dr. Bernard move his car.

"Carol, I'll show him into the living room," my father said. "Can you put on a pot of coffee?"

But Roger Bernard remained outside, spontaneously picking up the basketball. He said when he attended school he was the only one who followed the NBA. He said he hardly followed the English Premier League. He didn't see why basketball wasn't popular in Europe. And why shouldn't they be able to compete? The Soviet Union was able to. I laugh now thinking how things would change over the next couple of decades.

"I suppose he wasn't any good at soccer," said Frank afterward. But I was quite impressed. Frank had fed him the ball and he made three shots in a row from beyond the foul line.

And then after a long frank chat my father remarked that he should have been an American because he was born of revolt, flourished in dissent, and was quite remarkable in the laboratory through experimentation.

I should add that I looked at him in the same way as everyone else. Today I would never dream of telling my father about his true intention. It was only a few other times that I saw him again before he moved on, but because my father spoke of him often it was as though I knew him quite well. My father once suggested that he and Roger shared many of the same ideas and doubts about evolution. It would be anyone's guess whether or not Roger Bernard was misleading him. Anyway I know my father truly strives, as much as humanly possible, to distance his department's work from debates about God; and he knows the importance of evidence, and despite his natural tendencies understands the dangers of tradition and authority. Yet I know that he is less sanguine about the possibilities of science, and casts a fond eye upon revelation and whatnot.

I was glad I had that conversation with Brenda, but I had difficulty putting it all together. I had started to read novels at school that lurched wildly between bawdy comedy and tragic gloom, and still found it hard to understand how one is meant to respond to the characters. I was beginning to conceive however that the elements of real life possessed some of these same feelings. But I knew these people, all of whom were born within a decade of me, and they all lived in the Norfolk area. Of course, still trying to understand what it all means, I did not think that I could possibly have anything to do with this drama.

"You don't think the Humes should have gotten married?" I asked Brenda.

"From what I heard there's very little that Dotti didn't like about Roger."

"But look here, they get along just fine."

In the novels I had read or re-read since that tender age it seems that whatever happens to lovers in the end has been waiting to happen since the beginning of the story; and so the winding roads of fate ultimately weave both of their lives together. At the time the marriage seemed quite reasonable, and presently I know that Theodore Hume acted as if he were not going to live ten thousand years—death hung over him.

"The world can be very hard on a woman, I submit," Brenda said. She must have recognized she was talking to a mere boy and turned back to the dishes. "It seems to me you are getting ahead of yourself, young man."

"I think she did very well," I said wittingly. "See, I'm older than you think, aren't I?"

"All I can tell you," said Brenda, "is that when Dotti told Roger about her engagement and he did not react it hurt. You can't tell me that Dotti didn't love him."

"Then why didn't she marry him instead?" I begged.

"Such is the nature of the dating game," said Brenda. "I know for a fact that she was equally impressed but for some reason Roger backed off and didn't propose to her."

"So that's it?"

"As good as any explanation."

I bent down and took another look at the cherry pies in the oven. It was all very confusing.

"Has she ever asked about me?" asked Brenda. "I haven't talked to her in ages. Actually I haven't talked to her since she moved away after graduation."

"No," I said.

"Well, if I don't see her at church first, say hello for me next time you see her."

# SIX

I HAD MADE UP my mind that I was going to ask my father for permission to go to Kitty Hawk, but knew that it was no good asking him on Saturday night. The optimum time would be after church in the morning and the fact that I was scheduled to serve at the seven-thirty mass helped my chances, and if he asked me whether I had already agreed to go with them I was quite prepared to say I had. But if he grilled me on any of the details I would have to fall back and wait for another day.

In the morning, the sun already shining brightly, I walked out through the garage and jumped into the car and my father, having to do something for my mother at the last moment, caused somewhat of a late arrival. Just as we were rushing across the parking lot of St. John Apostle Church, Theodore Hume approached us. He was alone and when he saw us came straight up to my father. I was startled at his courage.

"Good morning, Dr. Cooper," he said. "I wonder if you remember me. Ted Hume, I used to live across the street from you. I started going to church here."

My father was a very opinionated man, and although sure-footed and quite capable, he tried to preserve an appearance of neutrality.

"Oh, yes, of course. Good morning to you."

"The chapel near the base is quite limited. Dotti and I like it very much here."

"Chapel of the Immaculate Conception?"

"Oh, yes, say I see your son has his own jet ski now. I was wondering if you would permit him to come along with us to a jet-ski race this afternoon. We're going down to Cape Hatteras, to participate in the races there."

"It's very nice of you, but—"

My father was going to refuse, but Theodore Hume interrupted him.

"I think it would be a good experience. He might have said something. We had talked about it briefly. Anyway I thought he might like to see firsthand an officially run race. Perhaps one of your other boys would like to come along, too. We'll take good care of them."

My father was taken aback. He tried to project a tolerant mindset and the respectable proposal that Theodore Hume put before him was such that he quite forgot the reason behind his animosity toward the young man.

"I suppose it would be all right," he said. "At what time do you expect to get him back today?"

"Well, the races start at two, and there is always a little congestion on the causeway. I do not anticipate getting back much after sundown."

"I need to go now," I said, and to prevent from being delayed beyond the proper time hurried into the church.

# SEVEN

I HAVE YET TO develop a theory why Theodore Hume paid attention to me. I was rather shy, quite content to be on my own, and if Theodore Hume felt concerned about me or it upset him to see me out there in the bear-sized Back Bay nature reserve alone it must have been incidentally. I am not going to hide behind such superficiality as whether one should or should not help someone in need. I never asked for help, and he certainly did not offer any. I submit that perhaps he was amused by the way I behaved according to my own free will. Perhaps it was also a strong willfulness on my part to gravitate toward the intensity of the Navy SEALs, and what he represented was in opposition to my father, and when, with a trace of courage, I proceeded to ask him a hundred questions about jet-skiing during our first encounter and he said in so many words it might interest me I took him at his word and tried it. I think he must have seen what kind of person I was, and found it easy to put himself in my shoes.

After my father had once allowed me to go to the races with the Humes (and nothing terrible happened) he made no further objection to my association with them. Mostly we went for rides on Lake Tecumseh; now and then to some local hot spot where the waves boomed fantastically on the beach. I do not know if the weather in Virginia Beach was better in those days or if it was only a conjuring trick by meteorologists, but I seem to remember that whenever we took the jet skis out the sun would shine magically. I began to feel a strange new fondness for the glorious, green-and-blue nature reserve. We went for long, difficult rides and my stamina increased substantially. Theodore Hume led by example, and tips provided before each ride by Dotti remained fresh in my mind. My ability to use this knowledge effectively and readily became manifest in the execution of challenging maneuvers. Theodore Hume inspired me with his passion for this simple diversion and perfection of his own capabilities. I showed my family proudly the progress in which I was making, and I suppose the Professor thought that, whatever I was learning from the

Humes, I could do much worse by hanging out with Malcolm Brown who had been recently arrested for growing marijuana at the lake.

Because Theodore Hume was away a great deal of time, Dotti kept her position at the Rogue Warrior and on several occasions, not without a lot of pleading on my part, I was allowed to travel down to Cape Hatteras and spend the night. It was during one of these trips that Theodore Hume and I talked about my school, my academic interests there and my teachers, about the changing attitudes of kids and about many other related things. (He seemed discouraged by the recent turn of events in President Reagan's second term, using the word "landslide" and "undoing" to my puzzlement.) He was nonetheless impressed by my grades and congratulated me. I think he was the first person outside my immediate family who had ever done so and it made me feel good. I worked hard and resented it greatly when teachers told me what I could or could not accomplish in life. In fact I did not like my counselor because she defended the class pecking order and thus would not permit me to take any honor classes. The ones I wanted to take were mathematics and history and she remained firm even when I provided her a loud, point-blank letter from my mother. Mrs. Morton was her name, and, when I mentioned this to Theodore Hume that day, he said he would pay her a little visit. To this day I still laugh at the thought.

I then could not get over what Brenda Hoover had told me about Dotti. Though I knew already what females did when they dated, and was aware of their fastidiousness from manufactured soap operas played out at school, I did not possess any practical experience yet. I thought it indeed rather curious and I did altogether, without ambiguity, comprehend it. After all, I was going through puberty, and was quite aware of the forces of nature even though the young priest at our church explained to all of us altar boys that it was not so much the desiring, but in the consent of the desire that was a sin. Dotti seemed so true, her smile so pleasant, there was in her behavior something so affable and sincere, that I could not see her picking anyone else and above picking anyone more worthy than Theodore Hume. She was not at all the type of the silently disaffected women I had read about in Victorian novels. Of course, I also knew she wasn't "Buffy the Vampire Slayer" and she never spoke with a caustic tongue; she spread her wings now and then, and sometimes her strength surprised me, but I couldn't help liking her. I came to the conclusion that Brenda was a spiteful person.

When I saw her in Kitty Hawk, I happened to tell her that Brenda Hoover was our sitter.

"She said you played sports together and graduated the same year," I added, quite prepared to hear Dotti Hume say something dreadfully pitiful about her.

She looked away but her brown eyes glistened in the ocean's reflecting sunshine.

"I always liked her. She was a very good catcher. We used to practice together at the playground. I heard she might go to Peru to teach English for the Catholic mission there. I can't believe she is your sitter now. I wish I had the means to finish college. My mom said I should have taken advantage of my pitching ability and worked on getting a scholarship. Funny that our paths don't cross anymore."

"You'll probably see her at church," I offered.

"Oh, yes, I don't go."

"You don't?"

"Ted has been trying to get me to go with him, but it just doesn't interest me."

I was going to press her on the reasons why not. It very much interested me. Besides, the Humes were married in the church and they had maintained such a respectable lifestyle. It wouldn't be at all appropriate for me to question Dotti's predilection, and it would make it very awkward for her at the store. She seemed to have no appreciation of the things one should do and the things one simply shouldn't. It never ceased to amaze me, the way in which she spoke of funny antics in her youth that I should have thought she would not want to disclose to me. I did not realize that people I predominately knew were frauds in the sense of hiding their idiosyncrasies or making themselves out to be better than they really were, but looking back it does seem to me that my parents were preoccupied by the pretenses of their environment. They moved according to the two celestial poles of society. You never caught the men telling an offensive joke in public or having a good time on church grounds. The women put on their best clothes before each PTA and parish council meeting; they lived exclusively with kindred purpose so that newcomers or outsiders could not drop in, but when they entertained everybody would receive an invitation to the party.

Though despair and injustice overwhelmed the nightly news broadcasts, either nationally or locally, my parents made sure it did not consume the conversation at the dinner table. One of our neighbors separated and eventually divorced, but they never spoke of the tragedy, and though one of the boys I played with said it was painful, they took utmost care not to dwell on the public spectacles. We all knew that Mr. Blair who had helped serve the Holy Eucharist at mass was connected with prostitution, but neither my father nor my mother ever so much as hinted at the clandestine marital problem; and though everyone was polite and smiled at them, people often talked about them behind their backs at social gatherings. (Gossip among my mother's inner circle was Mrs. Blair's dieting and eating habits.) In the 1980's it was still not unheard of during a divorce for an angry parent to cut off his son without reconsideration or to send her daughter (who like most girls lived vicariously through her friends) to another school. I was used to hearing about all this and it seemed to me normal. What did shock me was to overhear Theodore Hume speak of picking up women at a bar in some distant land as though it were the most ordinary thing in the world. I knew he was away a lot and belonged to an elite group of special forces; that was topnotch stuff; and I knew that frogmen, in books and movies at all events, often did this and had thrilling adventures before they settled down and married nice local girls; but what was before and after was not clear and besides he had not told me what he had been involved in. In my young mind World War I and II and, sure as shooting, Vietnam, were real wars. But once when we watched *Full Metal Jacket* together, he mentioned quite casually, as though it were something that anyone might have done, that he had faced a situation much like on the television set during his first assignment abroad.

"I was thrown into a lion's den," he said. "After that I was quite content to be an officer, husband, and father. I only left to have a son or daughter."

He smiled as though he was satisfied or content. I did not know what to think; I did not know which way to look; I grabbed another handful of popcorn. Another time when we were driving through the small town of Mamie on our way back home, it being a hot Sunday evening and both he and I were thirsty after waiting in traffic on the causeway, he suggested that we should go into the gas station and buy a few sodas. He began talking to a guy at the counter and I was horror-struck to hear him remark that Hume had killed a man all by himself. The owner joined us and Theodore Hume was offered a cigar, and the first man said that he must have a beer with him, and for some time they all shot the breeze about offshore fishing and rental properties and how difficult it is after leaving the Navy after just one tour of duty. Meanwhile, I sat on a stool, curious and chilled by a cold soda bottle between my legs, and not knowing what to do with myself. As we went out Theodore Hume remarked:

"I love that poor bastard, Riley. He deserves much better than that. As I said to him, we owe each other our lives. I see that you are starting to understand what's going on and if you're discreet I'll share more with you. Did you notice the purple scar on his neck? Josh was slashed by our guide and because he was bleeding to death I had no other alternative."

Theodore Hume grimaced. He turned to me.

"We had a hell of a time, but of course you can't do it over; that is not how it works. One has to move on. Thank God I have Dotti by my side now."

But another surprise awaited him. It was almost the end of August and the summer was racing to a conclusion. It was one of the best summers of my life, but my brothers had grown tired of my happy-go-lucky enthusiasm.

"We don't want to here you bragging all day long," said Arnold. "Dad, will you tell Riley that he has become a loud arrogant boaster. It is really annoying."

"Well, Riley," said my father, "I do think that, since the Humes bought a townhouse and are good friends now, they might have us over for dinner or a picnic sometime soon."

One day I told Theodore Hume: "My dad thinks you should throw a party."

"Great idea. I've been living here all summer like a bachelor, and I'm tired of seeing all these white walls and empty rooms. A party is a perfect excuse to furnish this place for a huge gathering, perhaps on Labor Day!"

Of course, most Navy SEALs try not to commit to home ownership, knowing that they are away for months at a time and their address changes every couple of years. One way to accomplish this goal is by not decorating. Even if Theodore Hume did actually buy a place, as he did then after marriage, he knew in his heart that the home was going to be demoted to a glorified storage facility as Dotti kept her position in Kitty Hawk. (When she came home, he usually was gone on a mission.) Nothing brought this into focus more than social gatherings.

I told Brenda Hoover about the housewarming. I sat at the kitchen table just behind the counter and I could look up at her, but I was conscious of her demeanor as she rolled out the cookie dough that she was distressed or upset by something, and as soon as the next day I asked Brenda if she had seen Dotti.

"I saw here all right," she said with a glower.

"Did you stop by their townhouse?"

"You kidding?" She suddenly burst into tears. "You get out of my kitchen, young man. Did you come in here to provoke me or are you looking for something to eat?"

"All right," I said. "I'm going."

"I don't know what changed your father's mind, and what induced your mother to help that girl decorate. The idea of compromise infuriates me. I suppose Dotti has to get on Ted's program if she hopes to make the marriage work—even that assumes the belief that a serious commitment can work in a world of nomads and playboys, as I fail to close the deal myself."

I did not know why Brenda Hoover was so mad. I did not mention the party again. But the following week I happened to go into the kitchen to get something I needed. In my mind there were two places in the house with an atmosphere conducive for education, the soundproof cubbyhole in the basement and the table in the kitchen where the cooking was done, or else I could do my homework at the desk in the family room, where Frank camped by the television and played Nerf basketball until his prison term was over. That particular day I was doing my summer reading in the basement. We had dinner at about seven-thirty, so that after preparing dinner and setting the table, Brenda had little to do until my parents arrived. It was getting on seven and my parents were late. That was typically Brenda's time to leave and I expected to find her collecting her things, but as I entered I heard her talking and laughing rather loudly. Arnold lay claim to the kitchen table. I suppose Brenda was talking to him, but her manner of speaking was grownup and Arnold was bent over his book. She was talking to someone on the telephone.

The conversation continued as I turned to leave, then I heard something unexpected.

"Good talking to you, Dotti."

Stunned I hesitated and saw that Brenda was smiling. It occurred to me that she had had a very nice conversation with her old high-school friend.

At the party Brenda was a little unsure of herself, and not half so friendly as my finding her before. There was a good turnout from both the neighborhood and the church and the weather was amenable to the outside barbecue. Theodore Hume exuded that confident, cordial smile; he was perfectly at his ease. Dotti played her part to a tee. Guests floated easily between the patio and the kitchen and dining room. My father was pleased. For some reason I do not remember the interior decorations. I suppose because I had never thought to pay attention to that kind of thing before. Perhaps it was because my attention lay elsewhere. The theme of the picnic was somewhat unorthodox, and great fun for everybody, with a Hawaiian theme, and as a result our family had to get ready for the occasion. My mother took us boys shopping one day, and I selected a shirt with red parrots and large imperial ferns. My father wore a straw hat and my mother a long skirt with a flowery ruffle at the bottom. It was evidently the new clothes we all wore that made the day special.

"I love your dress, Brenda," Dotti said, meeting her at the door when she finally arrived.

Brenda smiled uncomfortably conscious, but did not look discomposed. It was of rose-colored silk, very loose at the waist, with sleeves and a long skirt with pleats. I came inside for whatever it was I wanted to snack on and as quickly as I could left them. I went out into the backyard and fell into a game of horseshoes. After dinner was served I walked down to the marsh and looked over the bushes at the stream. The moon had risen and the tide was high. Presently I spotted a man canoeing up the winding watercourse, but he stopped and floated and it looked as though he was putting in a fishing line. Then I realized that it was a ridiculous supposition and I was on the point of calling out to tell him so when he lit a green lamplight; I saw it was Roger Bernard. I crouched behind the bushes and began to wonder what he was doing there and at the same moment it struck me that he was waiting for someone.

The torches ablaze cast long shadows on the backyard and though I was hidden by the shadows I made sure that he could not see me. Theodore Hume was entertaining people on the patio. I waited a few minutes with keen interest, then I saw a fleeting shadow of a woman and heard the footsteps on the ground a short distance away from me. She came to the edge of the water and signaled to the man with a flashlight. It was very quick with three little clicks. I could not resist and looked up from behind the bushes and saw that it was Dotti Hume. My heart began to beat quickly, for I was only about twenty feet away from her. At the signal Roger Bernard began to row up the stream and within a few minutes he reached the shoreline and she stepped into the canoe. He took her hand and steadied the canoe for her. She gave him a little kiss before sitting down on the middle seat.

"Hurry up, darling," she whispered.

I had gotten down into a prone position to get a better look under the bushes but was concerned lest they should spot me. Yet I was more concerned for Theodore Hume. I felt bad for him and grew angry at the sight of them going off together.

"How much time do we have?" he said, still in a whisper.

"No, as long as it takes."

They floated into the darkness, he paddling gently, and she gazing back at him. Now I felt so mad that I could hardly think straight. I stood up and walked slowly back to the house. I was so ashamed and affected at what I had witnessed that I did not want to join the party. Instinctively I felt I should tell Theodore Hume about it, but that would only cause trouble. I knew fully well that I could not say a word to anybody.

"Who's that?" someone called out.

"It's me, Riley."

I saw my parents sitting on the patio. Theodore Hume was stoking the flames in the open-hearth fireplace. Arnold was on his left and Robert stood behind him.

"The smoke should drive out the mosquitoes from the backyard if we're lucky," he said.

"There you are. I was looking for you. I told Ted you might want to light the fire."

My father stood up and turned to me and I immediately addressed him. "Sorry, I was just looking at the full moon. When I saw it I went down to the water to check it out. You know the man in the moon is just like the Mona Lisa—the eyes follow you everywhere. Actually, I wanted to see the stream that runs through this area. I can't believe how wide it is here. But if I were smart I certainly wouldn't have walked out there because it is very muddy. Look here, I got a soaker."

I was anxious to excuse myself. After all I had said great things of the Humes and it was an unenviable situation for me that he might now already know this and tell me so. I did not want to remain here in this mess.

"I bet you were bitten alive," my father said instead.

I smiled. Notwithstanding his holier-than-thou face was dead-on and chastising.

"I don't hardly know why I didn't feel them, but now I can feel a thousand bites on my arms and legs. It is the best part of the month and I will say for sure, the moon never once makes me feel bad." And then my mother came over and told me with all sincerity on her face about all of the sugar in that tart Brenda Hoover made for this special occasion and where I could find it. I looked around for Brenda but did not see her, and then back at my mother. I could not help but think of what Brenda was trying to tell me. I remember her comments about Dotti in particular, and this turned my thoughts to my mother. Was Dotti thinking only about herself or about the future? I know my mother remembers everything: how she used to wash me in the kitchen sink before my bedtime, how she used to put lotion on my sunburned shoulders when I was a little kid, and how I used to make things up to fit my world order (which in an odd way was my parent's world order in miniature). She was still as pretty as the picture of her on her wedding day.

My father looked back at her and perhaps into the past and his funny lopsided face grew nostalgic.

"Excellent, mom," I said after scratching my arm. "You know, I've just gotten back my appetite. You said there was some leftovers in the kitchen?" I looked back and watched Arnold and Robert who along with other neighborhood kids were getting ready to toast marshmallows.

"You might have a few s'mores instead of the pie," my father remarked.

"I'd rather not," I said frowning. "I don't eat Girl Scout treats."

"Say, Riley," Theodore Hume called out, "I'd like you to show these guys your invention. I think they'll like it. You can show them how to assemble the entire s'more on the stick and cook it all at once, you know, so that the chocolate melts."

"Sure, okay."

# EIGHT

**M**Y JET SKI broke unexpectedly; it turned out to be a kettle of fish. Without savings in the bank for the needed repairs the season came to an abrupt end. I was not entirely upset, for the new school year created different priorities now and besides I did not really feel comfortable being around the Humes after seeing Dotti hook up with Roger Bernard. I was not so much astonished as confused. I could not understand how it was possible for Dotti Hume to want to be with another man, but I allowed the reality of marriage to gradually course into my limited understanding of life. Ideals entered my consciousness largely through the spousal relationship of my very own parents. The meeting between Catholic beliefs and broadminded American culture contained an element of dismay arising from originality. As is true of all young recipients of culture, I was at once attracted and repelled by the the great unwashed masses. In addition, perhaps a unique quality of growing interests, I was enormously sensitive to world currents. The result was that not only was I seeing thousands of direct actions to this kind of behavior in the American mainstream, but the cunning and the duplicity and the bad faith, dominated my thoughts like no other. Perhaps Dotti Hume's activity was normal; I never could quite understand what this might be, but I knew that the consequences were disastrous. On the other hand, it had not looked as though she had decided willingly to trade up to Roger Bernard's celestial orbit even though I could not get out of my brain the sight of them rowing off together under the full moon. Notwithstanding it aroused in me a new sense of sexual freedom.

During the school year I saw the Humes only twice. On both occasions I spotted them in church. At midnight mass on Christmas Eve they took communion from the very priest whom I was serving and then I saw them during the Stations of the Cross on Good Friday. I suddenly felt very embarrassed again, but when I looked at Theodore Hume I could not help smiling at him when our eyes met, for there was nothing in his countenance that indicated a defect or a guilt. He looked at me with those coarse blue eyes of his in which there was an animal's playful roughness. He rarely looked back again, once was all that was required, as though it were a secret handshake between fellow comrades, and he always held back a big smile; and there was honesty and goodness in Dotti's face and an innocent sweetness and though then I could not have expressed this, I felt something was wrong. If I had put it into words at all I think I should have said: she looks as cool as a cat and he resembles a lion as in courage and ferocity. It seemed plausible that Theodore Hume was not aware that Roger Bernard was standing below the balcony. There must be an explanation; I did not believe what my eyes had seen.

Then the day came when I had to pick up my jet ski at Marston's boat repair shop. The owner had taken my money and I walked to the outside enclosure with him. Frank followed us around to the back in his pickup truck. I had saved up money for this special day, reaching my goal just a week before, but I felt rather upset by the extra amount still owed. It was a necessary engine part and Mr. Marston neglected to call me about it. I took it in stride and the old man knew fully well that I was good for it. Suddenly I heard a voice: "Getting ready for the season!" and Theodore Hume appeared from out of nowhere.

"Good to see you, Riley," he said. "Are you picking up your machine today?"

"Oh, well, not today. I'll have to pick it up another time when I get some more money together."

"I see."

"You can," said Mr. Marston, "if you want, son."

His response cheered me, and at the same time the thought that he finally stated what was on his mind upon seeing Theodore Hume speak to me gave me confidence. I tried not to let the hostility I felt harden my reaction to the extra charges.

"I expect I shall be able to pick it up by Memorial Day," I said. "I don't want to be in debt."

Theodore Hume looked at me with a dry smile, reading between the impenetrable lines on my forehead. There was something in his eyes I had recently learned, and his voice reacted almost like an unconditioned reflex with a short laugh. For a couple of minutes while he engaged Mr. Marston I was afraid to speak up. I was concerned that he might find fault in the situation. The two men talked on, Theodore Hume was obviously a good customer of Mr. Marston's, and I stood there without saying anything. Frank beeped the horn and waved to me. Then I excused myself and walked up to the pickup truck. Just as I turned back Theodore Hume stepped forward and grabbed my arm.

"Here," he said. "No need to pay me back."

He pressed some money into my hand and walked away. When he disappeared around the corner I saw three twenty dollar bills. I did not know what to do or say. I was glad enough to have the money to pay off my account, but the thought that Theodore Hume had felt obligated to give me the money filled me with wonder and embarrassment. I could not possibly accept anything from him. It was a fact that I would have to deliver papers the rest of the month to come up with that kind of money, but it was my job and it was an affront to take such a gift. At first I thought to run after him and return it, then I composed myself and thought it over for a minute. The new part was not only necessary but a prudent investment (understanding that from the discussion) and I felt sure that he was merely concerned about my well being and, of course he was preoccupied about the risks one takes and the perils associated with the ocean; it would be rather odd to run up to him and return the money so I paid off the account in full and later that day called to thank him.

When summer vacation arrived, however, and I had tested my jet ski on Lake Tecumseh, it was essential that I stop over and tell him about it personally. In that beautiful little lake we alone seemed to have a connection with the past which was beginning to stir my dreams for the future. But I could not seem to ever run into him there, and it was a long way to their townhouse on the other side of the neighborhood. But the weather was perfect, a golden sun turned up the heat, pulling you to the great outdoors, and the first people of summer who had an urge to get a taste of nature were propelled along by their passionate desire like marching bands in a parade. The weather pattern persisted; then a Bermuda high conveyed more blue skies and hotter days, which typically came to the Mid-Atlantic region much later in the season, now was an imposing structure that weighed upon the area without remorse. I still thought there was a good chance of meeting him at the cool lake though and a few days before the Fourth of July I had Frank take me to the lake.

As far as the horizon Lake Tecumseh was deep blue, but the parking lot, empty and baking hot, made it less likely of meeting Theodore Hume by chance. The temperature must have been over ninety. I had Frank take me home by way of the Humes. In the driveway I spotted his black four-wheel-drive SUV, and behind it was Dotti's jeep. I had overcome my shyness but was somewhat nervous. The garage door was open and Theodore Hume stood at the workbench. There was a bright blaze of reflected light coming off the windows of the pickup truck and at first he could not see who it was; but in an instant he recognized us.

"Hey guys, over here. I wondered when you were going to come around." Then he called out: "Dotti, it's the Cooper boys."

There was a reply and a warning not to come out to the backyard but within a minute she had come into the garage and was still adjusting the top of her bathing suit.

"Well hello, Riley," she said. "And Frank, right?"

"Yes, ma'am," replied Frank.

"Oh, please, stop. You can call me Dotti. Isn't it unbearable, the heat? You boys must be thirsty."

She opened the refrigerator and helped us select a soda and opened two lawn chairs for us. It was somewhat cooler in the garage, a tidy space full of tools, with a jet ski standing in the middle; Theodore Hume had his own now, which I hadn't seen at the lake, and it looked as if he were working on it. The sunlight coming through the back door was bright. At first, dazzled and then balled over by Dotti's skimpy bikini, I did not look directly at her when she welcomed us. Then I saw two other women in the backyard, both topless and very good looking. I immediately took a seat and opened the soda offered to me.

"How are you?" she said. "I hope you had a successful school year. I bet you are happy it's over. I always was. Nothing more delightful. What grade are you boys in now? Frank, I reckon you're going to be a senior."

"No, I just graduated."

"No kidding. Well, congratulations. I suppose you're heading off to college."

"No, no plans yet."

"You should reconsider," she said.

"I'm going to be a junior."

"My God, Riley. How time has flown by. You boys have really grown up. Haven't they, Ted?"

"Oh, you bet. I want to show them my fishing gear if that's okay with you."

"All right," she said with a smile. "I have guests here, but let me know if you need anything. I'll be right outside."

I thought his statement was somewhat abrasive, that is the tone of voice, but I was directly taken in by his project. His constructive ideas were now in the ascendant.

"Well, guys, I'm getting ready for the long weekend. Let me show you what I'm working on here."

"I didn't realize you bought a jet ski," I said.

"This summer, I am in pursuit of finding an alternative. The guy you met, I believe last year, inspired me to buy my own and move forward with fishing from a jet ski."

"Oh, yes, I remember him."

"We call him Jet Ski Max. My job provides for little time and most of my fishing is done with advanced planning and always in a large group," he started. "But I have a preference to go out alone. Besides, owning a boat is just too much for me, especially to put in the water alone. Not to mention it takes too long to get to the fishing spots."

Theodore Hume pointed to his jet ski, which was laying just to the left of us, slapped it and began to talk again. He had purchased a used Yamaha, the largest, the two-seat model; he told us he was looking at size, stability, and engine reliability. He said that his priorities were changing and that he would now have to rely on friends or the Navy for his racing endeavors. His choice of jet ski was a little different: it had to be easy to trailer, easy to launch at boat ramps, and it needed to be very fuel efficient and offer low maintenance and cleaning costs. Even so it was equipped with 215 ponies. Like Jet Ski Max, he had installed a marine battery that powered a built-in VHF radio and fish-finding device; presently, he was fitting out the area behind the seat with a large cooler with rod holders and a cutting board that would offer him quick and easy access.

"My first test run was in six-foot waves and with the exception of getting a little wet, I had no problems." Then he added, "I hope to get her ten miles offshore."

He had a passionate voice. I was already aware of it. Whenever there were large waves at the beach, or I watched him prepare to fly off a ramp, he always grew very excited. He would tell everybody to stay put, so that it should not seem that we needed to follow him; but after a triumphant or dramatic act he asked us if we wanted to try it. I would bashfully admit that I was not yet ready, and back at the lake I was hesitantly prepared to give it a go. Then one day a fellow Navy SEAL remarked that I was quite ready for my first jump, but Theodore Hume broke in and said that *I* had already accomplished it, which took the pressure off of me. His passion, combined with his authority and sensitivity, made it that much easier to go for it. When he spoke it was not intoxicated, it was infectious. Another time at the annual competition in Kitty Hawk, he won a tremendous race, and though the people on the beach had cheered loudly, the average person had not realized the gutsiness in it. Perhaps there wasn't, but the trait of showing courage and determination in spite of possible loss or injury was something to behold. Anyhow, before the next competition he was asked to be a little more heedful about the way he conducted himself. (A tropical storm was heading up the coast, likely to go out to sea, but the life guards were very concerned about losing racers.) The next day when we went out together he led a few brave souls around the course and even Roger Bernard joined in lustily. I held my own and afterward was complimented for the way in which I handled the rough conditions.

When he was finished, assuming my best manners, I stood up and touched the watercraft gently.

"Have you taken it out on the lake yet?" I asked.

"No, I hope to get it out this weekend though." He paused to think. "You know, Riley, this rig should be ideal for both deep and shallow water."

"How about marshy areas?" I asked.

"It only needs two feet of water."

"I have an idea. Why don't you take it down to the creek behind your house and try some fishing out there. I believe the creek gets wider at the arm of Back Bay. It's sort of like a water passage where the tide meets the river. The fishing is always pretty fair there."

"Splendid idea, Riley."

"Hey, you may very well get the trailer stuck in the mud," chimed in Frank.

"Oh, yeah," I said, frowning.

"No risk, no reward," said Theodore Hume. "That which is necessary is never a risk." He turned back to the workbench for a moment and when he found the tool he was looking for said with a playful tone of voice: "You know, it might be better to take the maiden voyage from the boat ramp at the lake."

"Probably so," I said, smiling.

"You know, no matter how much thinking and innovating I conduct here, two common denominators hold true. Frank, can you guess what they might be?"

"Gosh, I don't pretend to know anything about fishing boats," began Frank.

"What do you think, Riley?" interrupted Theodore Hume with a smile.

"I don't think anyone need be ashamed to have built a machine that is safe to operate," I said, "and the second is that you love fishing off it."

"Well," commented Frank, "I've known the Back Bay National Wildlife Refuge since I was a boy and I think one must be prepared for the unexpected."

"Which is?" I begged.

"Alligators."

"There are no alligators out there!" I cried.

Theodore Hume laughed loudly but it was not a laugh of ridicule or derision.

"By God, you make a valid point, Frank."

"Oh, stop talking nonsense," I said, looking at my brother angrily.

"Of course, we know fully well that alligators can't necessarily survive this far north," Theodore Hume brokered, "but the fact is that life is not so evenhanded. Some people don't play by the rules. I for one have no intention to be set back by anyone who wishes to do harm to me."

"What does one do then?" I asked.

"Plan for dangerous encounters," he said.

When Frank and I left, he with the soda still in his hand, I asked him: "Did you understand what he was talking about?"

"Kind of—"

"So, the jet ski must be safe, fun, and take him to the fish, but what else?"

"No, protection is number one, whereas the other things that you mentioned are purely incidental."

This in my mind was some way from the point, but I did not care to let on that, though I was practically grown up, I had yet to realize so little about the true nature of man and what he was quite capable of doing to another man.

"Unless you have to I am not going to say anything about going over there today. The Humes are really cool, but dad still doesn't quite trust them."

"I know," Frank said. "It's all crap."

"Of course they're all right, but did you see the two women in the backyard?"

"You bet," he responded with a big smile, "if dad saw them, I'm sure he would have a conniption all right."

I was glad to know how my brother felt. Frank did not wish my father to know anything that he was doing and was quite aloof about my friendly terms with the Humes. I could feel sure at all events that he would not mention it when we came home.

The unaffected way in which my father reacted to one who has been now so long accepted as one of the greatest war heroes of the American Period should have raised a red flag. Of course it was speculative, but it was the manner in which he generally kept his distance that bothered me. The next day I went to Old Dominion University to help carry some boxes home and walked past the office of Dr. Bernard, who was going to spend the summer at the University of London, which, according to my father, he had suggested as it might help him make progress on his research project, and I was told that he was very unhappy about it. I was quite relieved not to run into Dr. Bernard. But we were met by a Dr. Lerner, a tall man with an indisposed demeanor; he always bothered me very much because he maintained a stylishly arranged haircut and wore reading glasses that sat down on the end of his condescending long nose. He was a good example of the children born between the beginning of World War II, in 1939, and its end, in 1945, whose members were too young to have experienced the Depression or the war, but too old to have participated in the turmoil on campuses in the 1960's. He was a close colleague of my father and I was immediately on the defensive, for he was calm and laconic but asked pointed questions, and it made me feel dimwitted. When he came to visit, my younger brothers imitated him, and my mother would always reprimand them upon seeing the antics: "Robert, stop that nonsense." And then Arnold would jump up on the sofa and give her a risible look and say: "But Dr. Lerner is very funny; we always know what he'll do next. And of course he doesn't." I could hardly grasp that my father shared that same quiet burden of psychological reserve when discussing political problems and family difficulties.

But we all found it very entertaining to hear Dr. Lerner talk about the women in the department he considered the most dependable. My parents had a picnic on Independence Day, and a select group of people they knew from the university was invited over to our house. My father had been at Princeton, but nearly everyone he brought with him seemed to be gone. Dr. Lerner knew Dr. Joyce Webster and adored his former secretary Susan Woodson. My father considered it treason when the latter left, and he was surprised that Dr. Conrad, who called himself broad-minded and even-handed, had preserved a great deal of affection for her. The generous flow of alcohol probably led to the uninhibited argument about it. My father never knew of the office romance and said he thought it would stir up gossip and give him all sorts of trouble that he would rather not have to make amends now. Dr. Lerner answered that he wouldn't think she was the type to make a lot of fuss. She was a woman of the very highest quality, a niece of Dr. Chambers, who was one of the original members of the department, and whatever you might think of the situation, he was quite certain that she had left for a rather large promotion (and he, Dr. Lerner, was quite willing to admit that there were parts which had better have been left unsaid). Dr. Conrad had an affair with Dr. Webster, too. She was of very good training and it was strange that she left the research she worked on.

"No great loss," said Dr. Lerner. "I think Joyce intended to take some time off from work anyway."

"Mrs. Long is very reliable," said my father of his new secretary.

"Very much so," said Dr. Lerner.

It was then that Dr. Lerner asked about the Humes who were sitting at the adjacent table.

"You know we invited folks from the parish," said my father.

"He's a big fellow," said Dr. Lerner's wife.

"We're trying to civilize him," said my father with a dry laugh, "but there is only so much one can do when you consider the field of work he's in as well as the rather remarkable circumstances he must contend."

"Military type?" probed Dr. Lerner.

"Indeed, they're friends of Riley's," said my mother.

Everybody looked at me, and I felt uncomfortable.

"They jet-ski together, and after Riley took lessons from them he bought his own jet ski." My mother smiled at me and then added: "Dotti is quite accomplished and is an instructor down at Nags Head. I'd like to think Riley has learned as much from her as from Ted, her husband, who by the way won the championship last year. Isn't that right, Riley?"

"Yes, mom," I replied.

"Carol and I think they're good people," my father said.

"That so," commented Dr. Lerner.

Consequently, as soon as dessert was brought out and Dotti went inside the house, I joined Theodore Hume and asked him if I could help test the jet ski. I always found Theodore Hume amenable. The turn of unfaithfulness had made me condole with him in his cause and when we took the modified watercraft to the lake I looked at him differently. I did not reveal my secret, but I got over it; I think it gave me a great deal of satisfaction to know that I was helping him create a means of escape. But one quiet weekday morning it occurred to me that I, finding Roger Bernard pull into our driveway, might mention that I was helping Theodore Hume on a special project. I went outside and stood quietly nearby as my father spoke to him of assorted research being undertaken by scientists at Cambridge University, who managed to identify and date the genomic events since the human and chimpanzee split. My father could go on for hours at a time and soon forgot that Roger Bernard was heading to the airport and was already late for his flight to London.

"What about Kitty Hawk?" I said to Dr. Bernard, who finally halted the one-sided conversation.

"Oh, I will miss it all right."

We chuckled. He had a certain way about him. At first I liked him and empathized with his difficult position, but he seemed so at ease with my father that I was ultimately forced to conclude that his unfaltering courtesy was more contrived than genuine. He was always deferential, fluid and even obnoxious; he surprised me in his quickness and I always seemed to be one step behind him; but we laughed together for a moment and this disposed me badly toward my father. I couldn't help myself, and the young professor was forever going to be considered suspect as a result of the great scheme to unseat him, but I always thought my father took in good part Roger Bernard's intractability at the expense of his own lofty departmental responsibilities. I should add here that my father had an interesting childhood. It amused us (especially Frank) to hear him tell stories about growing up on a farm in the New England hills that made him sound like Huck Finn, and when he spoke of his ingenuity we roared with laughter; however, he was right-angled and constant and the way he dressed for work was always the same to me. (I had never been to one of his classes nor heard one of his lectures, but that was my impression of how he might have portrayed himself to the student body.) Dr. Bernard's demeanor had softened recently, and as a result my father found himself less and less affronted by it all. But Dr. Bernard was persistent, so I carefully listened to him bid farewell to my father in his buttoned-down shirt, and watched him drive off with the top down in his sports car.

I typically visited the Humes after dinner, once or twice during the week, but I always turned around if Theodore Hume's SUV was not sitting in the driveway. (I drove right by their house if Dotti was home alone.) He would be working on his jet ski, listening to a ballgame on the radio with his rather tone deafness, until ten o'clock or so; there was a smile on his face and he always cheered when I arrived. We worked on several of the modifications together. My father and I had worked on several home projects together and I had become somewhat proficient with tools when I obtained my own jet ski. My father took a long time to complete the efforts, and though of course he demanded perfection, when my mother grew impatient with us, especially if we had gotten in her way or caused too much confusion, I used to disengage and retire to the television in the basement.

I did not have the same level of impatience while working with Theodore Hume, but he had a natural sense for teamwork. His method as a rule was rather imprecise, but when it came to getting it right he was quick and alert. If a problem came up, we spent the rest of the evening exploring various options until a solution emerged. Ordinarily he did not speak very much, unlike my father who talked a lot, but when, after an item was completed, he took the trouble with a pleasant cheerful cooperative nature to point out to me the correct way as well as the mistakes, and he was not only coherent but succinct. When Dotti returned home, she would tease him as he would tease her. He would smile at her moodiness, for they very seldom argued in front of me, and sometimes he would end the discussion with a witty retort. They behaved very much like lovers, but not like good friends, and I should have quite forgotten what I learned about them and what I had seen but now and then she came out to the garage and gave him a big kiss that embarrassed me. Her eyes were weighted and provocative, as though she were carefully approaching a beast in the wild, and in them was a naughty, heart-shaped smile. Then I would notice that his face seemed suddenly to swell and he worked with some distractedness. I looked quickly away, afraid that he would notice my regard, but he was intent on the lingering feeling or else was ready to finish up for the night.

The hour or two I spent with him in that hot, incandescently lighted garage passed like lightening, and as the summer drew nearer to the end I was seized with dismay at the thought that I must spend the next nine months dully in school.

"I don't know what I shall do without you," said Theodore Hume. "You sure you don't want to modify your jet ski?"

"Maybe next summer."

I was glad that he still encouraged my excelling in freestyle riding and facilitated my entering races. While I was appreciative of the offer I did not want to make the permanent changes to my watercraft but this made for an amusing give-and-take about the merits of jet-ski fishing.

"How about going down to the lake with me on Saturday?" he asked.

"The weather ought to be all right," I said. "We can ride in the afternoon when the fish are resting on the bottom."

"Ha-ha. If you would just try it, I'm sure you will never go back to casting a line from the shore."

"All right, we'll see."

# NINE

**W**HY SHOULD THE imagination of a man twice his prime remember such trivial matters? I was riding a big wave and I could see a large crowd cheering for me on the beach. I had grown stronger and I had bought a new bathing suit and vest at the Rogue Warrior, made of black synthetic fibers and very cool, and I had bought a new pair of sunglasses on the boardwalk before the contest at Ocean City. I wanted to go and tell Theodore Hume immediately I had won and I was full of emotion that the seat belt holding me in made a red impression on my shoulder. The trophy made me feel quite satisfied. (I had already begun trying my luck at two local races to test my newfound physical ability.) On our way through Nimmo I thought to ask my father to drive by the Humes to see if they were home. I would have liked to stop by and show him the hardware, but I knew that my mother wanted to get back and Arnold and Robert were getting a bit unruly. I had all sorts of electrifying things to tell him about the race. I had won the preliminary heat in the morning and I had landed a jump in an exhibition. I planned to enter a race up in Dewey Beach in a few weeks on Labor Day and I was surely going to have a field day with my finely tuned jet ski. Though time was running out before school started, the summer was peaking and there was a good feeling in the air. The neighborhood, with its deep green colors embraced by the sun and its wet borders loose as though formed with a paintbrush, felt like a landscape by Winslow Homer, defined by directness and realism and splendid color—now thinking back; then it felt like nothing other than home. When we came to our street I noticed that the trees were almost black.

"Finally," Arnold said. "We're here."

Down the street several boys were riding their bicycles. The moon was just beginning to show itself. I walked around the house and let myself in by the back door. My mother was already in the kitchen by the refrigerator preparing a late dinner for us. I shouted to Frank and he came up from the basement, a little lethargic from the physiological condition of being alone for the entire day, and threw his long body back against the counter. He said all the right things:

"Nothing happened" and "No VIPs stopped by unexpectedly, and I cut the grass in the backyard."

I hit my brother on the arm and I stood in front of him, with my legs apart and my trophy behind my back, and was going to reveal it to him with great fanfare. Instead I decided to merely put it down on the kitchen table. Then I went to the family room to see what was on the television, and up to my bedroom to change my shirt.

When I came back downstairs to dinner, and my father brought inside the grilled steak, Frank said to me:

"Sweet, good job, Riley."

"Thanks, man," I replied.

"Say, you won't believe what I heard today. I went down to Wal-Mart and ran into Brenda Hoover, and she told me something that might interest you."

My mother looked up and my father stopped carving the steak for a moment.

"Your good pal Ted Hume left his wife," he said.

"No way!" I cried.

"Yup, rabbit, run. He took all of his things and hit the road last night. Apparently they hadn't been getting along and they hadn't been talking for some time now. She still has that place down in Kitty Hawk."

"How awful," said my mother.

"Shameful," said my father, "but it all goes to show you, boys. The lesson here is that he sunk himself, and nobody of good faith can be sunk except by his own hand."

I was shocked. I lost my appetite.

"Just as well," added my father. "I was hoping something good would come out of the friendship but I don't want you to think that we subscribe to that kind of behavior."

"Of course not," I said.

"Best that you stay away," said my father. "Trouble will undoubtedly ensue."

"Yes, sir."

"I don't want you to get caught up in the mess at all."

"Brenda told me Dotti will be leaving," said Frank, "and I suppose the house will be left vacant like the one down the street when the Emersons foreclosed."

I did not think this was quite logical, but was pulled down too much to argue.

A few days later Brenda Hoover stopped over to say hello to my mother. She was preparing to visit Peru with the church and was very excited about the trip. As soon as my mother stepped away I asked her what she knew of the situation.

"They were ill-sorted," she said. "They was like oil and water with their different dispositions and everyone thought otherwise. It was always going to be hard for them to make it work and when they were apart they would seem all but the better off. Many of my friends think Dotti's ugly situation was a direct result of Ted's caddish behavior. And he goes to church every week when he's in town. I don't know how she could have been such an idiot."

But it was evidently of her own bias she was speaking and not of the Humes that I knew.

"I don't know more about it than a man in the street," she continued. "It's like shampoo down the drain. But I blame his behavior partly on Dotti. He seems to have a lot of fans, and perhaps this enthusiastic crowd contributes to the rotten atmosphere that allows for his behavior. It's like a new Paleolithic age where tens of thousands of years of society have swirled into oblivion. Cro-Magnons are once again dragging women by the hair into their caves—and women love it."

"Oh, come on."

"Well, look here. He's brainwashed you. Before, guys would never behave like this, but people still seemed to say, 'Boys will be boys.' I hardly agree that it's essentially harmless folly, like swallowing a goldfish. Nor do I believe in the Amish way of life. I mean what sane person would reject worldly concerns or disapprove of marrying outside the faith. Even our wonderful priests know that they are on the wrong side of many arguments. Oh, God, what am I trying to say? We have the license my mother didn't have while growing up, but are really screwing it up."

"So what about Dr. Bernard then?"

"What? Oh, please, he's a gentleman, besides he'd been gone to London, and when the girl finally got up the nerve it was no Roger or anything like that, but just a matter of personal conviction. And if you ask me, I call that very smart of her not to stick around here afterward."

I was much more shocked than before. I was certainly not brainwashed by Theodore Hume. The reader cannot have failed to observe that I accepted the state of their marriage as if it were a law of Nature, and though the reasons for the separation had seemed to me obvious, and the twists and turns of love were beginning to become more familiar to my young brain, I could not but think Brenda was mean and insecure not to consider Theodore Hume's side of the argument. The next day at Marston's I listened with keen interest when two young men spoke of him in my presence, and when they spoke of him as a colleague I said: "Hey there, I jet-ski with him"; and when they asked: "What did he tell you?" I replied: "Well, nothing much at all except that we were supposed to fish this weekend." The two men were noticeably relieved.

"Of course he was going to fish with you, kid," one of them said, "and I'm Batman and my friend here is Robin." He turned and exhibited a quirky smile which precipitated an immediate response from his sidekick: "Asshole."

"No, really. My name is Riley Cooper."

"Ah, yes, I remember Ted mentioning you. You were helping him with his jet ski, right?"

"You bet," I said proudly.

At that moment Frank came onto the scene and corroborated my story.

"To tell you the truth he's gone on a mission and won't be back for a long time. It's for your own good. I hate to see this kind of thing affect close friendships."

I felt very much cheered while at the same time let down by the news. If he took it upon himself to tell Dotti one day that he had been planning to go away for the foreseeable future, and it came to bear upon their plans together, I could easily see a God-awful quarrel. My mother would accuse my father of deception and untruthfulness and perhaps even infidelity and of not behaving like a decent human being, but I did not at the moment see what the reason could be. I knew the Navy well enough to be aware that he would not be able to tell her anything, and that I should be reminded of my own transgressions. I was just as glad not to see Roger Bernard involved. But a month or so later I ran into him face to face at Old Dominion University.

"Yo, nipper," he cried, calling me in a way I instantly recognized. "Just noncing about, I reckon."

"You reckon quite correctly," I answered with what I thought withering Monty Python quality.

As he bellowed with laughter I stepped into his office.

"I thought you were working in London," I said to start the conversation anew.

"The Professor tried to get rid of me for good," he said coolly. "Well, it looks as if I will be back here at least once a month. Now you should know what comes of living under an authoritarian regime. What I always say to my British colleagues across the pond is: the cause of America is, in a large way, the cause of mankind, but as to faith I say my own mind is my own church. I pity you Cooper boys, and know what you have to contend with every day—throttled even on Saturday."

"Oh, it's not so bad."

"You don't say."

"Yeah, he let me drive today."

But though he was smart about my father there was in his voice no aura of anger, but a rippling of joy emerged as though in his heart he were suddenly released from these contemptible, constraining petty contrivances.

"You going down to Kitty Hawk today?" I asked.

"Me?" His face assumed a look of utmost amazement, but his eyes glowed with sly hilarity. "Ha, what a man will put up with for a taste of heaven and you could not hold me back even with iron chains bound to my arms and legs. Your old man should know better for when people are well managed they neither look for nor want any other familiarity."

I had never seen Dr. Bernard more determined. Later that day I told Frank about the conversation and repeated what he had said to me because I did not quite understand the relevancy. I should have known Frank to say something quick and knowing, being the smartest (and laziest) in the family, but as I could not grasp his higher cognitive process and abstractions I just said that I must be getting along and with a nod let him be.

# MIDDLE PART

## Comrades in Arms

# TEN

**C**ONTEMPLATING MY YOUTH, while waiting for James Isner to arrive, I patted my furry friend on the head when I considered this unfortunate misunderstanding of Theodore Hume's personal life in the context of the immense achievements of his career. I wondered whether it was something akin to the way the military profession was not fully appreciated by my parents that he had not been given the proper treatment that the best critical opinion always ascribed to him. The historical effect of my father's own peculiar generation wasn't really talked about when I was growing up in Virginia Beach. He was for long thought to decry his ROTC experience, and indeed he gave you the impression of muddling through the compulsory experience; his language was labored, an uneasy mixture of counterpoints opposing ideas, and his restraint was such as to make my political attitude healthier and more amiable. Toward the end of my high school years, his manner, acquiring a palliative ease, became supportive and assailable; and then by graduation, going back to the period of his maturity, found that his experience had an unusually positive influence that imminently suited my situation. His prime belonged to a period when the military badge was no longer in vogue and there are many impassioned people from that time in America who have found their way into key leadership positions in the nation. His subtle opinions, his views that a country which strives and remains at peace must be ready to defend itself, rings true with me. It was not a mortification to him that I chose to join the Navy ROTC program at Old Dominion University.

When I was growing up, though Theodore Hume's work was worthy but mostly "black ops" of which only one or two were known by the public, it was very much a mark of group thinking to admire him. Among my friends Navy SEALs were thought boldly supernatural. Even my father thought they were a very good stick to beat the Philistines with, and that was well before al Qaeda made their grand entrance on the world stage. President Kennedy's divine inspiration already discovered that these unconventional misfits were Shakespearean, and who said that history does not repeat itself; and when in the late 1970's after an upsurge of trouble arose, the service chiefs got together and uttered shrill cries of ecstasy upon considering the wet and flavorful tactics of these creative men. This was a commodity that Theodore Hume had no difficulty in supplying. My own heart sank when during my First Class Cruise he led us onto the deck of a patrol boat and into the hold of a helicopter and I knew I was in for eight hours of excruciating pain at sea, in the air, and back on dry land. But I admit that I have always thought these protagonists were magnificent and their skillfulness artful or adroit.

Hume's strength lay evidently in his ability to lead the class of men he knew best: cowpunchers and steer wrestlers, field laborers and manufacturing workers, jacks of assorted equipment, unemployed jocks, computer hacks and able-bodied drifters. When he integrated young men belonging to a higher station in life even his warmest sentiments, I learned firsthand, would endure a certain level of discomfort; he made sure that his plain-woven teams were so unbelievably plain, members mutually supplying each other's lack, perfectly balanced, to fill out the whole unit; but at the same time you are not surprised that each man could easily bring forward another capacity, if called upon to do so. His men always were full of life. But here again I must say that this is an impression; the most popular Hollywood movies have shown that they are energetic types, spirited, rough-minded adventurers, and they can all be compared at some level with John Wayne or Teddy Roosevelt. Some people of course seem to think that Navy SEALs are habitually obsessed with violence and sex, but to represent them in such a way as being altogether devoid of a context that should go back to the country's first days seems to me really an excess of unwarranted criticism.

Meantime the Pentagon can force the world to pay attention to their immaculately groomed warriors, and the journalists may get all excited over the few who have broken the rules (where the result in the second case lasts longer); but I cannot help thinking that no warrior can make a mark on history like Theodore Hume without considerable risk. Yet even the hand-picked ones become jealous of popularity, for they know very well that posterity makes its choice not from among the most decorated of a period, but from among the most recognized. It may be that some great soldier, airman, sailor or marine which deserves immortality has earned a lot of medals and is highly regarded by the American public, but it is such that the battle in which he fought is immaterial; and it may be that posterity will disregard all the most worthy stars of our day, but it is among them that it must choose. At all events Captain Theodore Hume is in the running. His awards and decorations happen to bore me; I find them typical; even the two golden medallions with Minerva doing battle with Discord that once stirred my young imagination leave me indifferent now; but he certainly had impact. There is in his best engagements the flutter of moral excellence, and in none of them can you fail to be aware of the warrior's paradoxical quality. Right from the get-go he was praised or damned for his fight; according to the political affiliation of the person he was revered for his accomplishment or condemned for his over competitiveness—but *élan vital* has never ceased to excite America in this second decade of the new century.

The well-informed reader of this reflection will remember the vast majority of the lamentable headlines of the Iraq War played out at the height of Theodore Hume's career—later, even the surge in Afghanistan brought mixed feelings. Taking these unpopular campaigns as his state of affairs, I think he should be related by what was very well described in the *Aeneid's* opening line: "Of arms and the man I sing." No one who knows it can fail to grow nostalgic, which brings me back to the historical importance of men like Hume in the founding of the United States, by that independence and strong will, by all those virtuous and smart choices where mutually beneficial results were sought through others in unusually dire and complex situations, in short, defined in a way that valued people over technology, quality over quantity, knowledge over structured doctrine, and substance over theatrics. Herein I will not bring up to speed anyone who is not awake to this kind of style (even if widely read one may not fully appreciate the unique culture and nuances of the art), but let me just say that it is itself a thing of beauty. If some suggested that Hume was by way of being a crude, blunt person and that a snide remark here or there would have made light of this quiet, professional type it must be replied that it all can be traced back to our wicked Indian wars; but the first inhabitants of this great country knew well that Nature has given hearts to bulls, swiftness to hares, understanding to men, and that Beauty is more formidable than fire and iron. James Isner, when he was talking to me of Hume, inferred that, whatever his flaws, they were saved by the noble-mindedness that suffused his method. Now looking back on our conversation, I think it was this overmodest remark that most exasperated me.

Fifty-some years ago when Hume was born this art form was employed to fight Communism in Vietnam. And it was good form to support and politicians used this little country in Southeast Asia to embellish an argument or balance a position; then Vietnam and the Red Scare went out of favor (oddly enough with sex, drugs, and rock 'n' roll) and change came in and these warriors became whipping boys. That said, fifty years earlier the French had found the same result when they left their bloody imprint on this fertile land; they had also left their mark on U.S. military affairs that is relevant here. (Marcel "Bruno" Bigeard, one of the most decorated soldiers in France, was a paragon of a new type of professional warrior that arose during this period, but more about him later.) In Saigon the French had seen lurking in the shadows a nationalistic movement, but quietly gave a sigh of relief when leaders in Washington, D.C., consecrated their first military plans. We had our own plans during this expansionist age and what is more the unfair persecution of our missionaries would finally stop. Spiritually the West was on soft ground; but business was good there and then after World War II things turned for the worse, when Ho Chi Minh founded a coalition with the Communists, and established a republic in the north at Hanoi. The French were enraged and attempted to reassert their authority; the Chinese did not challenge this aspiring young man; and, while the British, who like us were also making money in the country, decided to help the French troops in suppressing the resistance. An agreement was finally struck, ushering in a period of hope, but then fighting broke out again; before long French ships were shelling Vietnam and in one coastal city they killed some six thousand civilians. Needless to say, boys being boys, the locals fought back and then retribution ushered in the prolonged and bloody guerrilla conflict known as the French Indochina War.

Men in power, each of whom is fighting so pleasing and competent a battle, bask in the glory in every manner from discursive to devious, from cold to charming; and the two sides, more or less saying everything to win popular support, but still defying dares while fashioning death or victory. They tell their people through broadcast mediums what they should think of life, culture and the world, and promote discord with an exalted negligence with self-reinforcing abstractions. It is the sum of human wretchedness, I suppose. My God, the force of inexorable mortality! The ideal has many faces and heaven is but one of them. I wonder if the origins of this state of motion is anything more than the cry of distress of those leaders who cannot make themselves free in our sad reality of suffering, and I wonder if their true passion for life, the divine gift if of woeful eternity, is anything more than greed. It may be so that the next generation, which typically accommodates itself more reasonably to the tyranny of fate, and the ruling principles of hate, will look for new ideas not in a flight from death, but in an eager acceptance of it.

As everybody knows, by the mid-1950's the United States was paying about eighty percent of the costs in Vietnam. The war escalated from a Vietnamese civil war into an international conflict in which we easily afforded and ultimately championed, taking the reins from the French and the British and thus carrying forth the torch for Western Civilization. The Soviet Union could never keep up and hence the American Empire was born. I do not know if others are like myself, but I am conscious that I cannot contemplate history long. Yet for me, a beneficiary of being on top of the world not a single complaint, but no dreamer made a truer statement than Lord Byron when he wrote *Prometheus*. Poetry has always given me the essence of human life when my mind shakes. I pan out with wonder to ponder with rapture for hours the view from above for clues of the big picture. Beauty is a kind of eternal punishment; it is as complex as life itself. There is so much to be said about it; however, it is as simple as a good piece of artwork: explaining that simplicity is how I make a living, except in so far as art criticism is concerned only with visual aspects and therefore with the human condition it is limited. Most people have an opinion with regard to the myth of Prometheus, still more if they had taken time out of their harried lives to ponder the complications of the rebel who resists all forms of institutional tyranny only to be punished forevermore by Zeus for his supposed crime to free himself. Should Prometheus be credited or blamed for playing a pivotal role in the early history of man? Did he serve merely to account for the mixture of good and bad in the individual or was he a proponent for humanity's advancement? These are the questions one must contemplate when defining the difference between war and survival, or more broadly humans and animals of the wild. But many people think in other terms when it comes to the human race—love, hate, generosity, egoism—because the human spirit is such a difficult thing to understand.

Religion tells us that our spirit is divine, but heaven holds our attention for only a little while. An old man who after seeing the Sistine Chapel asks his wife "So what's the big deal?" is not such an imbecile as he is made out by his accompanying friends. No one has ever been able to explain why *The Last Judgment* is more beautiful than a vase full of roses except by bringing in considerations that only an art critic might know. Truth sinks to triviality. Beauty is a limit which once surmounted means nothing more than the accomplishment. Art has many symbolic representations. That is why in the end we give up trying to distill the troubled stream from the pure source, in the realization that we live a bifurcated existence to which our spirit plays off. Little has been written about this latent hostility. I suppose that is why I am writing this book and perhaps the same reason why I am fascinated with Caravaggio's work. The human spirit is that impenetrable force which is equal to all suffering. It is only to the frantic people on treadmills that have no time to be curious. I know this is a bit silly: everybody has his own mindset when it comes to living.

But of course what the critics wrote about Captain Theodore Hume was unenlightened. His salient goodness was not the reason that he decided to steal fire from Zeus only to give it to mortals, nor his valor that made him the best frogman ever (my own opinion), nor the luck that made it so, nor his survival skills adapted to the windswept deserts, north of stormy oceans or east of blood-soaked shores; it was his firm will. A deep sense of vital principles is one of the most admirable characteristics of mankind and I think it may be safely stated that in no other country than the United States is this characteristic more pronounced. We took it from Europe. Still the love with which a Western nation bestows upon her heroes is oftentimes too passionate or extreme. Where did this madness come from and how did it ever come to be that an individual is called out? I remember seeing on the television how an entire country came together for the New York Yankees and still couldn't quite understand: "Gosh, Dad, but what about Hank Aaron's ticker-tape parade?"

I had already been acted upon by the forces of Nature, but my father reminded me that compared with the World Series those individual statistics mean nothing, and I know from experience now that Hank Aaron's *acte gratuit* (despite the snub) was of a singular good-natured deed. What is more, as a gracious example of society, it was the home-run king who showed us that it does not make one bitter even when considering that when at the age of seventy he saw his record broken by a younger man that did not play by the same rules as his generation. A man at the age of twenty-four who batted .322 and led the league in home runs and runs batted in, before hitting a walk-off shot to clinch his team's first pennant, was in my young mind a hero forever and worthy of a ticker-tape parade. But it is at this age, when he would be too young to be a mayor or a senator or the president of a Fortune-500 company, that he is prepared to lead men to victory. This is not so strange when you see that from the earliest times the young have been institutionalized by the elders of the group for battle because they are stronger and fitter than them, and before the young realize what nonsense this venture is they become the elders too, and it benefits them to preserve the deception. In my opinion this practice has undermined the very principles that our country is trying to preserve. Why youth should not be equal partners in societies used to bedevil me, but not any longer.

At one time I thought that the awards conferred among senior military officers when they had ceased for a decade or more to deliver the goods were largely due to the fact that the generals, having no longer to fear their authority challenged, felt it safe to recognize their own worthiness; and it is well known in organizational theory that to praise someone whose ideas are *not* different than yours is often a very good way of telling the lone wolves it's time to join the herd. But this is to assume that man is of the same nature as wild beasts and I would not for the world lay open here to the charge of doubting Darwin. After many years of considerable thought I have come to the conclusion that the real reason for the universal convention that discredits the youth of a country who exceed the thresholds of goodness is that wily intelligent people under the age of thirty-five are not dependable. As they grow older the deeds they perform in their youth for society are scrutinized by the elders and with every year that passes they ascribe greater merit to the young that conform with them. Of course, one must want it; one must keep in the good graces with the circle of elders. It is no good thinking that it is enough to accomplish great things in isolation; one must provide a platform for society to advance without undue consequences. Change needs time, and I suppose the circle of elders has no choice but to promote an environment that creates heroes for the purpose of growth and expansion, but fresh ideas must be such that if the apple cart is upset, you can pretty much forget about taking control of the reins.

If, as it's been beaten into me to think, social discipline is essential, few in the Navy have enjoyed his trip in a more flagrant way than Captain Hume. When he was a young Navy SEAL (having served operationally in an Underwater Demolition Team, SEAL Team, SEAL Delivery Team,

Special Boat Squadron, and in between assignments as a Navy program officer in the Middle East) his position in this narrow world was only respectable; the senior leaders praised him, but with moderation; however, the younger men were inclined to be earnest under his authority. It was agreed that he had natural ability, but it never occurred to anyone that he was right up there with Roy Boehm. Then when he came to an untimely death, an uncomfortableness set upon the Navy, like a light of faith when in the time of darkness that makes one believe, and it became plain that there had lived among them all those years a magnificent man of vision and none of them had suspected it. There was an upsurge of interest by the military at large (starting at the Special Operations Command) and a dozen or so scrambling think tanks, inside the Beltway, wrote convincing articles, opinions, detailed analyses, and even gossipy or long and expressive blogs on the revival that took place as a result of his work. These were circulated, wide and far, whole and in bits and pieces in discussion groups on the Internet and during conferences. His memoir was dissected, his philosophy was analyzed (duty and self-improvement, plain and simple), and his way of thinking was studied (adaptability, top-down and bottom-up simultaneously). Meanwhile, his two sons who were almost full-grown, were canvassed by prying, fact-finding journalists. Posthumously everyone agreed that Hume's legacy was at work every day, tracking down the nation's most wanted enemies in the Middle East and elsewhere in the world. This acceptance he gained was not to be until after he was slowly lowered into the desiccated ground in El Paso, Texas.

Now the military looks about and counts proudly all the men and women who have taken his place. A few hidebound senior Navy officials in the basement of the Pentagon and elsewhere are sitting up and taking notice, and they secretly feel that they probably should have seen the writing on the wall.

Though these reflections have taken a long time to synthesize they presently took but a few minutes to pass through my head. They came to me spontaneously, an inspiration and then shards of memory that belonged to a former time, and I have since tried to place them in a chronological order in my mind for ease of understanding and because I know the mind has a way of playing tricks. One thing that surprised me was that even though other things preoccupied me in the past I could remember distinctly what had transpired and even some of the words people said, but with vagueness what the record said. I know of course recent history, especially of Iraq and Afghanistan, but if I recalled it from memory it was hardly arranged in or according to the order of time.

I was standing in the kitchen and Riley Junior was sitting on the couch when a taxicab stopped at the curb outside, then his bark at the doorbell, and in an instant James Isner's stentorian voice telling me that he had arrived. He came in, confident, flushed, and bighearted; at once his broad smile impinged on an acclivity of resistance I had been building up from the suspended past. He brought in with him, like a Marine with orders to take the hill, the fast-growing and inevitable battle.

"I was just thinking about the past," I said, "and what qualities are especially important to the Navy and the Marine Corps now and you come to the fore."

"Well, hello, boy," he said, crouching down to stroke Riley Junior on the head.

"You have a way with animals, too."

"Oh, and a good day to you, Riley. You never told me you had a guard dog, but he seems to be a friendly little guy." When he asked about his name, and I explained how I came to own the stray and the coincidence of sharing the same name, he laughed; and when Jim stood upright his eyes converged on mine cheerfully.

"He goes by Junior," I qualified.

Jim looked down and his demeanor was quickly reciprocated. "Of course a man's best friend has an innate sense about certain things. All the people who have studied the progression of dogs from wolves are constantly reminded about the pace of this changing world and the implications of the shifts. It is a theory coincident with my visit, and I thank you for bringing up the reason I wanted to talk to you today."

"That so," I said.

"By the way, Riley, I'll always accept cordial compliments, but I haven't accomplished anything yet. Perhaps one day with your help. You know, I think one must start by looking at our General Krulak first, the visionary behind the Higgins boat and a great contributor to our collective understanding of Vietnam, and then at Nimitz and Rickover. Of course the Army and the Air Force have their champions. Personally, I don't quite see how in another twenty-five years or so Hume can help having the field pretty well to himself. It's just a question of separating the wheat from the chaff to determine the most worthy souls from Iraq and Afghanistan."

"Please, don't be so, so—"

Jim turned away and sank his fit body into one of my camelback armchairs, and I offered him a cup of tea instead of an objection.

"Do you want a nip of Irish whiskey to go along with it," I offered as I sat down across from him.

"No, I have to stay on top of my game today," he said. He looked around the room. "Nice, those your watercolors?"

"Yup. So what do you have for me today?"

He glanced at his leather briefcase and then at Riley Junior who lay in wait on the carpet next to it.

"Oh, I thought I'd better have a little talk with you about the project I'm trying to get started. It is rather difficult to explain over the telephone or through emails and whatnot. To be honest with you, Wanda Hume gave me complete access to Hume's military records."

"No kidding. Why didn't you just say so the other day. I know how to connect the dots."

Despite a hard stance I was inclined to accept what was plausible as true. Besides we were from the same tribe. I was happy to think that I had something of value to offer him that when made use of was not merely for his own personal pleasure.

"Well, I haven't really sorted things out yet. Wanda and I had several long conversations since my visit. She is going to do her part. I will also have complete access to his letters and emails. He seemed to have been a persistent writer. She's presently making copies for me now, but it's only one piece of the puzzle and of course I can't afford to rely on it completely. My department chair has so much more respect for a researcher or scientist if he questions everything. He said I've been scratching away at the surface for some time now, and my work to date has been awfully adorable, but limited. He's given me a license but I could never seem to take advantage of it."

"Until now," I said to complete his sentence.

"Yes, indeed."

"I think I understand your situation. You are trying to move beyond the ethnographic and archaeological evidence about warfare between groups of hunter-gatherers, geographical opportunities, economic and political integration, and the evolution of beliefs, by reexamining the sociology and human motivations that determine how opportunities are exploited, and you are jumping at the chance to exploit the life of an American war hero."

"Bravo. But of course he was fifty years old when I first made his acquaintance. I got myself invited to his birthday party and told him how much I admired *Gallantry in Action* and he told me in so many words to go to hell when I got up the nerve to talk to him. I got as far as I have gotten here with you. So I know nothing about the early part of his life and a little more about his military career. Wanda had little luck trying to get him to talk about those days while married and in any case she said that he hardly talked about work, and of course a lot of material has been lost in that unpublished manuscript. By the way, I'd like to make an effort to track it down. Say, I'll tell you the sort of thing I want to write with you, a set of discourses on the rise and fall of empires, with a lot of economic details that point to the paradoxical nature of human and societal virtues in Western culture, you know what I mean, and then a synopsis of the discourses into a best-selling book, but decisive and smart, of course, and although critical, fair and representative. Perhaps something business leaders will care for, too. Naturally it must be done up as a biography, and Wanda seems to think it won't be read by many people if it's too scholarly."

"A lot to ask," I commented.

"Sure, of course," said Jim. "I'm a professor, and you're a critic. It's obvious that I forgot the most important ingredient. An idea just came to me—a storyteller is needed."

I began to see where I really came in. Glancing at the briefcase, I wondered if Jim's efficaciousness was developed and rehearsed like a sales pitch.

"I asked you the other day if your writer's group was open to taking on an assignment and you said it certainly was—"

"I said what? You must be speaking of Joan Moaney?"

"Maybe so, nice lady," he said. "We had a long chat. I recall she's quite an accomplished writer. She said something about other writers who would be helpful, too. Can I take that as an affirmative now?"

"We only work for money—it's the American way."

"Then have you any objection to me looking for a literary agent?"

"My God, I think you are getting ahead of yourself."

"Oh, please," said Jim with a big smile, with a tone of an author who has been there, done that. "I think the first matter of business is to see about an advance."

"I thought it was a first draft."

"Ha, that's what they tell aspiring writers with no experience. After all, how are you going to solicit support from your colleagues without a healthy advance? This project will take a couple of years. It must have been obvious to you, and you were probably more observant and knowledgeable than I give you credit, so I see your point."

"You know, without the notoriety to back it up, I wonder if his personality would capture the attention of the public. Do you really imagine that if we went down to talk things over with Wanda, a proud but meek woman whose undivided motivation is to correct and cement her late husband's reputation, you would be able to persuade her to let you speak to both sides of the story?"

"Of course, I've told her that I am a serious man, not a political hack," said Jim, with a large laugh that took from his position any probability of solvency.

"Well, all I can tell you is that what chiefly bothered me about Hume afterward was his blind faith in institutions. He used to go to mass every Sunday—even over there when possible—and it started to make me question certain teachings in the Bible. King David was hardly a saint though idealized; and the Ten Commandments seemingly bear on only internal affairs."

"Well now. What exactly are you referring?"

"Oh, nothing really. You see, he was a man who led by example. He was rather keen on the rules of war, the real rules of war, but once he mentioned his frustration about two of his men who were charged with dereliction of duty and making false statements . . . ." I rambled on, though I could see by the look of Jim's expression that he was unimpressed by my weakening tone of voice; he listened, but he was a little bored by this story and its twisted irony, and it struck me that when he was bored he looked like my old man. I thought to finish the story and tell him that Hume had finally found this guy who burned and dragged three former Navy SEALs through the streets of Fallujah, and after they took him into custody he claimed that he was tortured by his captors, and he showed scars to prove it. I didn't know the facts, nor did I ever bother to look into it, so I let it go. But though I couldn't remember that Hume had ever said anything derogatory about the Geneva convention during any of my many interactions with him, I told Jim that I had a very acute recollection of his feelings about it. A little trauma was insignificant in his mind, that though it was a direct result of combat, with a smoothly blended field and valley at their backs, they used common sense to get the bad guys to talk to them under the hazy light of a warm spring evening.

When I looked up at one of my watercolors, I moved on to Afghanistan. From the air base, winding cracked roads ran between the great halcyon fields and clusters of sheep, goats or horses, real and with an Arcadian majesty like good old English country downs, only limited by natural springs and the old Mirab, which is different than our widely distributed laws based upon the *Magna Charta* and sacred texts and writings. And sometimes the road was only cart tracks, with jagged sedimentary stones, and the undulating treeless uplands extended for miles on either side so that when you looked up there were only pointed peaks below the blue sky. And as you rode toward the rocky border with Iran, cold air gave you a keen sensation that the world was standing still and members of another tribe were taking note of you. And as you traveled at a breakneck speed you had a feeling that you were on top and life would last forevermore. Although you were charged with such authority you had a lazy feeling of tedium. You were quite happy during the lulls, and if your guide from out-and-out panic suddenly told you to slow down and wait for the livestock to move gradually out of the way you either thought he was joking and sighed loudly or shot boldly ahead. This was because you razzed one another innocently and laughed at your own jokes. Now and then one would pass rain-fed flat areas with vast valleys behind them and in the flat areas were crops like wheat and barley or vegetables like peas and beans; and a little way from the road were simple brick houses, with their small shelters and outbuildings; and one would pass through poppy fields with the workers picking the ripening reddish orange fruit. I spoke of the citadel at Farah, which was one of a series of fortresses in the northern provinces built by the Greeks, the city being an intermediate stop near Herat, my base and the hub for traders both of today and in bygone eras. The history these people bore was ordinary but unfamiliar: there were the conquering forces of Alexander the Great from the west, Genghis Khan from the east, the Arab conquests from the south, Russia from the north, the fight for power and for equality in Islam from within, and there was the rise and fall of great empires from Achaemenid to Sassanid.

But of course all that could matter naught to my new partner, and he interrupted me.

"Did he ever talk of philosophy?" Jim asked.

"Yes and no. Well, I suppose he got his know-how from somewhere, but he never mentioned it. He used to read the classics. At the lake, when I first met him as a boy, I remember finding serious books in the back of his SUV and sometimes my dad and he would talk about religion, but my brothers and I used to interrupt them."

"Did you ever get into an argument or debate with him?"

"Not while growing up."

"I meant to say later when you were a Marine."

"No, not really. Although it was during my first tour in Afghanistan that I remember thinking he was a bit hard on me. I hadn't been having much success and he offered me some advice. Grudgingly, like any young Marine when confronted with new ideas, I listened to him but what he said made all the difference in the world. He said that Lawrence of Arabia is an imperfect model, but one who I could learn a great deal about the effects of our behavior, especially in the regions where there's a strange geography, culture and history, and he suggested that I shake off the notion that counterinsurgency operations should be led by the big Army. Oh, I took his advice and read Anwar Shaikh's books to gain a better sense of the beliefs of Islam and ways to exploit the fissures of the Arab national religion."

"I bet you ran into a little trouble with the doctrine department, but go on."

"Well, not then, that I remember; but when I was ready for a promotion a few years later I overheard one of my superiors saying that Captain Cooper had turned his back on the Marine Corps and the great tradition, the rise of faster armored vehicles and UAVs together with information technology, only to go exploit petty gossip gleaned from natives sitting around a desert campfire underneath the stars. It was Hume who told me that I best get out of my vehicle, that fear would only lead to failure. I was surprised at hearing him speak so forcefully, so frankly, but then was amused because a great big musclebound teenager who was assigned to me for a short while during the invasion in Iraq never missed a meal and played video games all day. I was the only one who knew what the devil was going on. Later on, back in Afghanistan, when we were working together, he remarked: 'Riley, you seem to be on the right track, but those knuckleheads you work for and their insular bases of operation, I think they are too detached from reality to get a sense of what's really happening on the other side of the border.'"

Jim listened to my brief account with attention. He nodded his head reflectively.

"Ah, yes, so goes the saying that our weapon system is the Marine himself, but there is a flip side to that formula. A key understructure of any country, whether old or new, is justice alongside a homegrown military and police force."

"Well, sure, but that would all come later on. We dug in while Hume put his men to work, and he made them ready to die for the cause."

"That's interesting," said Jim, leaning forward to pat my dog on the head. "Do you know how he did it?"

"More or less."

I could see that Jim was more than pleased with me now but asked: "But do you really think he moved his men to such a degree that it rubbed off on the locals, on their society?"

"Well, sure," I said, looking away.

"I see," Jim answered. "War is pure hell. Social integration versus disintegration. One must start somewhere. But I think I should have expected you to sing a battle song or hoot *Semper Fi* to respond to the unbreakable commitment, cohesion, connectedness in combat and in life, you know the sort of thing. It's a question that is being raised by some of my worst critics, and in response I quickly cite research at the Moscow Institute of Bionomics and Evolution. Initially, I spoke enthusiastically about our research on ants. Cornell has a very good research program. We found that Argentine ants don't fight each other, or rather don't fight ants from different nests—with one exception: they will if some are found to have eaten something they have not shared. Ants communicate with their feelers and the colony likewise communicates almost rhythmically based upon repeated contacts or interactions between ants. The misunderstanding is that Argentine ants live in one-big happy super colony when in fact they live in separate, competing, self-sufficient nests. The takeaway is that ant colonies function seemingly without central control, almost like genes that work with blueprints or programing. We are currently looking at scientific questions about ants and the human brain—you know, biological systems that function without hierarchy, such as the immune system. This research may one day be applied to the military, if they ever want to get serious about flattening the organization."

He laughed at his last thought and I responded:

"I'm sure you heard of Myrmidon ants being transformed by Zeus into selfless human soldiers."

"Yes, I've read the *Iliad*. Real ants, however, do not offer a lesson in behavior."

"Yes, they do."

"Well anyway, about thirty years ago the Russians began studying stray dogs in Moscow, and they found that their appearance and behavior changed over the decades as they continuously adapted to the harsh realities of the city. Like war without support structures, at the group and societal levels, dumping a pet dog on the street amounts to a near-certain death sentence. Their research points to a range of behavioral traits shaped by the situation that developed."

"You mean like that of wolves, their biological ancestors?"

"You bet," he said, "but in some cases the dogs are *devolving*. They found there are four groups: guard dogs are the ones who remain most comfortable with people and though they are still free they develop ties to certain individuals they regard as masters who feed them; the second group or stage of becoming wild is the dog that becomes socialized to people, much like beggars; the third group comprises those that are socialized to people but whose social interaction is directed almost exclusively toward other dogs where their main strategy is acquiring food from open rubbish bins—this group has flourished in the post-Soviet years because the pickings aren't so slim anymore; and that was the springboard for the last of the groups which are wild dogs whose range is extremely broad, and let me tell you they are smart predators—they know people, but view them as dangerous. I might have made something beautiful out of that—by the way, they're on my team now—but I'm still wondering if the theory will hold up with humans. After all, when you're drawing up man's portrait you must get the virtues right; you only confuse the impression if you put in things that are all out of tone."

"I can appreciate that."

Jim was silent for a moment and he looked out the window at the sky reflectively.

"I should have mentioned that a stray named Anton evokes a very strong reaction from Muscovites. Several years ago a young lady was returning home with her beloved terrier when they encountered Anton who had made the subway station his home. He was guarding it against drunks and other dogs, and started barking at the pair; but instead of walking away this woman reached into her jacket, pulled out a knife, and in front of rush-hour commuters stabbed poor Anton to death. I don't think it's necessary to dwell on the incident as it is not really of importance in the life of Hume. Anyway, the lady was arrested and forced into psychiatric treatment. You know there were some very typical reactions to this story in Russia. One would have thought that after a rather awful life like that a stray dog would be the last thing the public would choose to honor with a memorial, especially when it was an example of an extreme point; but they have a strong relationship to these dogs. A bronze statue of Anton now stands at the entrance of the station."

"I suppose the Russians, like us," I said with a smile, upon realization that the course of his argument had swerved, "can go nutty when it comes to dogs."

"No, I went to Moscow a few years ago and saw them everywhere," Jim continued thoughtfully. "You can hear them howling at the moon at night; and they do not look anything like the dogs here. Paying attention, I realized that they also acted differently. I saw one stray waiting on a Metro platform and when the train pulled up he stepped aboard and like everyone else scrambled to get a seat or a choice spot on the floor and then a few stops later exited. He had a wild aspect to him but was a rather easygoing guy. What am I trying to say here? The strays I saw sit somewhere between house pets and wolves as if the process of natural selection was reversing itself. One always thinks in terms of domestication, even when times are bad, but there I saw with my own eyes the first stages of the shift from the domesticated back towards the wild. My colleagues say it is virtually impossible to turn back biological clocks—but many of the dogs there cannot stand being confined indoors."

"Do you know what that means?" I said. "It means that for a very long time dogs had so little freedom that they jumped at the first opportunity to gain back their independence."

"Very funny, I was thinking of Stalin, but that's it; at any rate it's not a very pretty thing for our grand society. And then, you might find this amusing, I heard about a Metro dog with uncanny instincts about people, happily greeting nice riders but avoiding intolerable old ladies who typically oversee the automated turnstiles. Leo, a medium-sized stray with thick golden fur, oriented himself in a number of ways and seemed to have figured out where he was on the subway system either by smell or by recognizing the recorded announcer's voice. On Monday and Wednesday afternoons he could be found across the street from the Riga station, which is a short distance from the Bokol'niki Park where he hooked up with his girlfriend, lazily hanging out on a soft mat with a large bowl of freshly ground meat set before him. Of course, Leo was being taken care of, and, unbeknown to him, he was becoming domesticated, but he was still free to come and go at his own pleasure."

"Ha, there you go. Say I reckon they make living in the city more interesting. I might raise this up at the next city council meeting; you know we are huge dog lovers here."

"Well, one could say that even Americans are after local color and are interested in diversity. But the strays have some habits that are really difficult to cope with. Society usually prevails: it's kind of like triumphalism. Did you know that it was with great difficulty Hume could ever reconcile the Bedouin way of life?"

"You must be referring to his memoir," I said. "I read only the first few chapters, but he was born at a time when people thought it unworthy to be large-minded. He lived in a house that promoted taking the road *more* traveled by."

"You know, of course, he had a strange way of taking life by the throat and he didn't see why he should not hold it to be an inalienable right to go to hell in his own way. It was an amusing story about his being shanghaied by military police and sent to Dam Neck as punishment after getting into a fight with a fellow helicopter mechanic. I didn't think that was possible. I reckon it being his third fight in a matter of a week that had something to do with it. Then he said he made a mistake for heeding his father's advice about college. His old man worked for Union Pacific Railroad, doubted management types, and was quoted to say that the U.S. tolerates foreigners to the point of insanity."

"His parents used to take him to the peak of Mount Cristo Rey in nearby New Mexico, to celebrate feast days or take in the natural beauty of the Southwestern desert, and I think he gained an appreciation of the unique geography and cultural merging of the two countries," I said in defense of him.

"Conversely, if you read between the lines, I think it only wore him out to have to compromise so often."

"I don't know about that."

"Well, his parents didn't do much on the other side of the Rio Grande, and nothing would induce him to go to Ciudad Juárez when he grew older, and that was before the drug wars. It's strange, you know, for a guy who has always lived on the edge."

"His book points to the fact that he changed his opinion about the world," I said.

Jim pondered my point thoughtfully.

"All right, he was a curious guy, and curiosity is a trait that lends itself admirably to new ideas. Of course, all this is conjecture; I'm merely saying it to show you that in understanding his life I shall have to turn my thinking upside-down. I don't see how one can deny that he was a tad bit conservative, but on the other hand he had a natural tendency to take huge risks, and some of his personal habits were rather perverse, yet at home he was a good son and father and at work strangely biddable. I don't think the striking contradictions worked against him. I don't want to say anything that's erroneous, but I do think there's a certain amount that needs to be explained."

"Don't you think it would be better to look at constructive aspects of his life? He was a natural leader, a great communicator, and I think it's important to know that he had developed a close bond with his Muslim counterparts—whatever affected them correspondingly affected him."

"Are you talking about mutual understanding, compassion, trust?"

"Absolutely," I said. "But there's something else that needs to be explained, you know, the real motivation that drove him to perform so magnificently. A lot had to do with Dotti."

"Oh, Wanda would be furious to hear that. But, yes, it would be much better to show the man with everything exposed, his romantic side and his passion for mission despite his careless treatment of his responsibilities."

"And his personal notions for freedom," I added quickly, "and his ground-belief of wife, family, and religion."

"I hear what you're saying," Jim said.

"Well, if Wanda wants to maintain editorial approval, it's going to be much better to be allusive and charming, you know the sort of thing."

"And tender for her benefit. Of course his memoir was something less than the whole truth, very selective, especially in terms of opinions and remembrances of friendships, and no intimacies—and though Dotti was perhaps sorted out as a load-bearing truss, I know Wanda is upset by it. But you make a valid point. I need to tell Wanda it could backfire on her. And I ought to research and reflect on the comparative history that makes it clear that Western culture goes back more than a millennium, back to the opening up of Africa and the penetration of man into the Middle East and Asia. Well, I see this rather like a portrait of all creeds living there, with a good deal of local color, you know, and a certain center of gravity, and with a sort of social and economic interplay of the different races. It's a good way to compare our differences. In any event, you know what his world is about better than anyone."

He was absorbed for a moment in the idea of worldwide acceptance and acknowledgment. In his mind's eye he saw a book, rightful of a noble laureate, profound and elegant, published in a dozen languages with a thoughtful introduction by a champion of either capitalism or socialism who would lay out the key points and the fundamental implications in a humanistic manner for all the great thinkers of today, and I think he envisioned critics unanimously agreeing to his universal theory that would explain the evolution of both man and nations. But being because he possessed such great passion, Dr. James Isner could not, as I suggested much earlier in my account, help but consider this a proprietary business enterprise of his own.

"But how the hell am I to get credit for my contribution?" I said to his surprise.

"Oh, don't worry about that, Riley."

"I thought I best mention it now." He smiled and the thought I reserved while he was speaking came back to me: "I think you should consider bringing on a few Middle East specialists. Of course I can help identify them. But I see the first difficulty will be to understand who the Arabs and Persians really are. What I'm saying is it will go a long way and help bring light to Hume's work. You see, at the very outset, my first meeting with the people of Afghanistan, I found a universal joint or coupling of belief, almost mathematical in its limitation, and resistant in its tragic form. The origin of these people is still very much an academic question, but for the understanding of the military action in which Hume was involved their present social and political differences are important. It is known that there were well-developed civilizations there in prehistoric times. The Achaemenid Persian Empire first controlled the region and ultimately the Arabs became rulers. I really think that this period is crucial and needs to be delved into, because it changed everything. Socially, the people of the region seem to be divided into two groups: the settled townsmen and nomadic tribesmen. These two groups are not different races, but just men in different social and economic stages of development, with a family likeness in the way their minds work. This might interest you, as the second group is under severe pressure and it's coming to a head again. A long time ago some tribes found themselves driven to the very edge of cultivatable lands. Some clans were thrust by stronger clans into the wild, where unwillingly they became desert nomads to keep themselves alive. Opportunity, and their empty stomachs, persuaded them to start raising goats, and then sheep, and lastly they began to sow a little barley for them. So you see they were then no longer nomads, but townspeople, and they soon began to suffer from the selfishness of the clans they left behind. Numbly, they made common cause with the people already of good soil, to defend themselves but both realizing they too were wanderers; and so over time, the mark of Nomadism, that most deep and biting social discipline, was on each of them in a personal way, like your Argentine ants."

"I'm impressed."

"Well, it's what separates us from them. We vanquished Native Americans, but they are a people of fits and starts over there, and the shared experience is a very strong force. It is a cycle of courage and continuance."

"Yes, but go on."

"About a year after I had first arrived in Afghanistan, upon driving up into the hills, I checked out a ruin of the Greek period which my guide believed was made by a prince as a palace for his bride. The stones were said to be made with precious oils and flowers. My man Mahmas, sniffing the ground like a dog, led me from crumbing room to room, calling out, 'This is jasmine, this rose.' But at last his father who came along for the ride that day waved to me: 'Here, come and smell the very sweetest scent of all,' and so I went into the main section of the ruin and there looking out an opening with him, took a deep breath of the silent wind of the empty desert plain before me. 'This has no smell at all,' I remarked. He nodded his head and smiled at me. Right then I understood this creed of the nomadic tribesmen, which for a long time was hard to fathom, and was inexpressible in words. Many have turned their backs on modern life and deny themselves things that we consider all-important; they forgo material ties, comforts, necessities and complications to achieve personal liberty, unlike us; but perhaps like your Russian dogs, they only partake in simple self-indulgences: coffee, fresh water, and women. So these people that I was there to protect embrace with all their souls this pureness too abstract for Americans to understand, for the reason, counterintuitive but felt, that in the desert they find themselves perfectly free."

"Sure, I can't see why all that part of the story shouldn't be treated with the greatest possible consideration, even though many of them have been co-opted by our way of life already, but as not to neglect the resistance of certain things, with a sort of detachment from our own society, à la Lévi-Strauss if I understand what you mean, that would be rather important."

"I know it is a very tall order."

"As I see it now, there's an urgent need to get to the root cause. It can only be a question of getting just the right string to pull. What I like about your ideas is that you have combined the spiritual resistance inside the souls of many Muslims with a focus on traditional customs and beliefs—it's good stuff, I mean, most Americans think it's perfectly reasonable to innovate and to get rich. Autonomy, I think that might be it—and I think that this might be a case where a radical amount of autonomy is needed as a pathway to better results. And if you look at the military operation on these staggeringly low levels of engagement in the villages, I think it's because we're deploying the wrong management techniques. People don't engage by being managed or controlled. I know from my own experience that people engage if they get there under their own initiative. The objective is to demand some measure of compliance, but what you want more than anything is engagement. I wouldn't scope the problem more than I can afford, but I would suggest what is essential for the logical progression of the story. You know, however unpleasant a revelation is you can overlook its meaning if you put it into the wrong context, but I can do nothing unless I'm able to get Wanda to appreciate the underlying concepts and facts."

"Obviously she has her own ideas."

"Sure, but that is why I got the call. Man, we're not mice on treadmills with little carrots being dangled in front of us all the time. Well, sometimes we are."

My thoughts traveled to Afghanistan and Theodore Hume's adaptation of the old carrot-and-stick notion.

"Riley, this is what I'd like you to do for me now," he said finally.

I have learned from experience it is always beneficial to listen intently when I had nothing more but an opinion to offer or when I do not know how to appeal to the immediate interests or concerns of the person in charge. I held my tongue and smiled benignly.

"You know more about Navy SEALs than I do."

"I don't know that much. There must be other people in your vast network who can get you acquainted with the business. It is not as secretive as it used to be."

"That may be, but you after all are my friend and more important a friend of Hume's from Virginia Beach."

"Oh, I see. You mean that I'm a good vehicle to gain access to inside information."

"All right, if you feel that you must put it that way."

I saw that Jim was not inclined to beat around the bush anymore. I preferred it this way, for I am quite used to dealing with people in a direct manner.

"As a starting point, I reckon you saw much of him in Iraq."

"Not really."

"But you saw a good deal of him after, I believe."

"Yes."

"When you worked with him in Afghanistan, right?"

"I suppose."

Jim restrained his smile.

"I won't press you about the precise details. The outcome is quite clear anyway. You were fairly close to him then."

"That's right."

"How long did that last?"

"Almost a year."

"How old was Hume then?"

"Oh, forty-something. You must understand he had been already promoted to captain, with many responsibilities, so you see he left most of the work to his men."

"Got it, my mistake. Here's the thing, Riley. I want you to help me write the narrative."

"Say that again."

"I want you to jot down the story of the mission, from both Washington's perspective and that of Hume. It won't take you long and it will be of great value. I'll strengthen it by some reports and books already published. All I want are the facts. You can write it quite crudely, and nothing classified. My point of view is rather different. Comrades in arms, you know, become comrades in other things, too. My theory starts in an obscure cranny of evolutionary theory called group selection. I don't want you to be evaluative or anything like that at this point, but Captain Hume crafted a perfect plan, which was mislaid, and we owe it to his memory and to the American people to tell everything we know about it. For God's sake, he gets recognized twice in Iraq but gets nothing for his singularly most worthy effort. Frankly, it seems to me historically useful to recount the story."

Jim therefore appealed at once to my sense of patriotism because I knew fully well that the mission was a success despite its obvious failure.

"I suppose only idiots write except for money."

"Oh, I'll try to arrange something for you. I have some headroom on a grant being carried out on preferences in our Behavioral Sciences department. You'll fit in and perhaps it will lead to something beneficial to you down the road. Of course, in the meantime, I'll start looking for an agent."

"But why must I visit Wanda Hume?" I asked.

"Well, if you want to be an equal partner, you need to come along with me. It will give you a better appreciation of the deal I've struck with her. Wanda's concerned about keeping this very quiet, so as to protect both Hume and her own personal privacy. In the end of course, the book will be published, hopefully taking Capitol Hill by surprise, if you understand what's going on here."

"All right."

"I have not even discussed the details with my people, but I would suggest that you do what is necessary to get reacquainted with Hume's men. You know how it goes in the military, however heinous a subject is you can always dampen its offensiveness if you handle it with pride. But I can do nothing unless you get to the bottom of it."

"Wanda won't be able to handle the truth."

"Well, we talked it over. She's aware of the allegations, and ought to be able to deal with the unadulterated facts. Until just recently she worked for the Navy as a civilian and as a result has been exposed to a lot so if you feel inclined to leave out a few things it might not be a good thing."

"Well, we'll have to see about that."

"I've said my needs are somewhat different, but otherwise being there during the holidays would be an ideal time to talk of the past with your parents. I'm very interested to know what your father thinks about him. In addition, your mother should have some recollections of Dotti, and after all it's quite likely that you'll say things that you wouldn't happen to recall the outlying circumstances and she could perhaps facilitate, you know how a young person's memories get all mixed up but come back in conversation. Let's plan to go to a nice restaurant. And we can take a hike around that lake of yours."

"Sure, why not," I said. "By the way, do you want to stay with my parents? There's plenty of room at the old ranch now and I'll be there of course with you. My brothers usually visit with their families but I think we'll be all right."

"You sure?"

"My mother would love it."

"I'll tell you what I'll do. I'll visit after spending Christmas with my folks. I'll stay with you for a couple of days before heading back to Cornell. You can arrange matters with your parents, but I'll be flexible to accommodate Wanda. It will be a bang-up trip."

"Sounds like a plan," I said. Satisfied I laughed easily, and Jim looked seriously at his mobile phone.

"Christmas is on a Wednesday this year. I'll arrive on Friday, and we can perhaps get together with Wanda on Saturday afternoon."

"All right. Shall I come and pick you up at the airport?"

"Excellent, I'll buy tickets right now."

I know Jim has always been an earnest sort of guy, but he changed his mind about the whiskey, and before he left we made a toast to the brotherhood. Riley Junior and I walked him to the door. There I reminded him to bring along a good pair of hiking shoes and a poncho in case it rained.

# ELEVEN

**M**Y DEAL WITH Jim sent my thoughts back to my second tour in Afghanistan. Neglecting work that afternoon, it occurred to me to drive down to Mount Vernon and shoot the breeze with my old boss. Jacob Dirst was a veteran Army lieutenant colonel and our fearless leader when, a second deadly mishap led to the dismissal of our task force in the country, and at a moment's notice I was transferred from Iraq. He had secured a vacant house near Shindand for me. I worked out of the air base there for about three years, first charged to support military actions and then to support USAID reconstruction efforts in Herat Province. I lived out of the smallest of three rooms, in a wrought-iron bunk bed, and over me he slept when he was in town: his rule as to the use or otherwise of it. I shared the house with two junior reservists and we held true to our self-sufficient heritage. Lt Col. Dirst was a tall, progressive, combat-ready man, with very long legs and arms, a large head and the largest, the most subdued hazel eyes that I ever saw. He had thick whiskers of very dark hair for his age, in the afternoons and all day on Friday bestubbled in a nascent beard around the mouth and on the neck as you may see in old photographs of the Confederate soldiers. He had a forgiving nature (though I did not want to test him, for in the Marine Corps when you are subordinate you take the goodness people show you as a fluke) and he was an excellent manager.

No one could make quicker decisions than he. In Kabul he was up before first light to get the word out to his foot soldiers' outposts so that "they needn't drink their coffee simply starin' out the window, my Lord it's a hunky-dory morning"; and if he didn't hear from you by eight o'clock, a short email to get a rise out of you, a dry joke about military bureaucracy and the lunacy of war, the latter usually aimed at the overambitious CIA operatives trying to exceed their objectives, he'd say: "Come on now, there's my southeastern corner not up yet, e'll be late for the party again";

and he would come up suddenly on the satellite radio and ask for you by name and you would hear his jovial voice: "If you don't get out there at once you won't 'ave time to 'ave a say in the matter, an' I've got to break this fiendish cycle." He worked all day long and he whistled at his desk and he was loose and happy and smiling, it seemed.

His wife was much tighter than he. She had been a homemaker with a hand on all affairs, and preened and wore a perfect manner; she was president at the neighborhood citizen association, highly connected, and maintained a strong voice that was heard and responded to by their county and state representatives. Mrs. Dirst's only easing came after she had become exasperated by either irrepressible women or their raving four children and have a little holiday with her unmarried sister in Vermont. (Jacob knew it was time again when he saw her walking around the house talking to herself.) I wish I had the sense to pay better attention of their relationship (like Dotti Hume and her adoring husband), for Mrs. Dirst was a conundrum of the rebellion of man against fate. She had a gift of antipathy that never failed her, she had a naughty style and an apt and varied way about her, and she cared not a straw for conventional morality or the notion of letting her girlfriends be chastised. Yet she was a pattern of virtue and she would never be brought down by vulgarity like other women: marriage never should be founded on a spontaneous urge ("It's sex, sex, sex all the time with them, and afternoon pinochle and diet drinks and snacks, and chitchattin' on the telephone and talkin' for hours at a time on the front lawn, and I don't know what the point."); but in public she did not hesitate to remind her husband to obey what was called in my mind a woman's self-love.

One could have said of her what her husband privately said to me after her untimely death from cancer: "What I loved about 'er was that she seemed to be seeking God through me. Oh, Mary drove me crazy sometimes, but she never doubted me." Mrs. Dirst loved her husband, too. I think she assigned to herself that as her supreme vocation ("It's as it should be," she said, "I'm bein' a good wife but also helpin' the neighborhood and the church and what all."), because she inspired him with horror and it wasn't any different than the horror of his own carnality that he cast upon her. "When I think of Mary I cry," said Lt Col. Dirst to me one afternoon, "I won't cry anymore when I'm dead and buried down behind St. Clare's with 'er."

Lt Col. Dirst's nostalgia was cumulative and the stories of his wife who died while I served under him in Afghanistan was a great comic relief that went on every time he visited me.

"She was a tyrant, but I swear on the Bible I'd corked my mouth whenever she flushed red as a tomato. Though what she'd do when she got going was always the same. A few times she gave me thoughts of walkin' right out the door."

Mrs. Dirst had very nice legs and the question whether she had cunningly employed them to temper her husband was discussed for a year or so with an unimaginable variety of invention.

"But as I said to you last night, when she said, 'Oh, big fella, come on, take me now and 'ave your way with me,' I shouldn't 'ave remembered thinkin' bad thoughts about 'er."

I had seen pictures of Mrs. Dirst both on his desk in Kabul and on the mantel above the fireplace at his house in Mount Vernon. My last visit to see him had been in response to a telephone call in which he asked me to come and drink a couple cans of Budweiser with him on the back porch and announced: "I'm finally relieved to be out, that damn salt mine was killin' me, but right now I need you to help me with something out in the garden." He was holding the picture of her on their wedding day. Though Lt Col. Dirst must have been at least fifty when I was under his command, and that was about six years ago, I had no feeling as I rode leisurely down Mount Vernon Memorial Parkway that I should not find him in excellent health. He was unquestionably part of the memories of my life as the Harley-Davidson motorcycle that carried me along the Potomac River that fine December day. The final product of their marriage greeted me at the door. Hannah was now a woman approaching twenty-five who worked at the nearby Safeway grocery store, and her father had been repeating for as long as I can remember that Hannah would be marrying George Abbott one of these days. Hannah was the mainstay of the household that she had inherited toward the final days of her mother's life (Her three older brothers lived on the West Coast.), and she still spoke of the way her mother referred to her as "that dratted hussy of mine."

I was ushered inside the house and asked if a cup of tea would suit my fancy by Hannah, a young woman always intent on charming me, but still bearing on her shyly pale face the homely college student. Lt Col. Dirst was looking out the bay window when I was shown into the kitchen and he turned about slowly and smiled comfortably at me.

"Well, if it isn't Major Cooper. Whatever brings you down this way? Is the water boiling, Hannah? You will 'ave a tumbler of whiskey with me, won't you?"

"Ha, you were on my mind today, Colonel," I said. "But I probably shouldn't."

"Oh, I've got nothin' better to do except that I'm not so wound up as I used to be," he answered. "I take care of one or two things around the house each day. I cut down my Christmas tree yesterday, brought it in this morning."

"You need any help setting it straight?"

"No, of course not."

Owing to the rise of Veteran benefits, he was able to get more out of the flawed system, and I think in his own way he was doing just fine. But of course Hannah took care of him.

"Oh, you wouldn't believe this, first they tell me I 'ad to upgrade my cable, and then I 'ad to put in the fiber, and then nothin' seemed to work right but I must have a telephone. What it's all about I can't think."

"I says it's pretty much time Methuselah thought of getting with it," said Hannah, who was laying the tea.

"You 'ave your iPhone," said Lt Col. Dirst hotly. "When I die you can 'ave it all. The 'ell with your brothers. Look at me livin' with only dial-up Internet service and an analog converter box to watch television."

"Now and then George says to me I ought to move into his apartment an' look after *him*," said Hannah dryly, unperturbed by the decreasing circumstances.

"You two should be thinkin' about getting married. I dear say though, George might be smarter than he leads me to think. I don't know if it was the military or your mother that nearly killed me, I give you my word. The doggedness of it. All them demands comin' all the time, and the wife crowin' and the general cryin'. Maybe I confused the two. Ha, I don't know how I did it. When you lived a few years in peace and solitude you can't get back on the treadmill."

"Oh, you loved every minute of it," said Hannah, topping off her own cup. She winked at me, and I took a sip of tea.

A few feet away was a bird feeder and on it finches were perched, fluttering their wings as they ate, two squirrels were collecting spillage below, the sun sitting above a stately row of pine trees in the background that made me think of the hardy Afghan Pine that Persian nobility had planted throughout the country some 2,500 years ago. Lt Col. Dirst looked outside, it was Nature he saw though, and it soothed him as a steady candle flame soothes an elderly bishop.

I looked around the cozy, timeworn, untidy little kitchen in which he had lived so long; however, I knew there was really nothing I could do for him. I noticed a stack of library books on the counter. One of the books interested me.

"Tell Riley about your new girlfriend," said Hannah.

"I don't know if I would call Eleanor that, now you come to speak of 'er, except me pension and ambition ain't enough so as to go on workin' another twenty years for 'er."

I don't think I am a disagreeable person, but his reply, unexpected but so dry, made a sudden smile come to my face.

When it was time to go I asked if I could speak to him privately about military matters.

"Sure thing, Riley, and I'll show you my garden. If you don't mind, I might need you to help me come springtime. I'd like to add some space for a few rows of corn."

Hannah answered her iPhone, and in a moment, lightly cloaked, Lt Col. Dirst escorted me out into the backyard through his tidy garage. The garden was the same narrow dirt plot that I had created for him a couple years back and sweated in and there was the same bench and the same fence around the perimeter to keep the deer out. But the garden had been made ready for the grim winter; on the ground were screens and several inches of mulch to protect sensitive plants; debris and fallen leaves were cleaned up all throughout and dead annuals were removed from the nearby flowerbeds. In my experience I saw both ends of the spectrum upon retirement and the most common he demonstrated here to a tee, by maintaining meticulous order and by putting in vibrant colors from bright red to yellow to pale blue and white, which I readily perceived by seeing the ripe fruit of Northern Bayberry, Winterberry, and Common Snowberry.

"What was it you wanted to ask me?" said Lt Col. Dirst, not without some concern for me.

"Oh, Hume is in the news again. I can't quite figure out what all the fuss is about."

"Theodorus, he tried to write history."

"Of course, no matter, change is coming through Tahrir and not Herat, or Baghdad—"

I couldn't help stopping myself as I thought of all the years that had passed since I was commissioned, and of all that had happened to me. It was with Lt Col. Dirst that I had gotten shot in the leg by a stray bullet, when putting boots on the ground in the Wakhan Corridor. It was with him that I had tried to make a difference and experienced my first real success. It was under his command that I had been given the chance to work with Hume and his men, the Shakespearean heroes and their roving bands of freedom fighters, who were willing to work with outside infidels to weaken the Camp of Islam. I wondered what had happened to them since. Persians, Kurds, Tajiks, Uzbeks, Pashtuns, Hazaras, and others, young men learning our innovative new ways and willing old men expelled from the villages or thrown unexpectedly upon us because of social failures in their societies. The visit that day made me feel (as Lt Col. Dirst would have put it) really pissed off. All the hopes that had been kindled there, the bright visions of the future, the flaming passion of a new life; the regrets, the disillusion, the tiredness, but the unwillingness to accept the world as it is through the pejorative state of apathy (implying a shaking of the fist at Providence as in *Prometheus*); however, so much had been felt in so short a time span, by so many of us, the whole gamut of human emotion, that it seemed strangely to have acquired a troubling and enigmatic personality of its own. I have no concept why, but it made me think of middle school and Mrs. Morton with a stern finger pointed at me, when my wings were clipped by her derisive eyes. What I obscurely (and rather deeply) felt, was conveyed to Lt Col. Dirst, for he smiled loosely and with a characteristic gesture rubbed his black whiskers.

"My God, what follies," he remarked. "When I think of all the lost chances, I kneel down and thank God Almighty I came out a sane man knowing that I gave it my best shot. The amount of squandered men, money, and material. Sometimes I lie in bed at night thinkin' about it, and crack up. Well, it would be a crazy world if you didn't come out of that with something to laugh about, but you my boy, were okay."

# TWELVE

I HAD WORKED WITH Lt Col. Dirst for nearly a year before I bumped into Theodore Hume in Afghanistan. I spent all day in the field and at about six o'clock returned to the district of Shindand (the Green Place, formerly called Sabzawar in Pashto). I bought language books in Kabul and studied them until my mind turned to mud. Sometimes I read seriously for an hour or two, training manuals to improve my negotiating skills, for I was an earnest, toilsome, and industrious sort, and after that wrote tips for myself until bedtime. Other times I took much pleasure and satisfaction with my artwork. I do not know for what reason it was that one day toward the end of April, happening to get back early from the border town of Islam Qala, I thought I would walk into town to see what was going on, as I hadn't been there for several days. I liked Shindand for its prosperous bustle, but it had a sordid history that was pleasantly exciting and you felt that at any moment an adventure might instantly befall you. (In the fourteenth century for example, Tamerlane, who was angered by the town's stubborn resistance, had two thousand prisoners piled one atop another, and immured the still-living men with bricks and mortar to form a minaret.)

I strolled by the abandoned fortress and turning to the bazaar in a daydream was surprised to hear my name called out in plain English. I stopped and looked, and there to my disbelief stood Captain Hume. He was smiling at me.

"Don't you recognize me?" he cried.

"Yes, I do, sir."

"Ted, call me Ted."

And though I was grown up I was conscious that I felt extremely uncomfortable as when I was a teenager. But my feelings of embarrassment quickly dissipated. With my pitiful Christian construct for prudence I was still somewhat dismayed by his young wife's behavior some two decades before. Yet it still seemed to me dishonorable. I felt profoundly the disgrace I thought he must have felt at the time but I was glad that they remained married during all of those years—maintaining status, raising children, accumulating property, and ensuring personal happiness—despite the affair. We had a couple of encounters before and I knew their relationship was a touchy subject. Today I discerned that Iraq was still on his mind. Notwithstanding, I should never have looked away, my discernment presuming that he would wish to avoid the position of talking to me; but he held out his hand and shook my hand with hardy pleasure.

"Long time no see," he said. "It's good to see a familiar face every once in a while."

"I recall Fallujah was the last time but I remember you being in a hurry."

He laughed and I laughed, too; but his laugh was lusty and full-blooded, while mine was forced.

"I heard there was a to-do in Washington when they found out we'd stamped out that nonsense. I thought the Navy staff would never stop laughing when they heard about the outcries up on the Hill. What did you think?"

I was quick to get back in line. I wasn't going to let him think that I couldn't discern pettiness as well as anyone.

"Oh, you know how it is."

"Yes, of course I do, Riley. Good to see you." He took stock of me. "I see that you are doing well, look good. Why, you're here alone."

"Yes," I said, deflecting his scrutiny by turning to look up the street. "But I've got people working with me. Local experts, guides, about a dozen men and a few women."

"You make me feel proud. You were just a boy when we first met at the lake."

"I appreciate everything," I replied somewhat homesick. "You showed me how to jet-ski. Say how are your boys?"

"They're doing fine. Ronny is now twelve"—his smile widened—"and Parker is ten."

I was looking at Theodore Hume and almost asked about Dotti but caught myself. He wore a woolly pakol hat similar to that of a beret, and a gray collared tunic with baggy trousers called Perahan Tunban, and leather boots. I thought he looked very sharp. I had always thought that he had disliked stylish clothes, but I noticed now, without drawing attention to myself, that he was comfortably stylish. His eyes were bluer than I remembered and his red hair was like fire.

"I have a place in Herat," he said.

"No kidding."

"I'm heading up a new effort. It seems as if I've been here ever since the Cold War." He hesitated and then qualified: "We've been in Herat for only about a month."

"Well, I arrived last spring."

"Yes, I knew you were here, and I often wondered when I'd see you. Why don't you stop by tomorrow? I'd be pleased to welcome you into our tent."

"I don't mind," I said.

As we walked along he told me that he was now living in Fayetteville, North Carolina; his next bid to assume command of the Naval Special Warfare Developmental Group would be successful and he was expecting to get quite a bit as a leg up on his peers the next time around. He seemed to know most of the provincial politics and gossip, and I always thought that he had suspected right along that Dr. Roger Bernard was seeing Dotti back in Virginia Beach. I guessed that he had his own connections and would not need me as such. I noticed as we walked on through the bazaar that sometimes the men who passed us nodded at him. It occurred to me then that they must think highly of him. I began to feel important.

The bazaar was on a long, narrow uninterrupted street that ran through the center of town. The buildings here were all alike, of sun-dried bricks, plastered with mud and straw, solid and with vaulted storefronts. I suppose that they had been built to be inhabited by men of commercial enterprise in the unfettered frontier region, but the city had gone down in the world since its heyday in the early 1970's or had not been able since the widespread popular unrest in Iran (also known as the Khalq uprising or the Great Saur Revolution) to attract the right sort of customers; and its decayed respectability had an air at once furtive and shabbily dissipated, that made you think of what could have been if these people had seen better days. Even so the bazaar was crowded with sellers and pedestrians, and cars and gharries threaded through the early evening crowd honking at children playing together and donkeys that wouldn't move. We strolled past carpet shops, handicraft shops, dried fruit and mobile phone shops, shops that made colorful wool textiles and baked goods, bored-looking merchants inside their tiny stalls, sitting quietly or smoking, their faces emerging from the shadows now and then to peddle their goods to us. A couple of times Theodore Hume greeted shopkeepers he knew, sometimes in Dari Persian, other times in Pashto. I stood a few feet away, but after they shook hands and kissed on the cheek, he would introduce me as a friend or colleague.

"He's a good man, Riley. We need his support."

The next morning I drove into Herat. Hume and his men rented several houses in a quiet residential district not far from the airport. I parked my vehicle in front of a two-story house and looked down the conifer-lined street. Overhead a lone white cloud slid past a pale crescent moon in the blue sky. It was a pleasantly warm spring morning. A square-shouldered guard with a calm face approached me at the front gate and, upon taking my name, promptly opened it for me. He led me through a courtyard with blossoming holly trees and brightly colored flowers and I entered the sitting room. In a moment the guard brought Theodore Hume and he greeted me heartily. He wore a casual pocketed shirt that hung loosely over his worn bluejeans; he was unshaven and he looked more like I remembered him. There was something childlike in his appearance and I thought this was much more what I should expect a Navy SEAL to look like here.

"Well, what do you think of our little abode?" he asked. "It looks a lot better from inside, doesn't it? I think it is very spacious and comfortable."

He looked around and, upon taking an unlit cigar out of his mouth, thanked Ahmad.

"And there's a three-car garage in the back where we can work, and we've got plenty of space below for storage," he said, escorting me inside. "The owner was a buyer of produce for many years and when he died he left the house with all the furniture. The whole family is living in Jordan, but you can see everything's in good shape, look here." We walked through the living room and then into the kitchen. "You can see these people were doing very well before the country went to hell."

"Very nice."

"We do most of our own cooking and the guys really like working out of here," he added.

"Looks like you do, too."

"We spend a lot of time in bad conditions in the field; it's nice to come back to a decent place. I'd be the first to admit that I enjoy going without, but I know my men well. Though trained to ignore fatigue and hunger for long durations, it's too much to ask. Come on, I'll introduce you to some of them. We're getting ready for our next gig."

When I left that day it was with a very earnest invitation to come again. It appeared that they were going to be in town for a long while and all sorts of people whom I would like to meet were in the habit of dropping in.

# THIRTEEN

I **WENT.** I **GOT** involved. I went again. When the summer came and I traveled to Kabul and coordinated with Lt Col. Dirst my support to Operation Blue Skies (or Operation Apollo Unbound to our British friends), I got into the habit of going every day. It was my introduction to the art of balancing hard and soft military actions. I kept both undertakings a profound secret, and merely told people that I was involved in a brand-new NATO force protection mission. I was excited to work with people who were identifying and supporting a more progressive order of business in the community and who were willing to take risks, and I listened entranced to their private conversations.

All sorts of people came to the house in Herat. At that time the quagmire next door was still the focal point; the surge in Iraq was underway and little was going on in Afghanistan. I do not think anyone came was of any great importance; at all events, of all the teachers, merchants, craftsmen, scientists, big thinkers, and iconoclasts I met at the house I cannot remember one whose ideas has prevailed here today, perhaps someday; but the effect was cultured and full of life.

You found young professors who were looking for a break and middle-aged businessmen who deplored the fact that the Arabs were not a highly developed race, women wearing burqas arrived with their husbands all the way from Tehran and complained in a whisper aside that they felt good about nothing except at a wedding, former military men who on pressure consented to tell a little about the kinds of arbitrary (oft diabolic) orders that they had frequently enforced, and artists who were looking for work. I learned that Herat University seemed to have not only much potential as a research center, but as a networking hub, cultural enterprise, and, to our good fortune, an amenable president. Occasionally a university man added doubt, however, for in those days if a person of learning questioned the president it was generally because a spot of jealousy

135

or a little difficulty over what to do with his bright and highly educated daughters had made life in his own house a bit depressive.

We had changed all that, I thought. In regard to the practice of governing, one of the greatest benefits that the European wars in the so-called Dark Ages had conferred upon the world is the wide space between the clergy and the ruling class. James Fenimore Cooper (no relation of mine by the way) once wrote about the inclination of the United States in *The American Democrat*, that our great nation was sectarian, rather than religious. I soon found out that such a work in some parts of the Middle East would have gotten him executed. A retreat, even pulling in one's horns before being offered a cigarette, such as democracies cultivate mediocrity, since tastes, knowledge, and principles of the majority form the playing field, a maxim that is true in neither nature nor moral theory, makes a well-liked novelist more controversial (and more popular) here, but over there it might not have been enough for a reprieve, thus sending a stern reminder that there's absolutely no better path to the world of prosperity than theological virtue.

I have since sometimes thought that now the *Ulama* must inevitably and in quick order be abolished, and many of my fellow comrades think it would be a very good idea before the masses of men guided by freedom fighters once again exhibit their tyranny; however, it would be a graceful compensation that the Muslim people might offer the clergy a stake in the educational system in return of the surrender of their hereditary privileges. It would be a means of passage for those (too many) whom devotion to the public cause has been arbitrating archaic laws and in a wider sense by conducting useless scholarship, and a decent occupation for the rest who by the process of natural selection have in the course of time become unfit to do anything else but govern their impoverished countries. But this is an age of specialization and if this idea is fully adopted by the people it is obvious that it cannot but be to the greater glory of their own culture that its various administrative divisions should be parceled out according to the various ranks of the faithful.

I would think, therefore, that this compromise should yield a benefit for the lower classes of society and that the crowned heads of state and the village mullahs, imams, and maulvis—the last having attained only the lowest rungs on the ladder of Islamic scholarship—should devote themselves exclusively to providing everybody a solid eduction that includes mathematics, computers, and science. Hence primary and secondary education might be the principle domain of the clergy. In the West they have already shown their aptitude for this difficult practice of training children and young adults and their numbers are so small that trained laity could very competently supply the demand. To the Islamic scholars might safely be left the granting of academic degrees at colleges, law schools, and medical schools. Of course, we would have to provide advice and assistance. I've read that the Islamic scholarly system of *fatwa* and *ijma*, meaning opinion and consensus respectively, formed the scholarly system the West has practiced from the Middle Ages up to the present day, so it can be reasoned out that the Muslim and Christian institutions of higher eduction are closely related and thus this would be a good first step and evolve over time. Conversely, it is also quite reasonable to think that this is a highly risky venture because the resemblances in method had less to do with the beginning and more with the two religions having common problems (both cannot seem to reconcile conflicting statements about their own authorities, and both seem to be still safeguarding Revelation from the influence of Greek philosophy). It is perhaps not active or fast enough from an American standpoint, but it has a distinction that very well suits the adoption of our culture in the long run, especially our language.

The crown of freedom is enlightenment. It is the ultimate goal. It is the most important activity of the human spirit. It is the flower and reproductive structure of society. Yet the enlightened individual who wishes to create great things knows that the end *does not* justify the means; sometimes wise as he has become, even with so much experience from the journey, he will stop at nothing to get society to adopt his ideas, justifying a bribe on the promise that he has been good enough in other situations. Still the best of the body of Muslim clergy gaze at him like a pack of chimpanzees. He may not know why this is so but society requires a dense population of a certain scale and a certain movement where changes are linked to beliefs, traditions, and customs. It is evident then that the accomplishment of great things should be left to the masses, and the circle of elders should like to see that everyone's rights are protected by the most severe pains and penalties, for it is intolerable that the most innovative enterprises should not be allowed to fully develop if they are fair and provide a benefit for society. Here, too, specialization must prevail, and I anticipate that the heritage of the Arabs (like the successors of Persia before) will divide the realm of learning and applying knowledge between them, each confining himself to that aspect with which natural passions influence and talents have rendered him competent to succeed. Consequently, to start, I see the clergy of Sunni Islam advancing a rebirth in philosophy on the scale of the third and fourth centuries of the *Hijra*; the clergy of Shia Islam influencing literature of a rich and rhythmic character as they once were bringing forth in the time of *One Thousand and One Nights*; whereas I imagine that the supreme leaders and presidents of Iran and Pakistan respectively would be more likely to create new products and artwork for the world in the all-inclusive Samanid manner, and so it is almost necessary that the kings and crowned princes of Saudi Arabia should pipe in an aesthetic strain of the common folk on such matters as domestic bliss, cultural movement, and engagement with natural virtue.

If you say that this is somewhat formidable and remind me that the prudent ruler ought never to lose faith or make changes when by doing so it would be against his interest, but I tell you now the elders of the Middle East have already lost their countries. If, recalling the wise Machiavelli who said that it is a common fault of men not to reckon on storms in fair weather, you may ask me, when thinking that things often change only when adverse times come, who will think of stopping the uprisings, fleeing, or better yet hope once again that the people, enraged by the gall of conquerors, will repel them—I answer all of them (obvious enough, I should have thought). I recognize that the day is not gone when the romantic Bedouin of the desert commune to Allah the verses of the Koran and beguiled fathers croon over their boys' bedsides the choruses from Tha'alibi's *Yatimat al-dahr*. But my God, the age demands something more up-to-date. That said, I believe that the question remains about how far, not necessarily whether, Islam should be infused into the new or reformed governments. I suggest, therefore, before rebellion or revolution consumes the heavens, that the more nervous leaders should begin by merely tolerating new rhymes for children and better songs for grownups; but the progressive ones, those who are inclined to ignore orthodoxy, should begin to sponsor new entertainment for everyone to enjoy, from hipper music for the airwaves and comedies for television to gripping movies for theaters. Thus they retain in the hearts of the Muslim public that place which they have held on to now only on account of their one-room churches.

It was not at these meetings in Herat that I formed these opinions but later after watching the homegrown, bottom-up change coming that I reaffirmed very much to my surprise that Theodore Hume was an astute person. He had already realized that it was inevitable and only picked the wrong place. I suppose he thought what better place than the eastern parts of the Middle East where Islam was forged and the New Persian renaissance began, and though the Arab tribal background of Islam that had been completely transformed under the Abbasids into a universal religion and higher culture was ultimately snuffed out, he looked to the people to examine the ground from which these developments might arise again. He had never made any specific commitments to the visitors but his sincerity was genuine. The best judges of character admired him and the people who came to the house were agreed that one of these days he would take action. They came and went quietly because it was felt that here was a great and just warrior, and since the easiest way to suppress tribal rivalries in this neck of the woods is to kick another in the butt, they vilified freely all the provincial leaders whose own greed obfuscated their improving lives.

If, indeed, I had known as much about covert operations as I learned later on I should have guessed by the not infrequent visits of Commander Rick Wasson that the time was approaching when Captain Hume, like a rival tribal leader taking the time to understand things for himself and appreciate what others can understand and do for him, must forge ahead. I admit that when first I was introduced to this circumspect man from the Navy staff at the Pentagon his name meant nothing to me. Hume presented me as a young neighbor of his in Virginia and told him that I was a good man. He gave me a discerning smile, murmured in a soft voice something about the Marine Corps, and, accepting me at face value, went on talking with Hume in confidence. But I noticed that his arrival had created a wave and the conversation, which had been noisy and easygoing the previous day, was subdued. When in an undertone I asked who he was, I found that my ignorance was amazing; I was told that he was the right-hand man of Admiral Seton. After half an hour he stood, shook hands very earnestly with the few as he was already acquainted, and with a sort of impatient swagger left with his guide. Hume accompanied him to the front gate and put him in a bulletproof vehicle.

Commander Wasson was a man about the same age, weight, and height as Hume. Well, upon reconsideration, he was perhaps a tad shorter and somewhat older, but with rather strong features and artificially colored light-brown hair that made him look a little too youthful for his years; and unlike Hume he was supposed in his leisure to be a Civil

War buff; furthermore, he was said to be unhappily married, but now for the last couple years had been congenially dating Tina Allen, a clerk at Williamsburg City Hall and a well-known local authority on the British Colony of Virginia. He dressed accordingly in typical Afghanistan clothing, and wore a Perahan Tunban of contemporary style and cut. He gave you the curious impression of being fiercely loyal and you felt that if you disagreed with him (which of course my respect for his rank as well as something of quiet respect in his lofty position would have never allowed me to do) your noses would suddenly converge. But when you shook his hand it was like grabbing hold of a wet bar of soap. Thus the facade, notwithstanding its potent features, had something strange about it. When he sat listening to Hume it was as though he was a caged bird, with the yellow eyes grown mild, but enough of description.

Let me merely add that everything was submissive about him, his voice, his smile, his laugh; his eyes, which were round and slavish, ironically had the quality of being strong like a hawk; but his manner was as dutiful as the summer clothing worn here. Yet it was this purposeful, and unpleasant, characteristic that made him the wonderful friend he was to Hume. It was this that had gained him the trust that he now enjoyed. The whole team was aware of his friendship with the recipient of the Medals of Honor whose premature death a few years back had come as such a shock to him. Notwithstanding, he added value. Everyone had benefited from the innumerable purchase orders which he had written and which he was able to get funded shortly after returning to the Pentagon. What is more, the budget for research grants he was able to get through the bureaucracy revealed his angle of inclination for his dedication and his respect for Hume's judgment; he could never say often enough how much homage he obliged the Castle of Arlington, as seen by his quick sarcasm, his anger; and his self-confidence was such as some outsiders might think his arguments would not be strong enough to convince lawyers with mixed feelings, but that only added to the favorable reception of his efforts. But Commander Wasson was above the wholesale acceptance of company men. (His bad luck, as such, was one that upon first meeting Hume he had gone native during a long assignment with him.) Ultimately abandoning the traditions of the Naval Academy and unlearning the studies of surface warfare, he missed a promotion and consented to an unconventional life in which he showed quite definitely how great a part of the warrior's genius was due to his acculturation.

But Commander Wasson's desire to make a difference, his passion for the future, was not lost because the friend for whom he had worked so tirelessly for had not yet become part of American culture. My view of him began to change because he was a great reader of serious journals. Little that was useful to us escaped his attention and he was quick to share information with any person who might be interested in the fresh idea, divergent theory, new taste, or interesting tidbit. His passion, especially since joining the team, was now such that he was sure that visitors would not hesitate to offer the answers to questions he was fully prepared to ask. It wasn't long before Commander Wasson's quest for knowledge should in due course contribute to a long list of people who could help the cause; and when he found someone that struck him as a true leader, Captain Hume, himself open to suggestions for he was unable to identify anyone from the numerous people who came to the house, wrote an inquiring email to the person. Subsequently, having to clear matters with security before telling him about the concept for a business park tied to the university in Herat, Commander Wasson left the boss to have a discreet telephone call with the individual. They had developed a handful of good candidates, but that was not enough. Both wanted to build a "Silicon Valley" in *real time*, but both feared the unavoidable: success would depend on not only a magnetic leader, but an integrated community and, more important, the other, broader things that only the government could do, such as making Herat a place where the region's most talented people actually wanted to live, creating an environment full of opportunities for everybody, demoting tribal sentiments, clearing the way for the development of the land adjacent to the university, and implementing many other changes that would come in the form of tax breaks or lowered regulatory barriers to foreign investments, just to name a few. Admiral Seton hardly bade them to slow down and focus on the counter-terrorism mission.

Yet they were so circumspect and secretive indeed that with Ali Haddawy they almost missed the boat. His critics in the Pentagon who knew of him as a Mujahid wanted to see which way the cat would jump, and President Karzai who is an ethnic Pashtun from the south has always been suspicious of the Northern Alliance's motives despite their tangible efforts to uplift the country from civil war by throwing out the Taliban. But of Ali Haddawy it was almost unbelievable that he did therefore come up on the radar screen. Now that he is dead and so completely forgotten and the critics who doubted him would openly eat their words if they were not so thoroughly locked up on the classified computer networks of countless intelligence services; but the sensation he made in Pakistan was almost startling. Someone leaked to one of the largest newspapers in Islamabad the fact that he was backed by money and weapons from India in a kind of open give-and-take after Pakistan-based militants were implicated in the attacks in New Delhi. Then the most important newspapers in India gave to reviews of the fact that the Afghan militant groups among the southern Pashtuns were backed by Pakistan. Both countries gave it as much coverage as they would have to report of a championship cricket match. The most influential critics fell over one another in their eagerness to talk about it on the television. In Great Britain they likened Haddawy to Odysseus (for the rigid sense of his honor), to Robin Hood (for the similarity of his yeomanry ideals), and to Tennyson (for the romanticism of gathering together a band of his old comrades to sail beyond the sunset); and, viewing him as a man of the mean and renowned for his self-restraint and diplomatic skills, they thought of him as a genius and viewed him as the antithesis of the beef-witted Taliban (as evidenced by his deployment of a Trojan horse against them).

The accounting of the past (enter the United States into this dispute—not once, but three times) gives a hint of the "proxy" war between neighbors who have been at each other's throats since 1947, when the Muslim-imbued Pakistan and Hindu-imbued India were partitioned into two countries, the reason primarily being the region of Kashmir remained unresolved, but in our country this is unimportant. The Afghans knew better. Local officials were skeptical, and you saw Haddawy's ties to the United States, in the initial frame stories from the mujahideen's epic battles with the Soviet Union in the 1980's to glorious conquests of Taliban and al Qaeda in 2001—and throughout some of his men had survived. When it became known that the transitional Afghan government had accepted help from the Northern Alliance, and had recognized their good deeds (not his, the military-political umbrella organization), the tension finally diminished somewhat.

And all this happened as if it were in folk tales composed out of recent events like in ancient Greece. Homer's *Iliad* and *Odyssey* portrayed Odysseus as a cultural hero, but the Romans who believed themselves the scions of Prince Aeneas of Troy considered him a villainous cheater, and though Ali Haddawy's birthplace (Khujand, Tajikistan, once a Greek settlement in 329 B.C. on the northern Silk Road) was well known, twice

Herat claimed the honor of having raised him; distinguished elders of the Tajik tribal areas surrounding the city who for decades had retained bragging rights of his family's roots in their houses of prayer quarreled so bitterly over this matter that one dispatched the other dead in the street. The newly elected provincial government began steps to restrict what it saw as un-Islamic infighting that was very similar to that which had been seen before the Taliban came to power. Ali Haddawy was asked to dinners and invited to prayers by the new governor by name of Abdullah Khalis who ruled more or less autocratically. It was said that the two were blood brothers in one of the first battlegrounds in the Soviet invasion and together led a relentless resistance until their withdrawal a decade later; but I believe now Khalis grudgingly invited this former associate to Herat and at bottom only wanted to give the people the impression that they were still good friends.

It was not out of the question then for Theodore Hume to try to take advantage of this situation. Advisors close to President Karzai expressed concern that Khalis' strong-arming was affecting reconstruction and damaging the transitional government. A war of words followed, with many people (both men and women) protesting angrily at what they saw as a threat to their advancement. Stubbornly, the ultra-conservative graybeard shut down Radio Free Afghanistan, expelled a dozen or so dissenting journalists, and shut down the Internet provider in Herat; and then, to win back the hearts and minds of the people, he refused Kabul the millions in tax revenue collected from the long lines of trucks flowing across the border from Iran and Turkmenistan and placed one of his daughters of his first wife in a newly established Department of Women's Affairs.

Theodore Hume was certainly not going to upset him. I can only surmise and smile; he was using both the Afghan president and governor while taking full advantage of the corrupt institutions. He entered these relationships with some resignation upon a difficult and, especially upon weighing the evidence against us, a distressing course of action. Governor Khalis was testing his newfound levers of power. Still Hume was admirable. He lunched with Khalis and his cronies merely to meet the right people; he dealt with the military brass in Kabul on his behalf and one time made a contact for him that would lobby his cause before elected officials in parliament; just once he introduced him to an arms dealer in Kuwait who supplied him with weapons; on only a couple of occasions he turned a blind eye to farmers who were growing poppies instead of wheat; from time to time he saw that his efforts in the remote districts should appear better than the president's; and he took care that he should accept only invitations of which were approved even though Hume never went so far as to run everybody by him whom he had business dealings with, because he knew that he was a self-centered man and his own interests must not be encumbered with arbitrary rules and regulations. When later questioned, Captain Hume, had he chosen, might have said that he had done everything by the book that was reasonably right to do.

At any rate, Hume took action on tacit approval. Ali Haddawy went on about his business elsewhere; it was neither good nor bad for the country; it was very much like before the Taliban, but the Shia factions in Kabul had reservations about his behavior; the Hazaras with affiliations with Iran objected. Meanwhile, the Northern Alliance became part of the United National Front, which was led by a fellow Tajik who did his best to defend Haddawy while representing the different views of the seven factions, and he made sure that Kabul was mollified by transferring some of their military strength to the newly formed Military of Afghanistan. This transformed alliance positioned itself as a "loyal" opponent to the affable Afghan president much like you see in the political landscape in the United States. A few of the former faction leaders were however quite loyal, notably the Pashtun leader. The Northern Alliance thus had been effectively subsumed and the rise of the Afghan National Army reduced the threat of the former elements attempting to disrupt the transitional government. Only Ali Haddawy was inclined to stir up trouble by associating himself with old friends in India. He had never been accustomed to having to get along with anyone. He was quite unused to the democratic processes that were put before him; perhaps he missed his romantic, tribal lifestyle of war. Once or twice he secretly came to the house in Herat in a state of mind that anyone less knowledgeable, less attuned to the vices of this region, would have described as put off by the deeply corrupted alliance. He told us calmly that he was not quite himself that afternoon. He was under attack. Former colleagues were sharpening their blades; they threatened to hang him out to dry from two of the minarets built by Queen Gowhar in the fifteenth century, and, to quote the preeminent Salafi scholar, then to take him down while he was still breathing and lop off his head outside the beautifully restored Friday Mosque: they were quite naturally miffed that they had mistaken a staunch freedom fighter for an adulterated reformer and were determined that he should pay the price. Then, one day upon his return to Tajikistan, Ali Haddawy was abducted by armed young men on motorbikes in Badakhshan Province and Theodore Hume had a local man go there and search for him.

Commander Wasson at this point was perfect. He did not run the matter up the flagpole. Not a word leaked out. Hume might have been excused if he had felt a certain embarrassment because this man for whom we had affiliated ourselves had done nothing for us thus far. Commander Wasson remained quiet, loyal and sympathetic; he was a man who understood Hume and sought a patriotic Tajik to travel alone. In a village, this elderly patriarch found Haddawy sitting among about fifty men outside a mosque. The adjacent buildings brimmed with gunmen. For hours he argued with the captors, Haddawy's rival tribe, explained the Islamic bloodline and paid the bribe; afterward he turned him over to the NATO-backed provincial government in Mazar-e Sharif. Hume cut him loose after considerable thought, as thoughtful as the politics that he doubtless felt when Admiral Seton finally made up his mind to table the initiative for a while; he cut him loose with a fair amount of publicity, but with such consideration, that Ali Haddawy perhaps hardly knew he was no longer a candidate. But there was no doubt about it. Hume would say nothing against him, indeed he would still talk about him a lot, and when Khalis mentioned him he merely shook his head, and sighed; but his eyes were deceptive and his expression Janus-faced.

Theodore Hume had an intuitive feeling for true leaders and his passion for the cause so deep now to allow a setback of this type long to discourage him; and however great a lightening rod he was a man of too sportsmanlike a nature to cut off Ali Haddawy completely, and it was in this regard that I was able to provide some assistance. Meanwhile, between gigs, Hume continued to move in social circles in Herat, inviting people to the house and going to dinners here and there, even attending outings in the Saudi Arabian desert with Khalis, gracious always and sensitive to local customs, listening searchingly, but watchful, critical, and determined (if I may put it bluntly) to infuse revolution. Hume's sentiments toward Khalis were direct and not a contradiction to his faith; however, the fighting creed was nationality and status and position, not necessarily in that order, but of religious fanaticism there was none. What Khalis wanted was in essence what Hume wanted—so it played out with the two men.

It was about this time that Hume met his second wife Alexandra from Iran and formed a favorable opinion of her abilities. It is true that she was not seen in public much, but Khalis was warming up to him. Guardedly Hume offered her an ear at a private dinner party. He could not fail to be moved by her beauty when, in the subtle way of hers, she told him that it was shameful that her husband was turning back the clock against the people's wishes. He was amused and fascinated. It is always nice to be assured that you are on the right track. At long last, after probes and tests, he told Alexandra that he was seriously looking at the possibility of building a research park in Herat. He explained to her that he wanted to provide the spark that would help the city to rally, and with that the people would seek further changes to improve themselves. Alexandra knew that her city was ready, and spoke about the need to feed the hesitant, anti-capitalist left with facts and outflank the moralistic, anti-innovation fervor on the right. She asked him to a luncheon to meet people who might be useful to us. Then toward the middle of summer she secretly arranged to see him at a friend of a friend's home, and they had tea under the shade of Russian olive trees, and talked of friends dead and gone and love and family. When she came to the house later that night she had the air of a queen and was fully prepared to deal with her infidelity.

But Theodore Hume's manners were honorable. He was no less than what is stated, but showed much interest in her. He always complimented her on her appearance and flattered her very extravagantly for having allowed him to enter into her life and understand her needs. If Alexandra praised Theodore Hume, telling him with a touch of shame in her voice what a good thing it was to enjoy the companionship of such a nice man, it was certainly from Eros, and not because she knew that there is nothing that fires up a husband in a Muslim country more than to have another man mark down his ability to control the women in his own house; however, Hume was keen enough not to be taken advantage of by a clever woman. As I understood it she merely spoke to him of the simple things that her simple nature might be supposed to dream of at night, of respect and fulfillment and her two girls' dreams and how fearful she was for their future well-being; and he regarded her exactly as you would expect a man who was still technically married, which he was, to treat a lovely but disaffected woman with whom he had an ulterior motive.

He was respectful, playful, and gently determined to put her at her ease, in sum. It was strange then that Commander Wasson could not endure the relationship; indeed, he was the only man on the team that really disliked her. After he learned that she had spent the night he confronted Hume about the matter and even used "spy-bitch" and "prick-tease" that are part and parcel of the vocabulary in the Navy, and I never would have thought the two would come to blows over the matter, but did one afternoon. When anyone told a story about the two old friends one could only laugh at the way each man applied himself so earnestly. But he referred to Hume as "that damned old hound." It needed the most awkward form of dissuasion by Hume's higher rank to induce him to be civil to her even though the mission required it of him now.

"Don't be a fool, Rick," the men said. They all called him Rick and presently I, though still habitually commander, got in the habit of doing it, too. "If the boss wants to, he can see the woman. We found ourselves a genie. She can tell us what's going on better than anyone."

Though Commander Wasson kept his distance from me, due to his self-importance and paranoia associated with being left out of the loop, say, for his infrequent visits to the region, there was a little band that I became close friends. I was an unknown ingredient initially; they were a tightly knit team who trained together, but because of the joint nature of the mission, my being an outsider was quickly overcome. Of these I'll call out Mark Sykes (Navy), Lenny Abbas (Air Force), Billy Graves (Army Ranger), and Ryan Qajar (Army).

The first of us was Mark Sykes, a warrant officer, the most creative man on the team, and an elusively efficient mechanic despite his compulsion for classical music and art, of sculpture in particular. He nevertheless was fundamental to the team's success, and was always the first to offer a solution, and Hume's go-to man in a crunch. His ideas would have been woven into the fabric of our foreign policy in the Middle East like a Persian carpet, had he been able to dedicate himself to bigger and better things, and to focus all his energy like an Olympic athlete. One day in August, I discovered that he stormed out of the house because the boss wanted him to do something, or rather because he was the one who could be used to further the purposes of the team, if willing to do so of course.

Now that I look back I cannot get over my surprise that I should have had to be told by Ryan Qajar what was surely so obvious. When I first traveled to Afghanistan it never occurred to me to ask myself what women considered attractive or sexy, and when, thinking about it again presently, I recalled for the first time that Hume mentioned that women

147

prefer lanky men with fine beards of the type that was admired at the time in the region. I was interested but did not trouble to think much about it. I took it as part of the natural order of things, just as I took the sun rising over the mountains each day and the turn to the Kaaba in Mecca. I was quite startled when I saw Alexandra flash her eyes at Mark Sykes, and when she looked down upon making eye contact with him and he turned abruptly away, mine turned to Theodore Hume's (so much for going beyond what is openly said). Billy Graves' father was involved in the failed attempt to rescue the hostages in 1980, code-named "Eagle Claw," and he quickly asked her about her family, drawing attention away from the boss; whereas Lenny Abbas grew up under the Shah's autocratic rule in the late 1970's and, before his family immigrated to the United States, saw firsthand how the regime employed the secret police. (I assumed most recollections were passed on to him by his parents because he was a young boy at the time, but I figured that his stories were mostly true.) Distracted, Alexandra talked of the changes she wanted to see and told us what she thought was possible, and I listened quietly. When Lenny quipped in Farsi that evil begets evil, referring to Ayatollah Khomeini and his rise to theocratic power after the corrupt monarchy crumpled, and Billy laughed, we established a connection with her.

A week or two later the relationship between Mark Sykes and Alexandra had begun and we all considered ways to exploit it. I participated in the discussion but had little experience inside Iran. Plainly, the men conserved a palpable attitude, considering their history (eight killed and four wounded in the aborted operation), and thus a stake in the matter, but for the United States it all began well before with the discovery of oil in the early 1900's. Alexandra's family was a beneficiary of this period of time, when her family profited from the ensuing rivalry between Great Britain and Russia for power over the region. Then came our ascent in the 1950's, and it was when the Shah fled the country but had returned and forcefully reestablished the monarchy (with the help of the CIA) that things started to become unstable. However, it was not until the 1970's that things started to become unhinged in the country; the rapid growth of industrialization and modernization programs, accompanied by ostentatious private wealth, was greatly resented by the bulk of the people, especially in the overcrowded cities and among the rural poor. After the overthrow of the Shah's government in 1979, the new government made a major shift in its ideology; in quick fashion it revived Islamic traditions and nationalized industries and banks. Clashes occurred between rival religious factions throughout the year, and as oil prices fell arrests and executions were rampant. Then toward the end of the year Iranian militants seized the U.S. Embassy, taking fifty-two American hostages. But Theodore Hume dismissed our sad history impatiently.

"It has nothing to do with oil," he insisted. "Oh, for crying out loud. Let me be clear. Our goal here is to reestablish an equilibrium among the Arabs, Persians, and of course our interests. We blew it then; we really did. But I still can't comprehend the ease with which Khomeini consolidated power in Tehran. His tactics—and techniques—can only be compared to those of the invading Arabs when considering the ease with which they took Ctesiphon in 637. Before you knew it, the Sassanid power toppled, Islam replaced Zoroastrianism, and the caliphate made Persia a part of a larger Islamic world. Men, I'm not interested in preserving the status quo."

We looked at him without answering, but his eyes widened chimerically when he saw that we understood the basic idea.

Presently I learned that Theodore Hume and Mark Sykes had devised a plan for Alexandra that could be used to further the purposes of the mission. I also learned that Commander Wasson was in Iraq with the CIA visiting the People's Mujahideen of Iran, but when, showcasing my knowledge of this right-minded militant group in the Iranian Revolution, the Iraq-Iran War (on the side of the Iraqis) and recently in Iraq internal conflicts (helping us) and looking upon it as the explicative proposition, I asked if I might not travel there and meet up with him, Theodore Hume said that he wanted me to talk with Ali Haddawy.

Haddawy was a man of extraordinary intelligence and memory and of scholarship. I asked for a recent picture of him, but was told that he looked like a statue of Avicenna in which the distinction had been attributed to the Tajik State Medical University. He was a man of fifty-five and about my same height, slim; but he had a fine head of gray hair and streaming ponytail and an unkempt beard. He favored a mix of all different types of clothing including traditional and western styles, and was told that I should brush up on chemistry, microbiology, physics, mathematics, astronomy, philosophy, classical music, poetry, and the fine arts. He had attended Oxford University and talked admiringly of the old masters, especially Tintoretto and Turner, of whom I have always admired, and with contempt of Rembrandt and Rubens, whom I have always disliked.

I have always wondered what educed good luck! He spent a few years in Bangalore trying to make his way in a start-up drug company, failed, I suppose, and then drifted back to his homeland. I was told that he had secured a position at the university there, but when war broke out in Afghanistan, chancing to back a government that spoke to his own sensibilities, he dropped everything and looked for people who would fight the Russians. Both of his wives and five children had been killed about this time. I think he must have had a lot of charisma and endurance, for I have even now a very vivid recollection of the portrait Hume painted of him. I then wondered what he was doing. Was he back in the classroom and conducting research again or was he hiding out, in a safe house at some lesser known lake in the Pamir mountain region? I should like to think that Hume was right and he has at least found some peace now that his own country's civil war had finally ended.

When I at last coordinated matters in Dushanbe and got the green light, I spoke to him in unequivocal terms. Haddawy's apartment building was just off campus, one of a group of Sovietized complexes built during the 1970's, and you went in through a small unfurnished lobby. It was a Friday morning, a fine blue day, and I walked from my hotel through bustling streets. Haddawy lived in a small apartment with his new wife and baby-girl; there was only one bedroom and he slept on a large couch in the small living room, and a tiny kitchen where there was a pile of dishes in the sink and, I suppose, the tiny little deck overlooking the grayish city was the place where he smoked an occasional cigarette.

When I arrived his wife still wore a bathrobe in which she had been nursing the baby on the couch and they were having a cup of tea. Haddawy opened the door for me, and holding his tea led me into the kitchen.

"Please help yourself," he said.

We had spoken only a few words on the telephone, abbreviated arrangements just three nights before. It was not at all like I had expected. I did not know what to say with his wife present, so I said the first thing that came to my head.

"So you recently move in?"

"Last year," he answered with a big smile.

I reddened somewhat. I felt a perfect idiot. I had not then acquired the technique that I see myself now enables me to deal completely with errors, lapses, or the unexpectedness of strangers. (Why no one seemed to know about his marriage still amuses me.) If this were the place I could write a very neat little article for a military intelligence journal to enable the young men and women to trade in the contentment of their time-honored routines for the most diverse manifestations of the creative instinct. There is the intense "My God" that feels the power of the roughshod creator, the "I never thought I could do it" that makes up for the fear of embarrassment when you first set out on the uncharted journey, the risk so high that it is neither comfortable nor comprehended, the "Lay it all on the line" that expresses what you feel about it, the "Only way but the highway" of one who is impassioned, and the "Get out of the way" of one who is totally committed.

"The city has come a long way" was all that then I could think to say.

"The Russians aren't like what they used to be," he said.

"I like this city a lot," I said quickly, explaining myself a little bit. "Ali, are you going to the mosque today?"

"Good God, no! I thought I would show you around. We'll have lunch with a few of my men."

I looked into the living room to his wife and from her dovish but demanding face to the blue sky outside.

"Follow me, Riley," said Haddawy, "and let me show you something."

He opened the door and stood at the rail of the deck. He made room for me. I looked at him and then I looked at the open sky. I had such a strange new feeling in my heart. It was as though he was looking not at, but through the sky. I do not know if I remember thinking of the truth of skies then or on the airplane ride back to Herat. For when I think how little people know about the sky and in fact that it is the part of creation that God had done more for the sake of pleasing us, or talking to us, or teaching us, than in anything else in Nature, but in as Wordsworth has given the chasm of the sky above is Heaven's profoundest azure. Subsequently, whenever looking at its exceeding depth, I see now not a flat lifeless color, but a deep, quivering, transparent body of penetrating atmosphere. Sometimes the effect of the sunshine is pleasant, sometimes dynamic, sometimes terrible, never the same for two moments together. So what is the truth of blue skies? Sometimes I think of the deep abyss and reckon the sky is almost human in its desire, almost spiritual in its compassion, almost divine in its profuseness, and yet its burden to what is immortal in us.

I never exactly learned Haddawy's interest in Turner (an artist that lends itself admirably to good discussion), but reckoning the stories he told me of what he had seen in Afghanistan, and scraps of Tajik secret history, or family affairs, recalled now as well as I could for myself, I think he must have wondered about what kind of ideas can be received from great works of art. I do not know if he dabbled in oils or watercolors like me. He certainly had none of the aesthetic tendencies of the creative people whose living spaces were for the most part exhibits of their artistic endeavors; he lived rather like a Spartan. Haddawy was passionately fond of the open sky, and would often provoke recollections of masterpieces, judging and rewarding the best paintings. We shared the same ideas of Nature, and what is necessary to the distinguishing of excellence. It is this faculty of perceiving in which men, even the most uncivilized, must always be seeking, even without the benefit of reflection, because none can estimate the power manifested in victory, and he had already been in battle and personally measured the strength required to overcome evil.

"So you like our fair city," he remarked at last.

"Well, the sky is bluer in Herat."

He knew what I meant, but the word had resonated like a gunshot in our midst. I felt at present that this man I had come to Tajikistan to examine—the leader who would bring the operation to full effect. He was in essence a simple man. He had by nature a heavy, quiet outlook, but when he stood outside on the deck this solemnity became on a sudden infinitely active. Against the open sky Haddawy took on a different quality and he looked very powerful and marble-like. His dark brown eyes were opulent, changeable and his thick beard and benighted white face were like a tall statue against the brightness of the sky. I told him that arrangements were in place for his protection via the U.S. Embassy. He stood like a prince looking out across this domain, lost in forthcoming military campaigns, but so surprisingly calm, that further explanation was meaningless. This mere mortal had already experienced American power or force before; however, he knew that he must put his people's future in the hands of that dreadful and supreme power the Greeks called Fate. He stood confidently, perceiving the riddle of human life—purification by suffering—but without another direct word on the subject, he disclosed to me his faith that this was not the end.

# FOURTEEN

T HEODORE HUME TRAVELED stateside to Fort Bragg and to Virginia Beach on his return, and I, having little to do in the afternoon, was glad to help out with one or other of the side efforts. He wanted to improve the lives of nearby villages by adapting our private Wi-Fi network in Herat (presently used to communicate among ourselves) and told me to work with Mark Sykes. I would sit with him in the garage and read the manuals on the hardware recently shipped to us (a new hub to exploit the hot spots in television gaps seemed like a novel substitute for Radio Free Afghanistan), and he would bounce ideas off me or a few of the other guys to extend the range; and Lenny Abbas, though he was a communications specialist, behaved as if he wasn't, and ignored us for the most part and continued to set up and test the hardware or laughed at us in one or other of his foreign languages that were becoming more familiar to me.

Lenny Abbas was a joker and a smart one, but he was difficult to understand and so was often out of step with the rest of the team. He was about my same age but looked no older than twenty-eight, a man with a baby face and a dry way of speaking that made what he said sound comical. Mark liked his straight-from-the-shoulder replies, the confidence with which he provided feedback by speaking the truth, the recklessness with which he would put an alternative idea on the table that he hadn't fully considered, and the ease with which he jumped about to get out of a hole during the discussion. He was cheerful, immature, unassuming, loud and perhaps a bit cocky. Mark told me that once he had set up a telephone patch through a Serbian radio tower and then placed a call from the roving E-3 Sentry/AWACS whose airmen transferred the call to his girlfriend in Italy in order to tell her not to wait up for him but would see her in a few days.

He seemed just the right sort to go with Mark Sykes into the city and meet up with Alexandra at a restaurant off the beaten track and spend the night talking, but it was only on the first occasion that he went along for the ride. Subsequently I performed the security detail. (My ideas of specialization finally caught up to me.) I used to fetch her after I had completed my tasks and she hers with Abdullah Khalis, and we would switch cars and go to a restaurant, where Mark Sykes would be waiting with a bottle of black-market Italian red wine. We went here and there, being warned of the need for precaution, sometimes to a private residence if there was a particular friend she wanted to see; but her favorite was the Desert Oasis. It was discreet and the service was very good. We ordered drinks and took turns smoking from the pipe. Alexandra looked around with delight at the dark gilded room, every table and private alcove tenanted with fashionable denizens of Herat.

"I love the Desert Oasis," she said. "It's so hip."

I discovered that she was well read. She liked cultural anthropology, but only of a certain kind, the families of royalty and of close family relations of kings and pharaohs; and she would tell us with wide-eyed wonder of the strange things she read. She had a wide familiarity with the various households of King Tut and there was little she did not know of King Rama V of Thailand who sired more than seventy children—some from marriages to half sisters but most with dozens of spouses and mistresses. Her preference was technical and she ranged from CT scans of mummies from ancient Egypt to DNA-sequencing tests of new discoveries from Inca Peru; then there was the long list of recent findings from the royal families of Europe. She knew the wives, and all about them, from half sisters to first cousins.

"I like to read about scientific things," she said. "I don't much care for historical accounts."

She nonetheless liked to gossip about polygamy in Herat and I thought it was on account of her disenchantment with Khalis' entire view of the world. (Presently he was courting a very young woman from Koshk.) Polygamy, of course I knew, predated Islam, but Prophet Muhammad elevated it and sanctioned it into law. She seemed to know all about the rival wives and their children, especially the struggles for power within the households of certain clergymen here. It was something an outsider would never recognize as people who are born into Islam don't talk much about the pain, uncertainty, distrust, envy, the plots, the tensions and the ambiguities of this custom.

"I sneak out every other day or so to visit the university library," she said. "Just for a couple of hours, you see."

"Sneak out?"

I was dumbfounded.

"No, well, slip away," she said with a giggle. "I don't know whether or not I am missed. Heaven knows. They prefer not to see me. I stay away from her as much as possible."

She was a great storyteller. Often when, Khalis being away, we decided to ride up into the hills at the edge of town at which point we waited for the sun to rise. She would always be the one who did the talking. But her voice was tender and diffuse. It did not exclude from me certain private thoughts that amused me apart from the stories; it included me in a permeating affinity as opposed to the many departures.

I was talking about her once to Mark Sykes in the garage and he said to me that he could not understand how she had turned from the fresh beautiful-looking Cleopatra whose arrival then practically everyone acknowledged into the mad schizophrenic house cat I had always found in Washington, D.C. He was not the first who had reservations. "Of course she has a very pretty face," he added, "but she's not the sort I very much like personally." Then Lenny Abbas said: "Dude, I think she really likes you, but it's a pity she isn't your type."

"I can't explain why," said Mark Sykes. "I reckon I prefer blonds."

I forgot what my comment was, but I know it was lewd.

"All right, Riley. That shows you Marines don't have any discipline." Everybody laughed. "Well, I thought she was a goddess till I saw her without the veil. I suppose she has certain qualities."

"You will have to take one for the team," I said.

"Ha, damn you, maybe I will."

Everybody laughed again.

When Mark Sykes talked to Alexandra in front of me she listened to him with a timid attraction. A little flush came into her pale cheeks. I think that at first when he spoke to her of her beauty I thought he was just making fun of her; but when I found that he wasn't, when he sculpted a bust of her in silvery translucent alabaster in the backyard, it had a particular effect on me. I was a little amused, impressed of course, and a little surprised, but it did not change my mind about him. I could not forget all I had read about great artists and what I had seen in myself. I wondered about Theodore Hume, too, and the lasting impression she made on him. I used to watch him with her. She was not exactly over him either; she continued to ask about him and made her visits to the house quite clearly when he was available; and when she looked at him it was with that mischievous, expectant smile which I had now discovered held such a mysterious beauty. Sometimes when we were sitting side by side at the Desert Oasis I looked at her face. I do not think I was in love with her. I merely enjoyed the sensation of sitting quietly beside her and looking at the dark peaceful nature of her timid brown eyes and the round face and dark richness of her complexion.

Of course Mark Sykes was right; because her beauty could be realized, it was limited. Having read Stendhal, I knew there was more than one type of love. Incidentally, the strange thing was that this quality enhanced her beauty and gave one a much better appreciation of the strange culture. She had the virtue of a cool morning when the blue light appears momentarily from the unclouded desert sky. There was nothing lost in the impermanence of the moment; it was as sublime as the desert under the moon as it lay calm and lustrous on the horizon. Mark Sykes' sculpture reminded me of Carrier-Belleuse's *Fantasy Bust of a Veiled Woman* with its gracefulness in which there is still an attractive force and its light flickering beauty in which still pulsates the blood in a man's heart. Her charm, harmony, simplicity, radiance—along with the way everything about her came into relation—was powerful; the desert sky was commanding—it channeled the infinite and the inexpressible—and by contrast was intimidating. Sometimes, feeling my eyes on her, she would turn around and for a moment or two look at me. She did not speak. I did not know of what she was thinking.

Once, I remember, I fetched her at the airport, and the necklace on her blue burqa, indicating to me she was concerned, told me to return to the car. She mixed in with the crowd. I stepped out and opened the back passenger door of the car for her and she spoke so calmly that I felt anger that this subjugation is silently feared. I played my role. The fashion of the day still set women apart from men and apart from the community; the traditional clothing in Afghanistan is really unique and beautiful because of the different colors and fabric and the handmade embroidery and design, but the law restrains it, confines it, grooms women for submissiveness. Later at the party, she would remove the head-to-ankle drapery and reveal a dress with matching trousers, a head scarf, a purse and flat shoes known as paizar. When she wore the burqa, abaya or hijab, I was reminded of the delicate sisters of St. Joseph and there was something amazingly attractive in the way her personal manner contrasted with the virginal beauty of her gowns. That day I could not persuade myself that it was natural, and I remarked sarcastically upon the situation. But she had a dimension that I think set her apart: the sureness of her walk, faintly seductive, was already liberated. Ironically that was the effect it gave.

"I've got a secret weapon," she said behind the veil, as we drove swiftly through venerable old pines that lined the road into town from the airport.

"Really?"

She laughed, held up a little silver vase hanging from her necklace and extended it to me.

"Rub it and see," she said.

Later that night when we had walked the last few blocks to her house, and I was leaving her at the back gate, when I whispered "Open Sesame" and she laughed a little, an expression of mirth it was, I leaned forward against the door.

To her delight the door swung open.

"Come here, silly," she said.

She gave me a French kiss. It was a wet kiss, and it was a kiss of passion. Her eyes, those very big brown eyes of hers, gazed at me long enough for me to be conscious of her beauty and her desire and her hunger. Then she closed them, but without motion, in silence, pressed against me then pulled back from me and disappeared into the garden. I was so affected that I had not been able to chase after her. I accepted her kiss manifestly. I remained affected. I turned and walked back to the car. I seemed to feel still in my mouth Alexandra's sweet kiss. It was not flirtatious or audacious, but urgent and natural; it was as though she kissed me because she needed me.

# FIFTEEN

I DID NOT SEE Alexandra again for more than a week. Mark Sykes became ill from food poisoning and was sent to Kabul. We had a top-notch medical center at the airport there. Then Theodore Hume asked me to make the rounds with him. The Wi-Fi communication system was a hit with a few key village leaders and great leaps in the technology was to be had, so we made up our minds to push the range to the extreme.

We had a group meeting back at the house and then assembled an implementation plan. In the Navy and Marine Corps there was no orderly way, and, when the purchase orders were funded (Commander Wasson coming through for us again), there was a mad rush to get the job done. We were hot and breathless and somewhat frantic when at last we successfully adapted and tested surplus satellite dishes that would work perfectly for our long-range Wi-Fi connections. Next we conducted experimental trials at the Herat airport to link villages separated by difficult geography. Atop the tower Lenny Abbas' face and back perspired profusely. He was exhausted, as it were with an emotion at once ecstatic and loud. (I express it awkwardly as we were all involved, especially Mark Sykes for distilling the idea, but I do not know how to describe the huge contribution Lenny gave us.) Theodore Hume put his hand on his wet tee shirt when he climbed down and in the early-morning light he personally thanked him. The low cost, unregulated point-to-point connections were so good that our system could also be used to extend the city's mobile phone network to the villages, but for the moment a celebration was in order.

We had steaks and beer back at the house. Unfortunately, the prototype was like a firecracker on the Fourth of July that gave its notice to the city. At midday there were already rumors floating about the university campus and affluent parts of the city of an organized protest, but we had already devised a cover story; in hindsight, a mistake, as men are apt to deceive one another in general matters but rarely do so in specifics.

"Khalis is getting awfully paranoid," he said suddenly, when we gathered together later in the afternoon.

"Aren't we all," I laughed.

"Couldn't we do something special for the old bugger?" Billy Graves offered.

"Rather."

"Social media, who would've thought," commented Ryan Qajar.

"What now then, boss?" someone asked.

"Why don't you guys look into building up the team for the roll out. I need to attend to other business today."

In those days I knew my way very well about Herat, not yet a completely safe city for Americans, and otherwise westernized persons, but poor and in many quarters quite dangerous like many urban areas in the United States; and so after we had finished our meeting, leaving the house with Lenny and Billy (who was armed suitably), I drove them to a computer repair shop in one such district on the Hari River. It was late and the only person there was the owner sitting at his desk inside. Rahmon was a Farsi-speaking Russian soldier in the 205th Motor Rifle Division before deserting; he had fallen in love with a local girl and married her, staying here after the war ended. I knew that he spoke English fairly well and took up a conversation with him. I had met him by accident one day in the market and was impressed by his technical savvy. A young man came in and purchased two cartridges for a printer and, upon putting them on his bill, promptly left the store. We talked casually about IEEE 802.11 technology and then about things in general.

Our way back to the house led us through the bazaar and as we stopped in traffic I asked Lenny Abbas:

"What did you think of him?"

"Smart guy, no doubt. He looks trustworthy. What about his ability to hire competent help?"

"Oh, he has associates."

"We need to follow up then."

"I'll introduce you to the USAID representatives now."

"Sounds like a plan."

Afterward I drove back to Shindand and because it was already half past eight went directly to the house. I turned on the lights in the sitting room. One of the guys living there with me at the time came out of his bedroom and smiling broadly gave me a message. Then he vigorously scratched his balls and took a cup of water from the cooler, but he was very sleepy and I had endured a long day that began at one o'clock in the morning and there was no energy in the tank for even smalltalk.

"You might want to call that number tonight," he said.

I put the message up to the light. The telephone number was Alexandra's and I held the message up so that I should be able to dial it on my mobile phone. She let it ring out, whereon I put the phone back into my pocket, and, taking a drink of water, brushed my teeth over the sink in the corner. I spit into the toilet, rinsed my mouth, and began to get ready for bed, and as I was intent on getting some sleep decided not to try again. When I had sat down on my bed, she returned the call; she did not say anything important; she spoke to me shyly, still with that sweet voice of her goodnight kiss. I reclined on the bed. The room was very small and the walls were made of cardboard. I kicked off my boots and softly spoke to her.

Alexandra lowered her voice in response to me. I do not know why I should have behaved as I then did; it was not at all how I had been trained to behave on such occasions. A sob broke from her taut throat. I do not know whether it was because I was coming on to her and lonely (not lonely in spirit, for I spent all day in close contact with the team, but lonely in the body) or because my desire for her was growing only stronger, but I tried to control myself. I began to feel terribly ashamed of myself, for she was married; then she began to sob loudly. I could see her in the darkness and immediately apologized to her.

"Oh, no, honey, it's not you."

"What's the matter? Don't, don't cry."

I knew right then there was a problem and began to worry for her safety, but she reassured me that she was okay. I asked her about Khalis and then I asked her about her girls; and she spoke forcefully and her voice rocked me back and forth as though I were a lover who must be coddled. She went on and on and I listened intently to her. I closed my eyes and kissed the white pillar of her neck and as she spoke to me I kissed the soft spot behind her ears; and she responded to me and slipped out of her clothes and lay down next to me. When I put my hands on her back, I could feel the tightness of the skin and I held her for a moment before making love to her; then we kissed each other and I slipped away into a deep dream.

It was she who awoke me when the new dawn peering through the dark shades revealed the starkness of the tiny room and the M16 rifle against the wall.

"You must get up," she said. "I am your wake-up call this wonderful late summer morning."

"Good morning, Alexandra."

"You fell asleep on me last night."

"I did?"

"Yes, my fellow friend."

"I'm so sorry."

"Seriously now."

"What is it? Oh, I know you wanted to tell me something last night. Are you okay? You can stay here."

"No, I'm so beside myself I could cry sometimes, but I am going to be a big girl and hope *you* will believe me. Nobody else seems to care what I do, think or know."

I listened to her talk then let her go. She spoke rather quickly, with the stoic voice of the Afghan women whose deep understanding and powerlessness embody the tragic condition of her country. I was unable to comprehend her, the tragedy she foresaw, the destruction of Herat and her own demise. I got out of bed and looked out the window. The wheat field had the bright hues of twelve noon. A small plane came down and landed at the distant airport. My two housemates were getting into their beaten-up pickup truck. I needed a cup of coffee.

I dressed in silence. I did not go into Herat that day, but logged onto the computer network and I read through several recent analyses of the insurgency in Afghanistan. I called up Lt Col. Dirst and when I told him about the possibility of a Saudi-influenced insurgent group coming to Herat and stepped him through the complex web of subgroups and possible alliances to suggest to him a new threat he met my concern like an ordinary man who doubts nothing and suspects nothing. I stepped outside and stood looking at the empty fields till I felt the hot shining sun. I felt as though the stability in Herat was in jeopardy if Khalis allows this new group sanctuary here. The severity of Alexandra's warning was conceivable: young men coming in from all over the Middle East need a secure space to train, organize, rest, refit, hibernate and, quite possibly now, fight. I called on my sources and put them to work straightaway.

Apparently, as Khalis grew in reputation, power, and dominance, the neighboring village tribal leaders, who at first had not thought how great a danger this new governor might prove to be to them began (too late, however) to see their mistake; and now wishing to correct the problem, they sought to unite under the auspices of a league against him. That afternoon they sent word to us that the clergy resorted, among other measures which they were accustomed to employ under Islamic law, to the establishment of a dictator; that is to say they gave the power to Khalis, who without consulting anyone else in the administration except for his hand-picked department directors and a few loyal members of the Provincial Council that represented the fourteen districts in Herat Province, decided upon a course of action and began to carry it into effect with his special security unit whose command reached to the Hezb-e-Islami group. This manifestation, which on former occasions had showcased our ability to quietly overcome hard problems close at hand, was presently lost to us in all the critical events that ostensibly occurred during the week Hume was away, and he was pissed. Upon this development, first, I must comment that when those terrible blue eyes of his are aroused, that is to say, from something considered fully within his authority, and has become so great as to fill every thought with wrath, he behaves prudently for the most part, rather than to destroy the first thing that crosses his path, for he knows that to destroy the transgression the problem only increases, and accelerates the damage. I must comment, second, that he seemed to be in a bad mood to begin with, since returning from his stateside trip, and it was more difficult to confront these feelings at their origin here, as it seems natural to men always to favor the destruction of things in times of war.

I wish now that I had not started to write this book in the first person singular. It is all very well when you can expose someone that you admire in a just or charitable light, and nothing can be more discerning than the undistorted spirit of a hero that in this manner is quite effective; it is pleasing to write about old-fashioned American virtues when you see in the readers' eyes the glowing patriotism and on his smile the enthusiastic grin; but it is not so pleasant when you have to expose this beloved comrade as a plain damned scoundrel.

At the time I read in the *Guardian* an article by a widely known critic in the course of which he remarked that in Iraq we were fighting a modern Thermopylae. I wish he had not made such a pronouncement because things were heading south in slow motion there, but he merely threw out the statement with just the same chagrin as General Walter Bedell Smith, then-Undersecretary of State, when he made his celebrated observation about the French (a close ally of ours at the time) at Dien Bien Phu. I was much concerned and forthwith asked Lt Col. Dirst (who reads everything, even the intelligence reports he writes introductions for) to recommend to me some books on the legacy of French efforts to reassert its influence over their colonies in Indochina and that battle in particular. On his advice I read *The Centurions* and its sequel, *The Praetorians*, by Jean Larteguy, from which I learned about a group of paratroopers who slugged it out in the jungle, their brutal march and survival in camps where they acquired the Communist's unconventional methods of war, ultimately employing them themselves when called upon to fight an insurgency closer to home in Algeria; after that I read his memoir, *The Face of War*, from which I learned that the war in Vietnam was more about democracy and popular perceptions than about the quest for a triumph of arms; then, putting my high-school French to use, I read the *Manuel de l'officier de renseignement* (Intelligence Officer's Handbook) by Bruno Bigeard, from which I learned everything about *quadrillage*: the block warden system used to spy on citizens, report their activities to the local secret police office, and torture suspected people to gain information on insurgents. Billy Graves went to his locker and showed me these same concepts in a translated version of the seminal book *La Guerre moderne*, by Roger Trinquier. In no other works could I fathom anything to the point at issue here. All the same, I can find only one reason why certain governments, such as the Fourth Republic, Nazi Germany, Argentina (the list goes on and on), and now my very own country, have justified the use of these methods as a necessary evil that many people hotly criticize. In a nut shell, I suppose as the United States has grown more worldly, with greater responsibilities, we became more conscious of the complexity, coherence, and necessity of war and thus began to rationalize these kinds of activities; this indeed is the only excuse for a highly developed society whose thoughts should have been more properly turned to productive matters, such as expanding trade and improving infrastructure for business enterprises. Regrettably, as the center of economic gravity shifts from the Atlantic to the Indian Ocean, mortality becomes a thought, taking possession of us, especially those who claim to have faith; and since as we grow older we feel ourselves more and more like earthbound mortals I should not be surprised to find that with advancing age the United States grows less and less inclined to do than past times has worthily provided her, even though a virtuous character abides throughout the nation.

# SIXTEEN

**S**TILL **I** **HAVE** a recollection of warm sunny days that replaced the tired air of Afghanistan when there was a longed-for newness, when our tactics alone seemed a bit too blunt or severe for the quiet villages, and when our heavy-handed counterinsurgency strategy was squeezing the life out of the people. Actually, this was fallacious reasoning, and yet I found myself more frequently neglecting my informants and going with Hume and his men on their daily rounds. The Italians on point duty for NATO in the province gave us a stare as we came, sometimes of suspicion; but sometimes also there was a wink of comprehension in their eyes. We would meet with one of our many village attendants or "block wardens" on the way through and Captain Hume gave my arm a friendly little tug when (chiefly for show but I was eager to make a good impression on him) I placed a few dollars on a colorful rug or in a skinny palm. Hume made me feel valuable. I had a great admiration for him. He was easy and confident. He had a placidness of temper during the meetings that communicated itself to the elders we were visiting; you shared his pleasure in the passing moment.

Before I became involved with the covert mission, I had often asked myself and others if the special forces were the salvation of the military. Now my band of brothers laughed at me.

"Light, adaptable—and fast, you know that."

I wanted to ask them if they thought the special forces was something the Marines could do, but I vaguely felt that this was a question that might precipitate more laughter. Though I knew the notion of a Marine special warfare contribution was now being considered again—it was resisted by many colonels—I had a notion that many of them held the traditional belief that Marines should support Marines, and thus the Marine Corps should not fund a special warfare capability. At any rate we stood up our first unit at about this time, a developmental but strong fighting force, which would answer directly to the Special Operations Command, and more important would provide us a way to learn how to become more innovative, more flexible. I was relatively old then, at least I felt that way, so it was not something I considered joining; these guys seemed young to me even though I knew that they were all about my same age. Yet it gave me a little thrill of satisfaction that Samuel Nicholas would be proud of these actions to improve ourselves, not bad for an organization that is famous for her exploits in the First Barbary War. It also gave me a little thrill of pride to think that I was Alexandra's darling. When I used to look at her chatting and laughing with them, I glowed with satisfaction. I thought of the afternoons we passed together at the house and was inclined to laugh at the other guys who were ignorant of my great secret. But sometimes I thought Mark Sykes looked at me in a playful way, as if he were enjoying a good joke at my expense, and I asked Theodore Hume uneasily if Alexandra had told him that she was having an affair with me. He of course did not take her seriously, and nothing really had happened between us, but I wondered if there was anything in the relationship that might hurt us. I told him that I was afraid that Khalis suspected something; he looked at me with those blue eyes of his that always seemed ready to smile.

"Ha, don't worry about it," he said, as if he were Faraydun in the *Shahnama*, the Book of Kings. "He's screwing us so keep up the good work, all right."

I had never been intimate with a source, but Hume looked upon Khalis as a greedy and wicked old man (which of course he was) and though he had always been civil he considered him from another tribe. I thought it could only be my luck that now he began to be a little more candid with me than before. But one day Lenny Abbas to my surprise told me the boss wanted me to go with them across the border into Iran and help out with an installation. I probed Alexandra about the situation on the ground over there.

"Oh, yes, my husband has cut a deal with Tehran, but you'll be just fine. Lenny speaks the language and knows the customs. He is a riot, and always cracks me up."

So I went with them. I made arrangements with the border agents (one of which was on my payroll) and Lenny made himself very funny. He had a sarcastic sense of humor and was very funny when he poked fun at Ryan Qajar, whom he loved like a brother; I tried to be serious for we had the truck filled with Wi-Fi equipment, but he was having too much fun.

He seemed to be a carefree guy. Subsequently, with grins and laughing innuendos aimed at the border guards in the rearview mirror, he gave me to understand that we were going to be staying awhile to set up not one but all seven communication hubs for the People's Mujahideen of Iran who would be sending men from inside Iraq to help target the insurgent camps. (The Navy would provide passage.) I could not but ask myself if he was playing with me because he knew I had talked to Alexandra and Ryan knew, too. I played along with them, but inside I grew somewhat nervous about the job.

Then near Tabas in the Yazd Province (formerly the southern part of the province of Khorasan), someone new appeared on the loosely paved road. This was an Azerbaijani Zoroastrian named Jimmy Elchibey, a computer hotshot from the CIA, who was quietly inserted along with their telescopic radio towers and solar-powered batteries. I do not know how the CIA had come to join forces with us and whether it was respect for Captain Hume that brought this guy to a lonely town in the middle of the desert, but it was certainly not that which motivated him to come. He was a tall, thin, dark man with a shaved head and brown crooked teeth, a man of thirty, but of an older appearance, astute, hardworking and jovial. He got along with Lenny almost immediately. He was paid very well apparently, for he maintained an apartment in Istanbul where most of his family was presently living; he was on the road for the most part, but spoke as if when there with this three brothers he would have a good-old time. I could not but like him. He was plain but quite impressive. I loved his fluent conversation in perfect but foreign English; I loved the cost-efficient way he prepared the sites for us; I loved the generosity with which he treated his day laborers. I found that Ryan disliked him as great as Lenny and I liked him; but he ultimately warmed up to him.

"Thankfully, he's not staying on with us." Ryan Qajar twisted his lips and raised his black eyebrows; with his shaggy hair and big ears he looked incredibly young. "The CIA is always trying to one up us; they want to be top dog."

"He's so terribly good though," I sounded off.

"Yeah, beauty of competition, I reckon," he said, kicking a stone.

For the next two weeks we set up and tested the point-to-point connections and broadcast network. On the other end, Mark Sykes worked through a problem of signal degradation outside Herat, by going around the rolling hills that made it difficult to establish line-of-sight propagation. We were all quite vexed and challenged by it.

"This has to be the record," cheered Jimmy Elchibey, triumphantly when trying out the multi-hop Wi-Fi chain. "I want to see everything while I'm here. It wouldn't be cool for me to leave until we test each of the hops and the effective broadcast range. I'm only here for a week more."

Later one night Ryan did not see the object of this dedication on his part.

"But don't you think he's too nonchalant," he said.

"Ha, I think he's good," said Lenny. "He makes me laugh."

"Don't you think the CIA's absolutely freeloading."

"Well, it pleases the boss and it doesn't do us any harm."

"I wonder if the helicopters are ready," I said, upon listening to the exchange. "It just occurred to me that it might be better to use their drones instead, but it makes all the sense in the world to work with them."

"I don't think it's so bad either," said Lenny.

"We shouldn't have anything to do with them," Ryan protested. "I mean, it's our mission."

I scratched my head. It was an unpleasant habit of ours.

"It's funny how different their people are from our people," I said.

Ryan Qajar was thankful when Jimmy Elchibey finally left us. But then Ryan was told to stay on with Lenny the day after and as a bone to assuage his frustration we arranged to dine in Tabas before my departure. Billy Graves met us there and I drove with him to the restaurant.

"I don't know why Ryan is so angry about staying," I said, content that I was allowed to return.

"He'll get over it."

"Is Hume happy with us," I asked.

"Very," Billy laughed.

I sat back with my hands behind my head. I have elsewhere remarked how much more rewarding the smaller unit is for this beautiful and indeed essential act in human intercourse than the battalion of present day, which reflexively refrains from behaving the selfless way. (James Isner would most likely agree with me on this point.) I looked out the window and saw my reflection on the glass. The sun was setting on the desert. The sky was like a piece of brilliant obscurity.

We arrived. I hung my beret-like hat on a peg and washed my hands in the washbasin (which was very large and open for everybody to use, with large bars of soap and cold water from a holding tank above; very common) and casually asked Billy about the roads.

"No problem," he said.

"We can transfer the spares after eating," I said.

"Yeah, I'm starved."

"The system is in good shape now. You said we should drive back tonight."

"That's right . . . . The boss set things in motion," he added after contradicting himself again. "Don't you think it's exciting. And look: showtime."

"What!" I gave his watch a glance. It gave us only five hours to get back across the border before the first missile strikes by our helicopters against militants in Iran's tribal areas. I didn't know if this was reasonable.

"It seems awfully tight. Do we have time for dinner?"

"We'll be fine. The boss told me to rent a house on this side of the port of entry, in Taybad." He dried his hands on a towel; he was happy as a Little Leaguer with a bat. "Do you guys let anything go to chance?"

"Not anymore."

"That makes me feel better. Whatever happened to the other guys? I told Lenny it was just outside town, but he doesn't listen to me," I said, trying to make my voice sound calm.

Billy chuckled with hilarity and his voice was loud. But I felt my breath go away and a shiver run through my heart.

"Won't Hume think it's rather funny, his men fleeing like rats from the rising floodwater?" I added.

Billy's eyes jumped around.

"You know what he is, he never misses anything; if he sees things turning sideways we'll know it straight off. He won't have it any other way." He turned to look outside. "He's a control freak. Say, here they are."

I tried to eat and in order not to show the throbbing of my heart I did my best to keep the conversation going on one topic or another. Billy Graves did not much mind what I said. He could only think of the delicious lamb chops and every other minute his eyes returned to the three of us who he insisted on getting a cup of tea so he could have seconds. He always looked at his food with an appetite in which there was something brutal and perhaps covetous. (I heard that he had once consumed three Army Ranger burgers while training at Fort Benning.) I was sort of angry with him. I thought him aloof and foolish.

"You look like a dog that's gobbling down its food," I could not help snapping at him.

He only laughed.

Lenny and Ryan took on the same mood as I and asked for the bill. The owner let his daughter return to our table with the change. Billy sensed the growing animosity and commented after she turned away that we had uncovered a plot against Israeli cities, and in an effort to foil the terrorist attack the mission was pushed up. I will add here that this is the point when things turned away from us. In hindsight, I could not believe that anyone would take a position as that of our policy-making critics; what did it mean but that Theodore Hume had been second guessed by a few preening congressional staffers back in Washington, D.C., day after day, all the time we were in Iran, and now when we were trying to preempt a possible attack on the West. How could they behave that way? Didn't they not see how it hurt us? Didn't they see how reckless it was of them? It forced us to act. It also gave Khalis a clear indication that we were on to him.

"Good thing he knows best," Ryan said.

"Oh, yes, he's got it under control," added Billy. "He said he wanted to give you guys something before he went to the mattresses and asked what I thought. Well, I said, I reckon they could do with heavier weapons and ammunition to match, but I never thought he'd agree with me like this."

"Like what?" begged Lenny.

"When we went into the vault, I asked the guys to show me the M60 machine guns, but he said: 'No, take the Rolls Royce instead, and all the ammunition you can carry.' And when he looked at the box of semi-automatic 12-gauge shotguns, he absolutely insisted on my taking a few of them, too."

I thought of Billy with his large mild face, his arms so tattooed, in the basement of the house with our big redheaded commando leader and his thick beard and authoritative voice. And then I knew that the intuition that I had refused to believe was true; I knew that when Hume went into battle with his men he went to fight with them just as he went jet-skiing with me. I could not speak; I knew that if I did I should indict myself. I felt nonetheless that Hume had seen the competitiveness in me all along. I used my determination to prevent the sapless worry from seeping out of my eyes.

We went on to another safe house. I could not bother with the weapons and inspected the spares. I could only feel the inevitability of the night; I could only see the night unfold one way. I could have taken the mindset of the others; it was Billy Graves who horrified me. How could he? It was not a coincidence that Captain Hume selected him to pick me up. But I had longed to have the chance to go into battle that if anybody would ask me about my long military career I would be able tell them something truly respectable. At last he told me what I already sensed.

"So you want to play cards with us now?" he said.

"I don't know."

"You come down with something?"

"I'm fine."

He gave me a strange look. I did not meet his eyes, but I knew they were scrutinizing with that scrutiny at once simple and playful that I knew so well from my exposure to the special forces. I reluctantly played poker with them that night until one o'clock in the morning. At the end of the game, since it was close to zero hour, we drove up to the nearest hilltop and Lenny Abbas checked the vitals of the Wi-Fi system. He did not speak until he came out of the truck, then said:

"Our friends are pushing video tonight."

"Looks like they got the green light," I said.

"We can't let them do that to us again," said Ryan Qajar.

Lenny lifted up the laptop and gave us a chance to look at the data moving across the network. He pointed out that the system expands Internet connectivity with meshing technology, thus enabling our hubs to communicate between each other and move data more efficiently. I was truly impressed by his software modifications. When the sun came up he jumped out from the truck and told us that it was over without a word. I took off my hat and coat. The CIA had launched at least twenty drone attacks that night from beyond the distant horizon.

"We need to bug out," said Billy, coming up to the truck.

"Let me check in first," Lenny said, looking away.

Ryan put his hand on Billy's back.

"Don't you think we should stay here a while longer? I reckon they'll be wanting to know if they hit the mark. We can't risk going anyway, don't you think?"

"Of course we can't leave now," said Lenny.

"Hume would have a fit if something went wrong," I added. "You can't expect this new technology to run all by itself. I've never been so lucky. It's a fact of life."

"And you can't expect us to believe that Hume gave permission to leave at this point," Ryan chimed in.

"We're vulnerable here," said Billy. "All right, let's see what he says, but he expects us to do what's required."

"He'll want us to stay."

I looked at Lenny now, with anticipation, eager eyes; he smiled at me, and I wish I knew how to describe the changing hues of the morning sky; it took on a luminous glow and the air moving over the vast inhospitable landscape was exquisitely gentle.

"Oh, you won't believe this. Why don't you guys read the email yourselves. Don't say the military isn't an adventure. Now we have Iran looking for us."

"Cars and tankers are being stopped at Taybad!" said Ryan.

"Well, well," said Billy. "I bet Tehran is second-guessing Khalis. We shall see how long he can go without that revenue stream and what will Kabul do about it? We'll have to see whether we are allies or enemies."

Billy put an arm around my neck and pressed his other hand into Lenny's shoulder. We read the email a second time. I only read the section below that outlined the number of dead Iranian soldiers, and the captured paramilitary men of the People's Mujahideen of Iran, and wondered if the battle would unfold as he had predicted earlier that night.

"Good thing you brought plenty of ammunition," I remembered uttering to him.

# SEVENTEEN

POLITICAL UPHEAVAL IN Iran and a sudden rupture in relations with Khalis heightened our concern about the likelihood of a quick return to Herat. During all this time I never doubted Theodore Hume would come for us. His plan occupied much of our day and in the evening of the next we were extracted by helicopters. We were, of course, told to go to the airstrip at Desert One, which was audacious and ironically amusing; he was there waiting for us with an unlit cigar in his mouth. He appeared very glad to see us and chatted with me for a little while of other things. (He wanted me to travel to Tajikistan and speak to Haddawy on his behalf about becoming the governor of Herat, and his willingness to marry Alexandra.) But naturally most of his attention was given to the pilots who were waiting for a signal to depart. I had a feeling that he was growing more and more restive; he was not the jovial, easygoing guy that I had met at the bazaar. Perhaps it was only my increasing sensibility that discerned as it were an invisible trait that separated him from the men he led and carried on with. It was as though he lived a life of the prince that made living every single day a little more difficult. We were asked to board the helicopter and in no time were back in Afghanistan.

The next day he traveled to Kabul. He met with senior military officials. He had already got to know a good many people outside the narrow circle into which his authority had placed him, and he was increasingly asked to meetings by generals who liked to gather about them innovative thinkers. Commander Wasson was asked too, but stayed in Herat; he said he didn't care for the Army. (He once remarked that these men did not quite understand that war in the desert was much like war at sea, taking place over a vast, often harsh landscape, where formations can be obscured easily; he added intelligence and agility were essential.) But after all they didn't really want him; they only wanted Ted. I think he was loyal and did what he was told. It may be that generals had more than once let him see how tiresome they thought it that Admiral Seton insisted he must be included; and after inviting him because it was politically correct, ignored him because to be working with the Navy here irked them.

After a lull the Hezb-e-Islami group began a terror campaign in Herat. We exchanged blows with them, tit for tat until our withdrawal. Ryan Qajar and Billy Graves got caught up in one such battle during a foot patrol one morning; as each tried to save the other, both were killed, brutally and graphically; and their lifeless bodies were dragged in front of the shrine of the renowned poet and scholar, Khwaja Abdullah Ansari. Captain Hume, angered with grief, swore to kill all of them in revenge. That said, it is not my business to criticize the boss, and of late much has been written about him as must satisfy the appetite of the ordinary American citizen; but I will permit myself to say here that Operation Blue Skies, though certainly not the most illustrious of his great career, is to my mind the most interesting and complex. (Hume chalked it up as a loss.) It has a cold ruthlessness that in all the sentimentality of Service academy schools strikes a fresh tone. It is beautiful and pure hell. It is the battleground where God and the Devil war for the soul of man. It makes your heart race, but it has a soft, pleasant feel that is very agreeable to the touch. Of all of Hume's battles or assignments it is the only one I should like to have been involved. Yet, quite clearly now, the instance of several unintended deaths (the unfortunate outcome of the lesser known block warden system to locate and target the insurgent training camps), terrible and despicable, and the armed drone attacks that followed it, cannot easily be forgotten by anyone who had participated in the operation.

It was this part that caused the sudden storm that burst on Hume's red head. For a few days after the cross-border bombing campaign it looked as though it would run its course like the rest of any bloody battle, namely that it would have substantial media coverage, favorable on the whole but with reservations, and that the collateral damage would be moderate. Mark Sykes told me he expected to get funding to expand the Wi-Fi communication network with conventional military operations and was talking with USAID of rolling out similar wireless networks in Kabul and other cities around the country. The media coverage in the Middle East was timid and noncommittal; then on the Qatar-based *Al Jazeera* television network appeared a violent attack. On a call-in show there was the unmasking of Saladin, the noble-minded leader of the Hezb-e-Islami group regarded as a close ally of Pakistan's powerful intelligence chief and his wife who was related to the Saudi royal family.

There was an account of suspects who were subjected to interrogation and sometimes the systematic use of torture. The show was described to me as gratuitously offensive, cruel, and soon other television networks followed suit. The more foolish purported that the United States was organizing a coup to remove Governor Khalis from office and some military officers asked themselves gravely if this was not a case of the sort that makes us all hold our virtues cheap. Of course the spokesmen at the White House and Pentagon denied everything. The wise Khalis had already begun to see through us as the sand escaped from the hourglass of our operation, and Hume knew that he never lacked legitimate reason to break his promise to him. Hume had often commented that it was always better to be feared than to be loved. And so unable to do both the result was presently plain. I tried to make contact with Alexandra but found that she had been locked away behind closed doors and that her premonitions about Khalis and his desire to forge a dynasty for himself were true. When after the fighting broke out in Herat, and things looked as if they would not be resolved, Admiral Seton was forced to send the entire team home. The big Army took control of the situation. A Marine Corps battalion came up from Helmand Province, and I continued my work from Shindand.

All this was naturally very hard for Theodore Hume, but he bore it with philosophic calm. He shrugged his shoulders.

"With resignation, I leave a mission I feel strongly about," he smiled. "And I leave unfulfilled commitments in the fight, commitments I hold sacred."

The dead were buried and he was supported in the succeeding investigation by the fidelity of his colleagues. To take account of Operation Blue Skies became a mark of aesthetic astuteness: to be shocked by it was to confess yourself a wuss. Needless to say, condemnation was universal; if here and there a courageous writer, accustomed to the more realistic tone of modern warfare, asserted that Captain Hume had never performed anywhere better, he was ignored. The doughty opinion was ascribed to the base desire to play to the far-right. Commander Wasson had no hesitation in saying that it was a masterpiece, and though the arrests, interrogations, and detentions that were sanctioned by the then legal authority became nonstandard and regrettable, his commitment to Captain Theodore Hume remained firm. It is strange (and somewhat instructive) to hear now, what people of the present day have to say about it all. Of course, I still believe there was nothing intrinsically dishonorable in the offering of my support upon invitation, but many nights, unable to sleep, I lay awake thinking about my actions. Alas, it would not be the first time someone has lowered himself to the level of the age, and furthermore to give credit to Rousseau's argument in his somewhat overdone *First Discourse*, someone had sacrificed his intuitive feelings to the "tyrants of their liberty." The desire for acceptance tends to inspire the worst in man. I can always hope—though history may never settle the matter—that people come to consider that we did some good.

# EIGHTEEN

**A**BOUT SIX MONTHS later, when the excitement over Operation Blue Skies had subsided and Theodore Hume had already begun an assignment at the Naval Special Warfare Developmental Group for which he was the commanding officer, I, working then with USAID and in my final year, in the course of my duties went one day to the student center of Herat University to await the provincial reconstruction team manager whom I was accompanying on his round of the faculty. I glanced at the five computer terminals at which no one was seated, for sometimes students, taking advantage of the convenience, checked the Internet and their email here. I was not surprised to find the system down again. I checked my mobile and was surprised to find it working and a text message from Commander Wasson. It ran as follows:

*I WILL TRY AGAIN AT 1800 HRS (AFT) TODAY WITHOUT FAIL. IMPORTANT. RICK*

I wondered what he wanted me for. I had learned that he had taken a position at William and Mary College in the history department, but he had never corresponded with me, and I had never really been friendly with him. I knew that adjunct professors were nervous at class-time and a warhorse, short of new fodder at the last moment, might think that I was better than nothing; but the wording of the message hardly suggested a desire for an update on the local situation in Afghanistan.

The foreign service officer for whom I supported was upbeat and long-winded. It was not till half past five that we left the president's office and then it took a good twenty minutes to review our findings. Commander Wasson called me precisely at six o'clock. It was just as I said farewell when the phone rang. But when I said hello and began talking he cut me short and began to explain why he needed to talk to me.

"I supposed the service was out again. It doesn't matter."

I let him continue with his train of thought.

"Oh, I think it's a good time for you, isn't it?" He paused for a second, his rough, rather brusque voice softened. "You have a minute, do you?"

I was worn out and hungry, for my lunch consisted of an apple and then later in the afternoon a cup of tea, but I did not want to stop him. I found a chair.

"Have you spoken to your father recently?" asked Commander Wasson, with a gesture towards family which had been always a way to display kindness, and now a military interest. "I know you have a good relationship with him."

I did. We used to talk often, but his question confused me and I wondered what point he was driving at. Though partly missed, in the first days my father was calling me practically every other week. Likewise, I was exchanging emails with my three brothers, especially Frank who considered the Iraq War to be a Babylon revisited. He noted the parallels between the British experience eight decades before us when they quit Mesopotamia; whereas, I reminded him that the lesson to be learned from them was that their pullout only led to more violence, the rise of a dictatorship, and a catastrophic unraveling of everything they had tried to build there. In any event, my father hardly ever called me now that I was coming home and I do not think I had received an email from him in about a month. I told him so.

"Have you heard from Ted lately?" he asked next as though I were his best friend.

"I haven't."

"No?"

Commander Wasson paused and I looked from the table to the clock on the distant wall and back again as though expressing my irritation.

"What is it I can do for you today, Rick?" I said, a faintly restless tone in my voice, in my impatient way.

"Then you don't know that Dotti left him."

"Say what."

The news took a few seconds to sink into my brain. I had thought the state of their marriage was improving, or good.

"I was hoping you might be able to help me, Riley," he said.

"I'm sorry."

"Ted is taking it very hard."

"My dad mentioned the Humes bought a new house in Nimmo but nothing more. Shall I make an inquiry for you?"

"No, quite all right."

I chose not to interpose myself between the two close friends. Commander Wasson cleared his throat and I placed the phone into the fingers of my other hand.

"Are you making any progress with the Wi-Fi system," he inquired casually. "I understand things are finally settling down over there."

"Well, somewhat. Karzai has managed to calm down the old bugger, but the seas are still rough. Have you been following the situation in Dushanbe?"

"No."

"Haddawy was assassinated this past week."

"No surprise there."

"Yeah. Is there anything I can do for the captain?" I asked finally.

"Oh, no," he said, before saying goodbye, and telling me to stay safe out there.

I was surprised at what he had said but not concerned or troubled; however reluctantly, to acknowledge the legitimacy of some of my feelings, I was disquieted because I could not make out why Commander Wasson had called me. He knew me much too little to think that the affair could be of any particular interest to me; nor would he have troubled to let me hear it as a piece of news out of the sports section. Since it was Sunday, while my housemates were out, I went to the telephone and called my father. He spoke for a few minutes to catch me up on family matters before I asked him about the Humes. I cannot believe that the congregation of St. John's provided him with such a thorough treatment of the situation. He had seen him at church.

"I saw Ted Hume sitting by himself in the pew on the other side of the aisle today. He was there early and before I took my seat in the usual place, since time permitted, I thought I would walk over to him and say a quick hello. He did not see me approach him; but I knew besides that he always acknowledged me at some point in the mass, being both regulars, as you know. Imagine my surprise then, no, my utter and complete bemusement, when as I approached I saw that he had been crying, his eyes wet and tears running down his cheeks. You know of course that he is a man of stoic indifference but was always smiling and in the habit of being forthcoming and friendly at church. Matter of fact everyone was accustomed to return his optimism before mass and when he came out of church an hour later he was talkative to people and always interested to spend a few minutes with Father Mayer. The Blairs were right, but confirmed by Brenda Hoover: Ted Hume had been issued a restraining order and he was beside himself."

My father paused for a moment to allow me to interject a thought or two. I let him continue:

"I did not know whether or not to turn around or proceed to interrupt him, but it immediately occurred to me that he may need someone to talk to that morning. He was kneeling down and turned slowly toward me. There was something wild in his eyes and distraught in his expression. I asked myself, knowing the fluctuation of the marital state myself, whether a difference of opinion had driven Dotti headlong from the house or whether he was still trying to get back into the groove of family life. He merely smiled and nodded his head. He did not seem to see me and the realization immediately occurred to me that he wanted to be alone. After mass I stopped him in the parking lot. 'Ted,' I said. He looked angry. For a moment I could have sworn he was going to confront me for meddling into his affairs. 'My apologies for interrupting you,' I started again. 'Oh, Dr. Cooper,' he said. 'Do you want to join me for a cup of coffee in the hall?' I asked. 'Not today, sorry,' he replied."

At this rate I thought my father would never finish his story, but I knew he would be upset if I cut the conversation short so I let him make his point.

"On the way home I started to think about the readings, relating them to my research, and wondered if Father Mayer was sending a subtle message during the homily. 'I am the Lord your God, who brought you out of the land of Egypt, out of the house of bondage.' You know that is Deuteronomy, and the succession of ideas that follow the biblical chronological sequence where Moses came down from the mountain and told the people what God had told him. To hear Father Mayer talk about it so passionately, the world has once again become the lawless chaos that was here on earth until God gave Moses the Ten Commandments. As with all things in life, there is nothing that can't be abused. In biblical days priests played the dual role as kings; they were the mediators between man and the gods. So Father Mayer made sure that we remembered that all of God's laws came from Moses. He told everyone to forget about scientists that have found other written codes of law that preceded the Bible, and he dismissed the Hittite Law Code, the Babylon Code of Hammurabi, and the Egyptians who had a law code as far back as 3,000 B.C. Of course, I thought he was talking to me. Thinking about it now, I recognize he was making reference to the wars and when talking about the fifth commandment he kept on trying to make the distinction between killing and murdering someone as if the Bible does not glorify violent killing and the slaughter of innocent men, women, and children. In Exodus, the same Moses who promulgated this law killed an Egyptian for hitting a Hebrew, and, in Numbers, we have the words of Moses after his army 'avenged' the Midianites by killing the entire male population and bringing back the women and children as prisoners. Being a merciful man he made for one exception: 'But all the young girls, who have not known a man by sleeping with him keep alive for yourselves.' You know, I always confuse the commandments. We skip over the regulation against graven images and as a result the Catholic version is out of sync with the Protestant version. So maybe he was speaking to the law against adultery; no, I take that back. Sometimes I find myself daydreaming when he goes on and on. My research, to sum it up for you, Riley, contends population density added to the social complexities that necessitated a commonly felt need to codify standards of behavior. It was the development of agriculture that ended the need for migrating to find food. When property became a measure of wealth, a lone farmer could not protect himself and his property from pillaging by raiders. So it became necessary to group together and pay for common protection. We found that the earliest tablets were tax records."

He paused again and invited me to make a comment, as his stance on evolutionary principles in explaining the spread of ideas and cultural phenomena had softened.

"Dad, you will have to tell me more about your work when I get home," I said instead.

"Yes, yes, very well," he said.

Realizing the connection and the occasion demanded deferential treatment, I said: "Many people think that all Catholics are drumbeaters. Our faith goes deeper, and I owe it all to you. By the way, is Roger still working with you?"

"He's left Old Dominion for good."

I gasped, but said nothing. I thought about disclosing my secret to him.

"He's gone home," he added. "Thank God. I had little time for him anyway. I should be frank with you. In a strange way I feel bad about his tenure at the university. 'You're well rid of me,' he said on his last day. 'Dr. Bernard,' I said, 'you're mistaken. I am a man of honor, of knowledge, and of ambitiousness, in that order. I wish you the best, and it was a great pleasure working with you. I will hold dear your contributions in the department.' At the farewell ceremony, I gave him full honors and in return he was very gracious. Riley, let me just add, he was nothing but a pain in the neck. His behavior was a public disgrace."

"You should have let him go a long time ago."

"He was tenured, irremovable, but as you might recall he did not confront my authority again after that little spat. He took full advantage of his assignment at the University of London in which we are collaborating. And I reflected also that there is no reason to slow a young man's momentum while at work on the creation of a great discovery. Ultimately, he began to put more and more of his energy into the soft sciences. Archeology, I would never have guessed. Whatever his affliction, he was willing to leave behind to us extraordinary ideas. You're probably wondering what I am talking about."

I did not answer. I began to perceive the contradiction that my father represented (tied to tradition and faith but working in the sciences to advance culture) and the way he treated Dr. Bernard was hardly fair but consistent with Mosaic Law; it became clear that he played by the new rules for promoting social cooperation and old ones for enforcing social conformity. I would never tell him so but he perhaps considered the function of religion is not to make men virtuous: it is to make them conform with their faith, which is coincident with the facts on the ground in the Middle East. I waited for him to go on.

"It was at the picnic on the Fourth of July you first met Dr. Bernard, wasn't it?"

"No, no, you're mistaken. I was introduced to him much earlier."

He almost laughed.

"Poor Roger," he said. "Of course no one can deny that it was a blessing in disguise, but I'm afraid you'll take it very much to heart. Unfortunately he's hurt one of our own." My father took a deep breath and spoke to me as an adult. "As soon as Mrs. Blair told us about the police coming to Ted's house I got Roger's resignation letter, but the dean said he'd been thinking about it for some time; that means that he must have finally found another position. Roger's finally got up the nerve and run away with Dotti."

I was astounded at what I heard from my own father and shocked and dismayed.

"You knew all along then?"

"Oh, they've been seeing each other for years now. It's almost a joke around here. But I never said anything. It's none of my business. Your mother didn't much like it though."

"I suppose so," I replied.

"A tragic situation."

"Yes, indeed, I still feel that he is nobler than the forces that are trying to destroy him."

"Precisely."

"Is there anything we can do for him? I reckon the boys are in Nimmo with him."

"No, Dotti took them with her."

"Dad, could it be possible?"

"I know what you are thinking—there is no reason to speculate. I see them occasionally. Ronny looks just like him, big-boned and redheaded; and Parker has reddish blond hair, but it is turning darker now."

"Well, I can see a battle brewing in the future."

"No doubt."

"I guess I should be moving on."

"Say Riley, I just had a thought. Why don't we have a big shindig on the Fourth? It would be great to get everyone together and celebrate your return."

"I'd appreciate that. Do you think you can entice my siblings to come?"

"Frank sent word a few weeks ago that he will be traveling with his family to Europe around that time. I will have to check to see if they can arrange a stopover. I reckon he won't mind breaking up the trip. It's such a long way from Australia. Your mother will make sure Robert and Arnold and their families are available. Arnold came to see us at Easter. He still loves the Windy City. Robert is looking for a new job again. He said he wants to stay in Boston."

"Yeah, he loves it there. Say what about the theme for the party? A most essential ingredient."

"Ha, why don't you suggest something."

"Sure, all right."

"So you're doing all right? What do you think of USAID?"

"Well, foreign aid workers are a different cup of tea."

"I understand."

"I'm not sure what I want to do next."

"You should consider graduate school."

"Funny you should say that as I've been looking into research opportunities."

"I will send you a few ideas to ponder this week."

"I appreciate it, Dad."

"Don't mention it."

"Well, good talking to you. I wish there was something we could do for the Humes. Let me know. Oh, say hello to mom for me; and so long, Dad."

"Goodbye, son."

But it was June before I spoke to my father again, even though I found the information he sent to me via email extremely useful and applicable to my experience (and merely replied to it by telling him so). As soon then as I could remove myself from the provincial reconstruction team I made my way to Kabul, and while spending a week there with Lt Col. Dirst I began to make plans to return to the states. At the new intelligence center he met me with a big deep-chested hullo.

"Well, looks like we are leaving on the same plane. I finally got me orders. I'll be goin' to the Pentagon for a final tour. Let us find a quiet corner and sit down."

We sought a place and found it.

"I must explain why I asked you to come 'ere," he said. "I've been tryin' to do something for you. All week I did not want to tell you, but I just got word this morning. I know you have your sights set on leaving. I did not want to run the risk of lettin' you down."

He told me the bare facts of his efforts to get me a promotion and I listened attentively. Now and then I nodded my head. But he could not hope to make me understand the commotion he had found at the various headquarters. The Army was beside itself for being without a relief. Nothing thrilling had happened here for years and no one could come up with a qualified person as a result of the focus on Iraq. The Army had had a great deficit. Of course the promotion would be forthcoming. About a month before he had hinted that he had to go over to Baghdad on business, and two days later a petition in the backfill was filed by him. It appeared that his motion had not been successful, his attempt to make a Marine into the overseer of allied ground operations met with no response, and he had been forced to find someone in every way he could. All kinds of rumors ran through the little country. Quite a number of officers who had worked with him were frustrated with the lack of confidence he had in them. The details were vague, for neither my housemates nor my colleagues in the other parts of the country knew anything of promotion matters, nor had I the knowledge to make what they told me comprehensible. But there was an email from a former colleague in Kuwait on the possibility. Lt Col. Dirst's wife had passed away and he had little or no passion for the mission. His four children, who were at a critical period of their development, were getting ready to spread their wings and fly the nest, but that too was unraveling on him. He had gone back many times with the intention of setting them straight, something like ten trips, he said, though how I remember that I cannot imagine; yet he had sent word to me each time he had left the country. It was supposed that the Army was going to find somebody; they always told him it was just a matter of days.

"I hope you take it," he said. "You ought to be a lieutenant colonel by now."

The indignation was shared. I could forgive them because I had always been so independent but loyal, because I had foiled them and disregarded them but responded with an unbreakable commitment, because I had neglected my dress uniforms but had been first to fight and did such a good job for them. But it was on the evening before my departure that Lt Col. Dirst dropped the bombshell. For the last two years I had been spending my leave on Crete at Souda Bay, and I had been taking some courses. The commanding officer of the base had launched an educational program with the Naval Research Laboratory, and on joining the Mitrou Project that studied crucial and poorly understood periods of transition in Greek prehistory I woke up one day realizing that it really interested me. I could have destined it if Theodore Hume had not found me that day at the bazaar in Herat, but that he should find me who had always looked up to him and whom I looked upon as a hero, that was the break.

"You can expect word from the commandin' general tomorrow," said my commander.

"I shouldn't be surprised," I said.

His efforts seemed a bit disconnected to me. I got up and held out my hand. "Why do these people in Washington, D.C., make these untimely decisions? It's all very funny, very funny. Thank you so much for what you've done for me. We know where we are here. The great thing is that it doesn't really matter to me now that Captain Hume is gone."

"I know how you feel, Riley."

The fact was, I have no doubt, that he was giving me not the smallest opportunity. He walked out of the intelligence center with me and put me into a bus that went down the road to the officers' club; then I walked back to my quarters.

I went my separate way. I took my father's advice and applied to the Zanvyl Krieger School of Arts and Sciences at Johns Hopkins University; my career with the Marine Corps was coming to a close, and when I had completed my fourteenth year I retired. I remember clearly to have heard from my father that Theodore Hume divorced Dotti. She relented and turned the boys over to him. He nonetheless was pissed about the whole situation, most certainly embarrassed, and the boys moved back in with him when the restraining order was dropped; but no address was given, no hint provided about Dotti's whereabouts, and we presumed she was living in London with Dr. Roger Bernard. Then one day a frustrated and angry Hume confirmed the use of torture in Afghanistan in the *Norfolk Daily Press*, where he was quoted to say it is a very useful device for its limited purpose, but he also claimed that he had not personally used the method.

# FINAL PART

## A Victory

# NINETEEN

J AMES ISNER AND I, as planned, met two days after Christmas at the Norfolk airport. We made time for a beer at the Scots-Irish pub in the main terminal. From him I now learned what had happened to Dotti after running away with Roger and getting the divorce from Theodore. Jim had in due course become intimate with Wanda Hume. Knowing him and thinking of her, I was not surprised to hear that he had spontaneously invited her to travel with him to a conference at Harvard University, sharing with her to the full their passion for her late husband, his military accomplishments and his John Wooden-like leadership and love of the men he served with on the battlefield. He had chaired diligently a session at the conference and when advancing technicality and decreasing depth had impelled Wanda Hume to sample the little shops in Cambridge, notwithstanding the many claims on his time he had gone regularly during breaks to talk with her. He was a good guy. Afterward he broke loose from his colleagues and friends and dined with her alone at the five-star restaurant inside the hotel conference center in which with disarming self-confidence he kindly showed due appreciation for her limited background and education.

It pleased me to think that his good genes should receive its due and unexpected reward, for Wanda Hume had found him kind and fascinating and over a nightcap told him much about Theodore Hume that could not fail to be of interest to him in the research work on which we were engaged. Rick Wasson, exuding a calm rage, not only sped down to Virginia Beach to see Theodore Hume when his traitorous wife ran off with Roger Bernard and the two boys what Jim could only describe by the French expression *guerre à outrance*, but stayed with him for nearly a week. (I immediately thought of Helen of Troy whose infidelity brought about the Trojan War.) He gave him the adoring consideration, the unfailing loyalty and the near-blind understanding of a man ready to die for another's sake, a comrade in arms who combined masculine vigor with feminine consideration. It was in his presence that Hume completed the first draft of the undiscovered manuscript. Rick Wasson was justified in looking upon it as his book, and, upon thinking about it for a moment after Jim mentioned it in passing before asking the bartender for two Scotch whiskeys, I knew right away that this was cogent evidence that he might be the possessor of the written material. Rick Wasson went on to London (with evil intentions of course, for I knew too well how military people were, to give occasion for retribution), and, when Jim spoke of a paperback of Machiavelli in his carry-on bag, this revealed to me that Theodore Hume was involved. He found Dr. Bernard in his classroom and returned later to see him, he acting very belligerent the part of avenger, where he could confront the man whom his increasing rage materialized.

It must be admitted that this description of increasing rage was very largely due to my prior interactions with him. Theodore Hume's great celebrity came only during his last years when he had retired from the Navy, but the repercussions of this affair were undoubtedly laid by Rick Wasson's untiring efforts in London. Not only did he inspire (and perhaps amplify not a little dirty secret from Afghanistan, for he was a man who spent his life striving to achieve his dreams) the first serious article about Hume in the *Foreign Affairs* journal in which the claim was made that he must be ranked with the best generals of American history, but as each article came out the sentiment passed from one extreme to another. Rick Wasson went here and there, seeing editors and, more important still, board members of right-wing think tanks; he gave parties to which lobbyists were invited who could be of use. He persuaded Theodore Hume not to give journalists any more material because it only stoked the fire; he saw to it that his ample military record should appear in Navy weeklies; he revised personally the manuscript Hume wrote. For the next year or so he was an untiring agent for his memoir, *Gallantry in Action*. He kept his image impeccably clean before the public.

Shortly after Rick Wasson's surprise visit Roger and Dotti took flight, but he did not find out about it right away. Six months passed before he got wind of their decision to move away. It was unwise indeed to pursue the vendetta at the time; Theodore Hume was still serving, but he never let it go. Private eyes were hired (and paid for with his own money to protect Hume); and if they happened to pick up a scent it was through him they sought direction, for while he remained charming before the public, Captain Hume would be uncommonly angry. As a rule these hired guns took direction from him. In any case, they could never pick up the trail. Revenge is not, in this view, a rational calculation of risk; it is, as students of the mafia sometimes deduct, a bit like gambling. But Rick Wasson knew exactly how to handle the situation and when the prying investigative reporters were nearly successful in uncovering the matter he could easily right the ship. After all he ran covert programs for the Navy. He was perfect for the job. All the while Hume never let on that he knew what was going on; likewise, Rick Wasson never let on about his efforts; even so he not only referred to Hume invariably as the admiral, but perhaps a little playfully and yet how manipulative addressed him in private as such. To the end he retained something jingoistic.

Then an unfortunate thing happened. Hume suffered a stroke and was sent to the hospital; for five days his life was in the balance. Rick Wasson did everything that such a good friend could do, and would willingly have cared for him himself, but he was too busy, he was indeed trying to make a mark for himself at William and Mary, and the boys with the aid of a visiting nurse took care of their father. When at last he gained strength, the doctors said he must take some time off, and since he was still extremely weak to report back to duty suggested that he should try a cruise. Rick Wasson thought that this was a good idea so that he could put his mind to rest and get the divorce out of his mind, and a neighbor agreed to look after the boys. Through the travel agency at work his executive officer found a ship departing Miami within the week that suited him. Let me move the story along. One would think that an attractive woman of thirty would have some reservations about an aging, ailing man. No, Wanda sought him out, consented to his advances, having already taken notice of him at church. He was of course attracted to her—and she to him; furthermore she impressed on him that she really wanted to be with him. She spent the whole first day tending to his needs, and, if not overnight, at least within the next couple of days, he gained back his strength, for Theodore was not of that Androgynous double and Wanda the other half embraced him. It was a perfect union.

About a week later Theodore Hume called and told Rick Wasson that he had married Wanda on the island of Barbados.

I imagine that never did Rick Wasson exhibit more preeminently his fidelity of love than in the manner in which he met this news. Did he drop the telephone to the floor and jump up and cry out with joy in an onrush of great relief and happiness? Did he turn on his best friend and call him a horny old fool? Did he inveigh against the greediness of women and the licentiousness of gold diggers or did he relieve his hurt feelings by shouting out a sequence of obscenities with which the early retired tell us the outranked are very well acquainted? Not at all. He congratulated him and wrote a nice letter to his bride telling her that he was glad to think now that he would have two loving friends instead of one. Theodore Hume begged him to do the same. (I suspect it was also at this time he told him to stop looking for Dr. Bernard.) Rick Wasson, being separated from his wife and always looking for his other half, embraced the idea that perhaps it was time for him to tie the knot with his long-time girlfriend Tina Allen. He never had anything but praise for the new Mrs. Hume. She looked a lot like Dotti, he said, but she was better looking; of course she wasn't quite, quite as confident as Dotti at that age, but Theodore Hume would only have been uncomfortable with anyone too independent. She was just the sort of wife for him. I think it may be not unjustly said that Rick Wasson was shamelessly satisfied to care for Theodore Hume, but was naturally inclined to get married himself; here was a case in point of two contented men who seek men are especially valiant and fine.

When Jim and I arrived at Nimmo, my father, neither limping toward nor obviously ready for retirement, was waiting for us on the driveway and Riley Junior who had heard the pickup truck came bounding around the corner of the garage from the backyard. I got out and reached down to pet him. My father had a proposal for us. I had learned from Jim that there might be a new relationship on the horizon, but I did not see how the two giants of learning could ever work together. Change rarely met me at the home of my youth, which was holding its own in the face of many new developments, and of course the Back Bay nature reserve was unchanged. Whenever I went there it received me with its old good-tempered fidelity: the strange fondness for my childhood sanctuary was a constant; I looked out and saw the same features; I walked around the lake and found boys with fishing poles and smiles on their faces; I'd ask them if the fish were biting; invariably they gave me a slightly funny look and said that they certainly are, but as that seemed to alter their interest in the matter I continued on with my walk knowing perfectly well that they wanted to be left alone. My father stepped forward and, holding a ready smile, in an easy voice said:

"Hello, boys; welcome, Jim."

"Hello, good to see you again, Professor," said Jim, extending his hand to my father.

"How was your flight, Jim?"

"Excellent, clear skies."

"And your Christmas?"

"Oh, excellent. The whole family got together this year."

"We'd like to prepare a nice meal for you instead of going out tonight. I'll put a steak on the grill, and your mother is baking a cherry pie for dessert—you can show Jim that new pub in town afterward."

"Sounds good, Dad."

In a little while sounded a timer and my mother in a very comfortable printed Yuletide apron, with a tidy mop of gray hair, came into the kitchen and showed me, upon opening the oven door, two very rustic pies.

"Delicious looking," I said, "but why two?"

"It's the same recipe I've always used," she answered with a smile.

"Appreciate you cleaning up Frank's room for Jim."

"Well, your father. He's been using it for storage."

"Yeah, I know. But I thought he might be more comfortable in Arnold and Bob's room."

"I'll go and ask him if everything is all right."

I accompanied her upstairs and knocked at the door. We were told to come in, and when I opened it I caught sight of James Isner standing by the window. He was reading a research paper. My father had absentmindedly left behind some of his old university work. He gave me a so-so look when my mother asked if he was satisfied with the room.

"Oh, very much so," he said.

"The bed too small for you?" she asked next. "Robert isn't coming in until Wednesday."

"I'm fine, really."

I began to feel that I had been a bit biased in speaking so constructively of my father's work at Old Dominion University and then putting aside in my usual way Jim's wise suggestion at the airport that I should let my father speak to him about some of his more relevant efforts. Most of his research was good, but this report on the origins of Old Testament priests obviously did not impress him.

Jim confirmed that he was quite all right and would be down in a few minutes.

"You can take your time," said my mother. "We won't be having dinner for a couple more hours, but I'll put some snacks out."

Knowing the football bowl schedule, I told Jim who was playing on the television. Then I went downstairs. I went out into the garage and found that my father had just purchased a case of lager beer and there was a row of bottles already chilled in the old refrigerator. And they were all different brands and types and I guessed that even after all these years my father's habit of serving his guests good beer had not faded. It was unusually cold. A chilly wind was blowing off the ocean and spots of rain were expected over the next couple of days.

I went back into the house and looking outside, in the space between the large oak tree and the garden, were a cluster of men and dogs standing about notwithstanding the playfulness of Riley Junior; and their eyes followed him around the tree, the reserved expressions of the two neighbors the same dry tone as that of my father—then the dogs engaged Riley Junior and the three men laughed. It was great to see that the two hearty terriers and the larger hunting dog shared the capacity to understand and behave according to the rules of right and wrong, and not only barking and wagging their tails wildly but showing an eager look so that my dog's invitation to play wasn't misconstrued. (Riley Junior's bow was highly stereotypical and communicated his intention to play fairly.) I sauntered out the back door and there was the leaves bagged, but the other side of the backyard where I had stopped raking earlier in the day to pick up James Isner with a thick carpet of yellow and orange and brown was unchanged; there was about three more hours of work left to complete the job and the assignment suddenly gave me a feeling of responsibility that dissipated when my old buddy joined me.

It was dull and darker in the backyard where the sun set on the front of the house. I was served a beer by the cordial Dr. Isner. I asked if he was doing all right.

"Absolutely," he said. "The room is fine; the bed is firm."

"Good to hear," I said.

The dogs came running by us and it looked like their roles were reversed as Riley Junior was now being chased.

"I heard the funniest thing on the plane," Jim started.

"What's that?"

"The girls behind me were taunting others across the aisle."

"That so."

"Yeah, apparently they go to rival colleges in the area. One of them began to chant, you know, like you'd hear at a softball or field hockey game, and the other girls joined in; it went something like this: We are the girls of Radford; we do not drink or swear, Nor-folk, Nor-folk!"

"Ha, I heard that before. You know, Radford is a coed university, been so for some time now."

"Oh, yeah."

Then my father joined us with a rake in his hand and I guessed that he was done for the afternoon. Riley Junior followed and sat down on the loose pile of leaves.

"I'll finish this up tomorrow, Dad."

"I've been meaning to get to these leaves since Thanksgiving but haven't found the time," he said.

"I always wait until they all come down," Jim commented casually.

"We've got a lot of trees back here and I try to clean up the yard a little each weekend. Besides, it's good exercise for me."

"Who were those guys, Dad. I can't remember meeting them."

"Oh, Jon Hendricks, the young guy with the cap, recently bought the Bekoffs' house, and the other was Mr. Murray."

"I didn't recognize him," I said.

"He told me something interesting about Ted, from when he was living across the street from us."

"No kidding."

I gave Jim some background information, from the days of my boyhood that I had spoken of before, but somewhat to my surprise I saw that it aroused no echo in his memory. He was very interested, however, to let my father continue with his thought.

"You ever do any charity work?" he asked Jim. "We get quite a few military families at one time and another. We always like to do what we can for them."

I told Jim that my father belonged to the Knights of Columbus and let him to guess on what rung of Jacob's ladder.

"I used to see him every Sunday," said my father. "He used to be very partial to attending the early mass but he never seemed to have time for any of the activities. Mind you, I don't say he wasn't interested, but he used to keep busy with work and *other* things. Women would slip in at night, and out of the house in the morning, usually by taxi, and his buddies drinking all night long. Your mother didn't half like his moving into the neighborhood; and you can imagine it's a bit of a problem for a man trying to raise four young boys. Well, one day I saw him down in the city at the Basilica's soup kitchen, and Mr. Murray just reminded me that he had seen him the weekend before. Again I hadn't really talked to him up to that time. But I was surprised to see him there. Anyway, as far as charity goes, I think it's a matter of being honest with oneself. I personally find a greater good in giving anonymously too because then the reason isn't about admiration from others, it's more that you feel good for yourself in doing it. For instance, I used to give to this homeless man who neither panhandled nor tried to draw some cash from me out of pity. I was glad to do it, for a couple of reasons. First, he had enough character to not try to make me feel sorry for him by staring and looking helpless, rather he tried to be invisible outside the university's gates and not get in my way. Second, I studied him before investing my money, by looking at the care of his clothes, posture, state, and well-being. I may not have known his circumstances but I knew the money I gave him would mean a lot to him and nothing to me. I sought no admiration or appreciation from him, and wouldn't have been offended if he threw the money back at me for suggesting the handout. I was merely investing in something I saw that I thought had worth. Unlike many of Norfolk's poor, he seemed to be a man who could turn things around and make a contribution. I wouldn't have given him money if I didn't see what I saw that I valued. Of course we knights always give support to anyone who comes through the door; we try to get them to a point where they can help themselves, but yes, I helped that homeless fellow. I haven't seen him since and hope he has done well for himself. Yes, indeed, Ted always said he liked it there. He said you saw good people there and he said he'd always felt obligated. Quite a character he was. He was still active when he suffered that coronary failure last year. I quite missed Ted when he passed. I was just saying to Mr. Murray I'd like to do something in his honor. Wanda tells me she gave St. Mary's outreach center a large donation in his name."

"I hadn't heard about that, Dad."

"Very interesting," added Jim.

"Well, I must clean up and see about helping your mother with dinner preparations."

James Isner and I stood looking out at the darkening backyard for a minute in silence.

"You know, Riley, your old man gave the bum money because he valued him. Even the way he spoke now of observing him and selecting him shows me that the bum embodies things that he thinks should be continued. This is a more subtle goal than that of hunter-gatherers, our ancestors, who developed this innate ability, but certainly an expression of his attempt to influence the community and the world, as we all do in some way. Your father's good deed could only go on within a group of people that has goals, and can make value judgments based upon another person's willingness to adhere to those goals. I think of this as a group's collective intelligence. When he saw the bum he helped him out because he saw helping him as helping a cause he valued."

At this point my heart quickened, finally perceiving the reason why Theodore Hume had helped me.

"And this is most clearly exemplified in war," Jim said. "Further, even to commune, let alone wage war as a collective body, selflessness is presupposed. Each individual recognizes the utility of his partners—or in aggregate, his community—in achieving his individual goals, and because the individual is faced with the prospect of an untimely death, or at least a finite lifespan, that individual transfers his actions to the furtherance of the group with the expectation that his comrades will carry on his legacy and his projects once he has died."

"So in essence," I said, smiling but not trying to bait my good friend, "community is the ultimate selfish act."

"Well, sure, that's one way to look at it."

"You don't think pure altruism is possible then?" I said.

"No, of course not."

# TWENTY

N**EXT MORNING IT** was cold and windy, but it was not raining, and I took Jim down the street towards Lake Tecumseh. I recognized the reflective blue body of water, the thick woody wetlands that has survived the decades—the sun in all of its magnificence becomes as much the landscape's focal point as the lake itself—but it was free of direct sunlight and any activity for that matter except for an innocuously parked Porsche. I felt like a young boy walking down that road which I had once considered infinitely long, or at least long enough to ask for a lift. I showed Jim the boat ramp first, and with Riley Junior propelling us forward we started around the lake. Suddenly a man emerged from behind a berm, stopped and turned back, and he looked at me curiously. He was a tall, balding, heavyset man.

"You Malcolm Brown?"

"Hey Riley, I thought that was you."

"Oh, I always come here when visiting my parents, and besides my dog over there loves it here."

"You don't say; me, too."

"What are you doing these days?" I asked.

"I'm a doctor—say, I heard you served in Iraq and Afghanistan. I would've liked to have served myself, except I had that run-in with the law, remember."

"Oh, yeah, that's right. What's your specialty by the way?"

"I'm a surgeon over in Petersburg."

"Damn, we could've used you. Oh, this is a Marine Corps buddy of mine, Jim Isner."

Malcolm nodded his head and smiled.

"Good to meet you," Jim said, acknowledging him.

"Well, I should be getting on. Good seeing you, Riley."

"So long."

It gave me pause, thinking about the sports car. He had turned himself around, got himself a doctor's degree and presently grown to respectability; I judged from the look of him that he had lived, in spite of incessant toil that goes with the job, in wealth. He had maintained the peculiar manner of the son of a football coach: hearty, potent and nonchalant. His life was going well. I had plans in my head for assignments and books, I was full of ideas for this project with Jim; I felt that a long life and fun still lay before me, and sure, I suppose, to others I must seem the venerable somebody that he seemed to me. I was so deep in thought that I had not the presence of mind to tell Jim about some of my jet-skiing experiences with Theodore Hume, or about the time he had taken us for a ride on the special operations craft; after a few self-indulgent minutes I began to talk enthusiastically about the past. We walked on to Back Bay, an ample, flowing body of water too far out of the way for the typical walker who took his exercise less seriously than did outdoor enthusiasts and too choppy for kayaking or canoeing on a day like this one. It lay on the other side of two weirs and a berm that separates it from Lake Tecumseh and was surrounded by wet fields. There was a bright yellow marker on a pole that announced that there was a trail now for the neighboring residents and gave the name of the congressman who was responsible for restoring the Bay Back National Wildlife Refuge. We followed it; the lake berm project was an improvement and successful and the winding trail followed the contours of the land in which I used to travel along as a young boy. "With less sediments and nutrients washing into the bay and lake," I explained to Jim, "water quality has gotten much better and the aquatic grasses are coming back." As we walked by the grounds of Dam Neck naval base I spoke to him how these grasses breathe oxygen into the water, provide habitat for fish and crabs, and are fodder for the thousands of waterfowl that seek shelter here during their great migrations.

We wandered about here and there. There seemed innumerable new streets of large houses on the fringes, but I did not know how the people afforded them for I knew about the prices. We went down to the ocean. It was deserted. There was but one man fishing a little way from the break wall. Two or three ships were sitting on the lustrous horizon and we gazed at them for a moment. Although the bottom had fallen out of the local economy and the aircraft carriers came to Norfolk no longer it was still pretty good here.

Then it was time to go to see Wanda Hume and we went back to the house. My mother told us that she had called to confirm the time of our arrival but looking at the clock I saw that we had plenty of time to take showers and get dressed for the occasion. Jim was sitting in the living room with my father when I came downstairs, engaged in a light, but worldly conversation, and I went out to warm up my most dilapidated pickup that Jim had laughed at when I had fetched him at the airport; it was reliable for the most part even though it panted and squeaked and rattled, with sudden angry jerks on the highway, so that I wondered if I should ever get to my destination. But the amazing, the extraordinary thing about my blue F-150 was that it never let me down and the exterior was in good condition and the interior quite clean, albeit the dog hair which I tried to remove every time I cleaned it. This was the price for having a dog; and I wondered in concern, if James Isner was upset by it, and reflexively apologized again when he jumped in. But this minor inconvenience could never overcome the pure joy and exhilaration Riley Junior got from the fresh smells of the great outdoors, and, seeing him looking at me with sad eyes now I knew that he fully expected to come along for the ride today. I got out and, taking him by the collar, led him quickly back into the house and then we were on our way.

"Now, Riley, let me do the talking today. Feel free to say whatever is on your mind, but please be pleasant. Wanda is still very emotional when talking about Hume. I really don't think she has come to closure yet. You know what I mean. I also wanted to tell you that there is nothing going on between us."

"I understand," I said.

When we arrived, Wanda Hume came walking around the house and came right up to Jim as we got out of the pickup truck.

"I was just out back," said Wanda Hume, as she took Jim's hand. And then with a smile: "Riley, thanks for coming; I want to show you something in the backyard."

She looked no older than when I saw her last. She retained her quiet hyperbolic demeanor. At her neck was a small brass crucifix and on her finger her wedding ring. Jim, I just noticed, wore a freshly pressed light blue shirt with a button-down collar; I supposed it was a token of sufferance for traditional views and values.

"I know you will appreciate it," said Wanda Hume, "and then we'll have some lunch."

We walked around the immaculately kept Neo-colonial house adorned with laurel wreaths and Jim was very talkative. She was not given to open expression and emotion, and withheld her opinion during his earnest expansion of our morning walk. He enjoyed the complexity of nature, especially the interdependency of plants and animals, and told Wanda Hume where she ought to go on walks and how perfectly lovely were the sights.

"Ted liked to sit here," she said, pointing to the lone chair. "I keep it exactly where it was when he was here. I recently painted it, but I haven't moved it an inch. You'd be surprised how many hours he sat in this chair, first thing in the morning with a cup of coffee and again in the afternoon, and of course he loved this old oak tree."

"Do you mind, Wanda?" I asked.

She smiled pleasantly.

"Please."

James Isner and I took turns sitting in the Adirondack chair. There was a clear view of Lake Tecumseh and beyond the lake a glimpse of the ocean. On the horizon was the eastern sky and the encroaching large clouds gave the appearance of powdered or tufted graphite. I do not know why the backyard seemed so strangely high; it had an unbroken view of the surrounding area. Wanda Hume watched us from behind and with a little smile, half playful, half sad, took in the panorama again when it was Jim's turn to sit in the chair.

"You know that Ted had a high opinion of you," said Wanda Hume to me. "He spoke about you quite often."

"I'm very glad to think that," I said politely.

I knew very well that he had not been one to speak of his men, even privately, and in a casual way I looked at her and pondered for a moment whether there was any truth in her comment. There was, I suppose. Then I took another look at the lake, the faint light of sky, and making a little effort tried to think of something else to say. No, it was indeed a proud moment and best to remain quiet.

We went into the house by way of the deck and Wanda served us a nice lunch, a hearty grilled sandwich and tossed salad, and we talked of the work on which Jim was engaged. He had a good relationship with her, but it was a particular type of connection existing between people having dealings with each other.

"When I returned from Boston," said Wanda Hume, "I began gathering together as much material as I could myself. Of course it's been rather difficult for me, but it's been very good, too. Rick Wasson dropped off some old photos that I must show you."

After lunch we went into the great room and Wanda Hume served us applejack cider and cookies. I noticed with what perfect style Wanda Hume had decorated the house for the holidays. The Christmas tree was stately and everything was new; even the furniture of Ethan Allen design seemed pristine. It suited the second wife of a distinguished naval officer almost more than it suited the first. The temple-like entrance, the large living areas, the Palladian windows—there was about them a vague air of faux finishing; they seemed to borrow loosely ideas from the past. I could have expected that there were more ideas to convey the traditional atmosphere in a smaller colonial home, but Americans are a spoiled as well as a pampered nation; and it is impossible to deny them desires at the cost of discomfort. I was quite certain Theodore Hume bought this wonderful house to please Dotti. We were just sitting down to look at the photos of Hume as a young man; Jim and Wanda were putting artful questions to incite me to open up. But I had nothing to offer. She asked me about my work for *The Imperium* magazine and then about the Caravaggio exhibit at the National Gallery of Art which had provided me work over the past year, and I surmised from her disinterest (and limited knowledge of the artist famous for his intense realism) that it was perhaps an overture designed to elicit a few more words from me. I thought to tell her a little about the man who painted his subjects as the eye saw them, with all their natural flaws and defects instead of as idealized creations, as exemplified by Michelangelo who perfected this accepted standard practice; controversial at the time, we hoped to get the same reaction from the public now by showcasing with high drama military artists from around the world alongside a few of his paintings that featured violent struggles, grotesque decapitations, torture and death. I merely told her that it opens in January, on the fifteenth, when suddenly the doorbell rang.

"Oh, sorry, excuse me for a minute," she said. "I hope it isn't another journalist. I never have a moment's peace."

"Well, why don't you say you're sorry you have guests?" said Jim, with what I thought a certain stinginess.

"Oh, I couldn't do that." She looked out the window. "Besides it looks like a young couple."

She opened the door, and James Isner and I stood momentarily, and one of them introduced himself: "Jason Boardman, Naval Academy," and then somewhat less confidently, "We're on leave this week and wanted to send holiday greetings." The other was "Sarah Hudson," and she had a basket of flowers which she offered to Wanda Hume with a smile.

"Midshipmen," said Wanda Hume. "Please come in, will you?"

Presently Wanda Hume ushered the students in. They were both of average height and weight, with cropped, dark hair and clean, enthusiastic expressions on their faces; they both wore their military uniforms and they both had flawlessly pressed shirts and pleats on their pants. They both wore dark blue jackets that were evidently new; they were both slightly embarrassed, but surefooted and friendly. They explained that they were taking a tour of battlefields in Maryland and Virginia during their break and, being admirers of Captain Theodore Hume, had taken the opportunity of stopping off on their way to visit Yorktown. The fact that they had traveled a fair distance out of their way did not go without notice with Wanda Hume.

"You must stay for a cup of tea then," she said.

She introduced the midshipmen to Jim and me. I was filled with awe by the way in which Jim rose to the occasion. It appeared that he had lectured before the Naval Academy and had recently brought them into the fold on one of his many grants. It had been a memorable experience. He did not know whether he had been more impressed by the unsparing hospitality with which the dean and his teaching staff had entertained him or by their keen interest in the evolution of altruism, parochialism and cooperation. He asked how Dr. Norm Clain was, and Dr. Andre Marshall; he had such a good time there, and it looked as though he had always wanted to go there but never had been invited before. Soon the young man was telling Jim how much he knew about his economic theories, and Jim was modestly telling him what in this one and the other his aim had been and how conscious he was that he had yet to develop a unified theory of economics that included biology, equality, and morality. He started to speak of globalization and cultural standardization when there would be neither a left and right nor an East and West. Wanda Hume listened with smiling patience, but I had a feeling that her smile was turning a bit tense. It may be that Jim had sensed it, for he suddenly broke off.

"But you didn't come here to listen to me," he said in his loud brusque way. "Isn't that right, Riley?"

They looked briefly at me and I thought he was going to start up again and disclose the reason for our visit, but he smiled at them and turned his regard toward Wanda Hume.

Wanda Hume looked down demurely at the photographs on the coffee table and the two young midshipmen turned their large dark eyes in which you could read their sympathy, their understanding and their respect. After a little more conversation—partly casual but also personal, for the students admitted that they were dating and they hoped to get to Colonial Williamsburg by nightfall, and here again Jim felt obliged, for he told them to look for such and such restaurant in the historic center—after this, I say, Wanda Hume offered to show them her late husband's wall of valor in the library, and of course, his chair in the backyard. Jim and I shook their hands, evidently bent on sitting back down, but Wanda Hume thought otherwise and gave us a little smile that was pleasant but firm.

"Please stay here, guys," she said. "I'll take them myself. I suspect they want to get going."

"Of course," said Jim. "They have a full schedule."

They bade us farewell and Jim and I settled down again in the plush sofa and armchair, respectively.

"Beautiful room," said Jim.

"Absolutely."

"Wanda has impeccable taste. She told me Hume let her furnish the house any which way she liked. Wanda said he was very helpful, but I suspect they hired a professional painter."

"I reckon so—the rooms are huge."

There was a pause for a moment as we sipped cider and ate cookies.

"You know, Riley, I finally got around to reading Clausewitz's *On War*, and found it very interesting. He's very astute in some ways. I for one can relate to the chapter that bears on genius, which is a word used in many ways, and he admitted that it is a very difficult matter to define but then proceeds to do a remarkable job anyway. While I disagree about his ideas of the soul's thirst for honor and fame, which he considered the noblest feelings that fill the human heart during the galvanizing revelry of battle, I still think he's right about courage. He conceptualized the hardest thing a leader must do when pitched in battle with his men is follow this faint light, which he expressed by the French phrase *coup d'oeil*; the other is resolution. Naturally, the first thing I thought of was judgment or intuition, but he said the two acting together, when combined with experience, has more to do with the rapid discovery of truth, of course in the area of military tactics, which by the way he considered for most people is neither readily seeable nor obvious even after long consideration and reflection. Here, he doesn't speak to strength and weakness. The mind must, he said, be aware to the feeling of courage from the start, and then be guided and supported by it, because in momentary glimpses where chaos and gunfire prevail one is influenced more by feelings than by thoughts. He didn't mean courage in the traditional sense, but one's frame of mind in the face of responsibility. Pure intelligence does not make a genius. He spoke of other factors, and even goes on to suggest characteristics of an ideal candidate for a field commander, but in my opinion these are merely secondary aspects or arguments for the genius in war. He was an extraordinary theorist and though a very good period piece I think he generally is still relevant today."

"Sure thing," I said. "Did you read the chapter on boldness?"

"I might have skipped over that one."

"Well, as I recall, he said it is the noblest of all virtues."

"How so?"

"You know the meaning underlying it as well as I do," I said, trying to remember the logic of Clausewitz's argument. "You know how it goes: the greater the risk, the greater the reward. That's one reason why I love this great country."

He gave me a quick look and laughed. Jim was not stupid.

"Yeah, we're big risk takers, willing to roll the dice, but in actuality risk and reward mutually support each other. You know, speaking of which, I think it would be valuable to create a role for your father on our project."

"Great," I said.

When Wanda Hume returned, having sent the midshipmen on their way, she bore under her arm a stack of photo albums.

"What a nice couple!" she said. "I wish young people took such a respectful interest in the military these days. I gave them a photo of Ted when he received his second Medal of Honor from the president. And they asked me if they could take a picture of the lake." Then almost in tears: "The Naval Academy does such a fine job. They said it was a real privilege to come here and finally talk to me."

"I'm going to Annapolis in a few weeks," said Jim, nonchalantly.

"Oh, they've studied your work. They say that what they like about your ideas is that they're so right." She paused. "Oh, I see you guys need a refill. Let me take your glasses before I sit down. I will be right back."

The first photo album contained pictures going back to the 1960's, a series of shots taken of Hume with his sister and parents, groups of boys from the neighborhood, among who I recognized a titan with blondish hair mainly because he was so large, baseball and football shots with him a little older, and then a few of a helicopter technician inside a hanger in San Diego, before becoming a Navy SEAL.

"This one has wedding pictures," said Wanda Hume.

She opened it up without any trepidation. The first picture showed Hume standing in front of the house with his proud parents. The next was of him with both of his grandparents. He was clean-shaven and wore a black-and-white tuxedo. In the next picture he was with his best man.

"And here's the bride," said Wanda Hume with great fanfare.

"Very pretty," said Jim to be polite.

"Oh, she was not," murmured Wanda.

We looked through the other albums, snapshots that had been taken of him when he came back to El Paso for the holidays and during summer vacations, photos when he wore a beard and others, all later ones, when he was both a family man and a full-fledged Navy SEAL. You saw his face had become maturer and more rugged. You saw the change in him wrought by experience, months spent in foreign lands, and by learning and achieved ambition. The stubborn innocence of early pictures faded gradually into a worldly man who had been almost everywhere. I looked again at his high school portrait and considered that I saw in his eyes a trace of that confidence that seemed to me so noticeable in older ones and that I had only a half dozen years before seen in the man himself on the battlefield. In the eyes you saw the same and everything else seemed irrelevant now. I had an impression that the real man, to his untimely death and alone, became separated from all others and the people who he had dedicated his life, and ultimately looked with confounding detachment at the sky that he had once understood. Perhaps Socrates' argument of the intrinsic value of a just society is still lacking. It seems that each time a solitary cry of rebellion is uttered, the response is more suffering. I don't know, but for as long as the West has been Christian, society's antagonistic perception and established pessimism concerning human behavior is based upon the assumption that injustice is as satisfying to man as justice. (We all know that only God can justify the endless and universal torture of innocence.) The strange manifestation of happiness by Hume and his men illustrates to me that man will be always ready for the great offensive against a hostile reality. I am conscious that in what I have written of him here I have not fully described his true nature, the living man, standing tall, grounded, with that searching and comprehensive mind; I have not tried to do that: I am afraid that would be too ambitious even for James Isner.

We came across a few pictures that someone, possibly a tourist, had taken of me with the Humes in Kitty Hawk. It gave me a rush. That was how I best remembered those days. Despite the unflattering wet suit, Dotti was full of life then and beautiful with the passion that filled her. She seemed to convey this passion for life to us. Theodore Hume would have died for her, and the Congress rewarded him by allowing him to return from Afghanistan bested, even though twice decorated in their name for conspicuous intrepidity at the risk of his own life.

"That's a good shot of you, Riley," said Jim.

"I remember that day very well," I said. "I spent the weekend with them."

"You did?" exclaimed Wanda Hume. "Your parents let you spend the weekend alone with them," she repeated, as if dumbfounded. "I can't believe it."

"Yeah, my dad finally relented."

Wanda Hume shook her head and shared an expressive look with Jim.

"I've heard a great deal about her," said Wanda. "I don't want to be hurtful, but I'm afraid I don't think she was any good for Ted and the boys, or *you*."

"That's where you are wrong," I said. "She was a very nice person to me. I mostly saw her in a good mood. I only had to say I wanted something and she would give it to me. She was very patient, too. She gave me many jet-skiing lessons."

"I heard she was a terrible housewife."

Jim burst out laughing and Wanda Hume stopped short of ripping up the old photograph. It was very clever on his part, and I added: "Haven't seen the boys around today."

"Well, they're visiting their grandparents in El Paso this week," she said after a pause, looking as though she had finally got the bad taste out of her mouth. "I know she really never loved him as I did. I mean, still do."

"The divorce was very painful," I said.

"For who?" Wanda cried. "You don't know the half of it."

"I'm just saying," I said.

"I understand you are divorced and have a daughter."

Jim laughed again and this time Wanda Hume without concealing her disgust threw the photo onto the floor.

I looked at her briefly. I have noticed that when I am most sincere people (especially to those with connections to Washington, D.C.) are apt to become angry with me, and indeed when after a lapse of a moment I decided to laugh myself. It must be that there is something naturally disarming in good humor or a candid chuckle, though why it happens I cannot imagine, unless it is rooted to the tongue of early man, or unless it is an expression of derision or contempt, but then you won't be laughing when the truth comes out.

I saw that Wanda Hume wanted to ask me something. She was not laughing along with us but composed.

"Do you think Ted really loved her?"

"Oh, I don't know," I said, thinking. "Well, I should say no. I should say that he had an intense combination of strong feeling and extreme callousness. He was angry and yet seemingly calm, and I think that when he had built up any remaining emotion he would transfer it to his men. You know, he put his life on the line for his men more than two times."

"Excellent, Riley," said Jim. "That's what this book is going to be all about."

Wanda was satisfied.

"I wonder what happened to her?" she asked.

"Well, we all know she married Roger Bernard," I said, thinking again. "And they left London. Of course, they just disappeared off the face of the earth."

"Yes, very strange," commented Jim.

"So you haven't heard from her?" she asked next.

"No, absolutely not," I said, belying the fact that I had recently learned from an associate that Dotti took another name, Lewis, when Roger became the administrator of the British School of Classical Studies in Greece.

At that moment the telephone rang in the kitchen. Wanda stood up and excused herself. Jim took a sip of cider and nibbled on a cookie, and I looked at the Christmas tree.

She embarked upon a conversation which, I gathered from her tone, was of a prominent and even a flirtatious character. I did not pay much attention, but Jim did, and since this person seemed to encourage her I began to meditate upon my assignment and the warrior's life. It is full of anxiety. First he must endeavor difficult training and the world's indifference; then, having achieved a measure of success, he must establish for himself a family. He depends upon both a loving wife, and a discriminating public. He is at the mercy of politicians who want to use him and generals who want to take him away from his loved ones, of street girls who tempt him, of mayors of cities and faraway towns who ask him to march in parades, of teachers in his hometown who ask him to talk to their students, of kids who want his autograph, veterans who want to swap stories and military contractors who want to hire him, of critics who ridicule him for mistakes and scholars who pick him apart for their own purposes and strange men who want to give him a loan, of creditors, friends, family, and his own conscience. But he has one comfort. Whenever he has anything on his mind, whether it be a harassing reflection, a grief at the loss of a comrade, unrequited love, family problems, wounded pride, anger at the betrayal of one to whom he has shown trust, in short any emotion or any perplexing thought, he has only to take a deep breath and keep everything in perspective. He must chalk it all up to experience and becoming wise. A warrior is certainly not a free man I thought.

Wanda Hume returned to the room.

"That was the Dev Group commander. I'm going to go with him and his wife to a party on New Year's Eve and he called to say he'd talked to Admiral Seton the other day. Of course he's retired, but he's going to be very helpful to us. He's working for a big shipbuilder, in Mississippi, but he's coming to Norfolk this week. Jim, you're welcome to come along with me. Is Tuesday morning good for you?"

"Oh, shoot, I'm busy—Riley, can you go?"

"Sure thing; have you ever thought of getting a secretary, Wanda?" I asked.

"Please." She giggled. "Not that I could use one. I'm quite capable myself, but I can't afford one. The way I look at it is this: I don't want to be known as a crazy woman. I used to cry all day. Some days were better than others; oftentimes I was mad as hell. I don't know what to say. I guess I'm doing much better now. It's been such a hard ordeal. I appreciate everything you guys are doing for me."

"Not a problem," said Jim. "We're here to help."

"Well, again, I'm fine. I'm being cared for, you know. Riley, I know your mother thinks I'm lonesome. Of course, for the longest time I thought I *was* alone. For one thing, I've always been sort of an independent person. My mother lives in Philadelphia, but we talk almost every day. Father Mayer and the whole parish have been just wonderful to me. And then when Rick came to me one day and said Congress was dead wrong and he should have been buried at Arlington Cemetery and there'd be an appeal submitted on my behalf in a few months and would I go see the Secretary of the Navy with him, well, what could I say? I was trying to do everything myself, with no luck whatsoever, and my husband having been always so demonized and living here by myself and trying to turn things around for him. It wasn't as if I was afraid of them."

"I wonder how you ever managed before," I commented.

Jim gave me a quick look and Wanda smiled.

"I sometimes wonder about that myself."

"In about a month," said Jim, "I'd like to get the team together for a kickoff meeting in Ithaca."

"Sounds wonderful," Wanda said with a smile.

Her eyes traveled to a picture laying on the coffee table that for some time had escaped my notice. It was an old faded photograph of Theodore Hume when he was a young man. It looked as if it might have been taken soon after his arrival in Virginia Beach; perhaps at the time he was living across the street from us when I first met him. It showed him in a diving suit, standing alone with a big broad smile, and a cigar in one hand and a knife in the other; there was a large shark at his feet; the ocean behind him went on for miles without reaching the horizon. He looked like a warrior on a limestone pediment of a Greek temple or ruin; what is more, the goggles on his head and the tip of his beard looked as if they were made of separate pieces; and there was some red on his hair and a light blue background that left ghosts of patterns in other colors. The picture led naturally enough to thoughts about Schliemann's quest for the truth of wars and of other things.

# About the Author

**W**ILLIAM MUELLER IS the author of *Rome Revisited, The Magnificent Man,* and *The Noble American;* each of his novels examines a basic aspect of the American experience. *Of Immortalized Warriors* links these books and advances ideas about freedom and the will of man to move the world. He lives in Alexandria, Virginia.